PURE HELL WITH A GUN!

"You got any kin you want me to notify, Vic?" asked Smoke Jensen.

"Notify about what?"

"Your death."

Vic was suddenly unsure of himself. He looked around him. "You alone, Jensen?"

"I don't need any help in dealing with scum like you, Vic. Come on, make your play."

Vic began cursing, working his courage back up to a fever. "Drag iron, Jensen!" he screamed.

"After you, punk."

Vic's hand dropped to his gun. . . .

BOOK YOUR PLACE ON OUR WEBSITE AND MAKE THE READING CONNECTION!

We've created a customized website just for our very special readers, where you can get the inside scoop on everything that's going on with Zebra, Pinnacle and Kensington books.

When you come online, you'll have the exciting opportunity to:

- View covers of upcoming books
- Read sample chapters
- Learn about our future publishing schedule (listed by publication month *and author*)
- Find out when your favorite authors will be visiting a city near you
- Search for and order backlist books from our online catalog
- Check out author bios and background information
- Send e-mail to your favorite authors
- Meet the Kensington staff online
- Join us in weekly chats with authors, readers and other guests
- Get writing guidelines
- AND MUCH MORE!

**Visit our website at
http://www.kensingtonbooks.com**

WILLIAM W. JOHNSTONE

WAR OF THE MOUNTAIN MAN

PINNACLE BOOKS
Kensington Publishing Corp.
http://www.pinnaclebooks.com

Dedicated to

Tommy & Emily Ruth Ervin

What man was ever content with one crime?

Juvenal

I had rather live with the woman I love in a world full of trouble, than to live in heaven with nobody but men.

Robert G. Ingersoll

1

"I don't like the idea of the kids on the ocean," Smoke said. "By God, I just don't."

Sally faced him from across the table in the house in the high-up country of Colorado. "Smoke, there is a new treatment available in France, and Louis Arthur has got to have it. We've been to the finest doctors on this continent. They all say the same thing."

"Sally, I'm not arguing that. I want what is best for Baby Arthur. But why do all the children have to go? My God, they'll be gone for more than a year."

She smiled at him. Smoke Jensen and Sally never had the hard, deadly quarrels that so many couples suffered. They were both reasonable people of high intelligence, and each loved the other. "The exposure to a more genteel climate—and I'm not talking about the weather—will be good for the older children. They need to broaden their horizons."

Smoke laughed as he picked up his coffee mug, holding it in one big, flat-knuckled hand. The laughter was full of good humor and did not contain a bit of anger or scorn. He stuck out his little finger. "They gonna learn how to hold a coffee cup dainty-like, with their little pinkies all poked out to one side?"

Sally laughed at him. "Yes. You heathen."

Smoke chuckled and rose from the table, picking up Sally's cup as well as his own. He walked to the stove, a big man, well over six feet, with broad shoulders, huge, heavily muscled arms, and a lean waist. He walked like a cat. His presence in a room, any room, usually brought the crowd to silence. His eyes were brown and could turn as cold as the Arctic. He was a ruggedly handsome man, turning the heads of ladies wherever he traveled.

He was Smoke Jensen. The man some called the last mountain man.

Smoke was the hero in dozens of dime novels. Plays had been written and were still being performed about his exploits. Smoke, himself, had never seen one. He was, without dispute, the fastest gun in the West. He had never wanted the title of gunfighter; but he had it.

There was no accurate count of how many would-be toughs, punks, thugs, thieves, and killers had fallen under the .44's of Smoke Jensen. Some say fifty; others said it was closer to two hundred. Smoke didn't know. As a young man, scarcely out of his teens, he had ridden into a mining camp taken over by the men who had killed his wife and baby son and had wiped it out to the last man.

His reputation had then been carved in solid granite. Smoke had become a living legend.

He had met Sally, who was working as a schoolteacher, and they had fallen in love. Together, working side by side— even though she was enormously wealthy, something Smoke didn't find out until well after they were married—they carved out a ranch in Colorado and named it the Sugarloaf.

For three years Smoke dropped out of sight, living a normal, peaceful life. Then he had to surface and once more strap on his guns in a fight for survival. He stayed surfaced. He would not hunt out a fight, but God help those who came to him trouble-hunting. As the western saying goes: Smoke could point out dozens of his graveyards.

Their coffee mugs refilled, Smoke sat back down at the table and they both sugared and stirred. Sally laid her hand on his. "Roundup is all over and the cattle sold, right, honey?"

"Yes. And it was a good one. We made money. Now we're rebuilding the herds, introducing a stronger breed, mixing in some Herefords. What'd you have on your mind, Sally?"

"I'd like to go with the children. . . ." She put a finger on his lips to stop his protests before they got started. "But I'm not. I know what the doctors said. And I'm never going to set foot on a ship again. But if we stay here, rattling around in this house, we'll both go crazy with worry. Let's wait until we receive the wire that the ship has steamed out, and then take a trip. Just the two of us."

"That's a good idea. The boys can run the spread; no worries there. You got some special place in mind?"

"Yes. It's a friend I went to college with. She and her husband just moved to Montana. They live near a small town about thirty miles from Kalispell. She's married to a doctor and they have a small ranch. I'd like to see her. She was my best friend."

"Suits me. We'll take a trip up there. It'll do us both good to get away, see some country, and meet new people. We'll take the train as far as it goes and then catch a stage."

"No," Sally shook her head. "Let's put the horses in a car and ride in, Smoke. It'll be worth it to see the expressions on their faces when we ride in."

"Sidesaddle?" he kidded her, knowing better.

"You have to be kidding!"

Smoke was with her. "All right, honey. But we're going to be heading into some rough country. I've been there. Cousin Fae lives not too far from there. We can take the train probably to Butte. That's wild country, Sally. Some ol' boys up there still have the bark on. And that's Big Max Huggins's country."

She smiled, but the curving of her pretty lips held no humor. "That's one of the reasons we're going, Smoke."

He laughed. "I was wondering if you were going to get around to leveling with me."

"You know this Max Huggins?"

"Only by name. We've never crossed trails."

She stared into her coffee cup.

"Sally, this town your friends have settled near . . . it wouldn't be Hell's Creek, would it?"

"Yes."

Smoke sighed and leaned back in his chair. "Then they

didn't show a lot of sense. Hell's Creek is owned—lock, stock, and outhouse—by Big Max Huggins. It's filled with gunfighters, whores, gamblers, killers. . . . You name it bad, and you'll find it there. Why did they settle there?"

"Robert—that's Vicky's husband—befriended an old man who took sick while visiting back east. Robert was just setting up his practice. Years later, he got a letter from an attorney telling him the old man had died and left him his ranch."

"And Big Max wanted the ranch?"

"Yes. But mostly he wants Victoria."

The next morning, Smoke rode into town and checked with Sheriff Monte Carson.

"What can you get me on Hell's Creek and a man named Big Max Huggins?"

Monte snorted. "I can tell you all about Big Max, Smoke. We got lead in each other about ten years ago."

"Over near the Bitterroot?"

Monte nodded his head.

"I remember that shoot-out. Is there any kind of law in Hell's Creek?"

"Only what Big Max says. Oh, there's a sheriff up there. But he's crooked as a snake's track and so are his deputies. I hear the governor keeps threatening to send men in to clean up the town, but he hasn't done it yet. Why the interest in Hell's Creek?"

"Sally has some friends who live near there. We're going to visit them. I'd sort of like to know what I'm riding into."

"You're riding into trouble, Smoke. Hell's Creek is a haven for outlaw gangs. In addition to Big Max's gang—and he's got forty or fifty men who ride for him—there's Alex Bell and his boys. Dave Poe, Warner Frigo, and Val Singer all run outlaw gangs out of Hell's Creek. The only way that town is ever going to be cleaned up is for the Army to go in and do it."

"Damn, Monte, it's 1883. The wild West is supposed to be calming down."

Monte shifted his chaw. "But you and me, Smoke, we know better, don't we?"

Smoke nodded his head. "Yeah. There'll be pockets of crud in the West for years to come, I reckon."

"Any way you can talk your missus out of takin' this trip?"

Smoke just looked at him.

"I do know the feelin'," Monte said. "Women get a notion in their heads, and a man's in trouble, for a fact. When are you and Sally pullin' out?"

"Probably in about a week. Who else do you know for sure is up there?"

"Ben Webster, Nelson Barlow, Vic Young, Dave Hall, Frank Norton, Lew Brooks, Sid Yorke, Pete Akins, and Larry Gayle. Is that enough?"

"Good God!" Smoke said, standing up. "You just named some of the randiest ol'boys in the country."

"Yeah. And believe you me, Smoke, they'll be plenty more up there just as good as them boys I just named. You're gonna be steppin' into a rattler's den."

"They do sell .44's up there, don't they?" Smoke asked dryly.

"Probably not to you." Monte's reply was just as dry.

2

That night, lying in bed, Sally said, "We don't have to go up there, Smoke. I don't want you to think I'm pressuring you in any way. Because I'm not."

"You think a lot of this friend of yours, don't you?"

"Like a sister, Smoke. She's had a lot of grief in her life and I'd like for her to have some happiness. She's overdue."

"Want to explain that?"

"She lost two brothers in the Civil War. Her mother died when she was in high school. Then in her second year of college, her father died. She worked terribly hard to finish school. Took in ironing, mended clothes, worked as a maid; anything to put food in her mouth and clothes on her back. I'd help whenever I could, but Vicky is an awfully proud girl. She and Robert had one child . . . that lived. Two others died. She can't have any more. Their daughter Lisa is ten."

Smoke waited for a moment, his eyes on the dark ceiling. "Finish it, honey. Tell it all."

"This Max Huggins trash has threatened Lisa several times, to get to Vicky."

Smoke thought about that. For about five seconds. He turned his head, his gaze meeting Sally's eyes. "We'll start packing up some things in the morning."

On the day they received the telegram from Sally's father, informing them of the steamer's departure, Smoke rode around their ranch, checking things out and speaking to the hands. His crew was a well-paid and tough bunch, who to a man would die for the brand. Some of them had been outlaws, riding the hoot-owl trail for a time. Some were gunfighters who sought relative peace and found it at the Sugarloaf. All were cowboys, hardworking and loyal.

"I still think you ought to take some of the boys with you, Smoke," his foreman grumbled. "Them's a hard bunch up yonder."

Smoke rolled a cigarette and handed the makings to his foreman. "You boys are needed here. There are still lots of folks who would just love to burn me out if they got the chance."

"They won't," the foreman said quietly.

"You boys take care of the place. You know where I'll be and how to reach me. We'll see you when we get back."

Smoke and Sally pulled out the next morning, Smoke riding a midnight-black gelding he called Star, and Sally on a fancy-stepping mountain-bred mare who could go all day and still have bottom left. Smoke led a packhorse with their few pieces of luggage and supplies.

They headed east, toward Denver, where they would catch the train. Sally had much experience with trains; Smoke had ridden only a few of them, preferring to travel in the saddle.

The beautiful woman and the handsome man turned heads when they boarded in Denver. And the whisper went from car to car: "That's Smoke Jensen! See them guns? He's killed a thousand men."

Smoke signed a half-dozen books about him and patiently answered the many questions that were asked of him, mostly by newcomers to the West, men and women making their first trip from the East.

One mouthy preacher lipped off one time too many about violent men who lived by the gun. Smoke finally told him to shut his mouth and mind his own business. The preacher's mouth opened and closed silently a few times, like a fish out of water. Then he sat back down and shut up.

They changed trains in Cheyenne and headed northwest, and Smoke had to endure yet another new bunch of pilgrims with a thousand questions.

"My, my," Sally said during a lull in the verbal bombardment. There was a twinkle in her eyes. "I didn't realize I was married to such a famous man."

"Bear it in mind," Smoke said with a straight face. "And the next time I ask for a cup of coffee, you quick step and fetch it."

Sally leaned over, putting her lips close to his ear, and whispered a terribly vulgar suggestion.

Smoke had to put his hat over his face to keep from busting out laughing. Sally was every bit the lady, but like so many western women, she could be quite blunt at times.

A fat drummer twisted in his seat and asked Smoke, "Will we see any Indians this trip? I've never seen an Indian."

"We might see a few," Smoke told him, aware that everyone within hearing range had their ears perked up. "But the tribes have pretty well been corralled. What we'll more than likely encounter—if anything—is outlaws working the trains."

"Outlaws!" a woman hollered. "You mean like . . . high-waymen?"

"Yes, ma'am. Once we cross over into Montana Territory, the odds of outlaws hitting trains really pick up. Especially this train," he added.

"What's so special about this train?" the lippy preacher asked.

"We're carrying gold."

"Now, how would someone such as you know that?" the preacher demanded.

Smoke ignored the scarcely concealed slur upon his character. "I saw them loading it, that's why."

"Well," the preacher huffed. "I'm certain the railroad has adequate security."

"They got an old man with a shotgun sitting in the car, if that's what you mean."

The preacher turned away and lifted his newspaper.

"Are we carrying gold, Smoke?" Sally asked.

"Yeah. And a lot of it. And not just gold. We're carrying several payrolls, too. For the miners."

"What are the chances of our getting held up?"

"Pretty good, I'd say. If I had to take a guess, I'd say we're carrying about a fifty-thousand-dollar payroll—all combined—and maybe twice that in gold. Be a juicy haul for those so inclined."

"They wouldn't dare attack this train," she kidded him. "Not with the famous Smoke Jensen on board." She punched him in the ribs.

"Your faith in me is touching." He rubbed the spot where she had punched him. "In more ways than one."

The day melted into dusk and then full dark, the train chugging on uneventfully through the night. The passengers slept fitfully, swaying back and forth in their seats to the rhythm of the drivers on the tracks.

Smoke sensed the train slowing and opened his eyes. Being careful not to rouse Sally, he stood up and stepped out into the aisle, making his weaving way to the door. He stepped outside and stretched, getting the kinks out of his muscles. On instinct, he slipped the leather thongs from the hammers of his six-guns.

Smoke leaned over the side and saw the skeletal form of the water tower ahead, faintly illuminated by the dim light of a nearly cloud-covered moon.

Through the odor of smoke pouring from the stack of the locomotive, Jensen could almost taste the wetness in the air. A storm was brewing, and from the build-up of clouds, it was going to be a bad one.

He looked back at the lantern-lit interior of the car, the lamps turned down very low. The passengers, including Sally, were still sleeping.

The train gradually slowed and came to a gentle halt, something most experienced engineers tried to do late at night so the paying passengers wouldn't be disturbed.

Smoke caught the furtive movement out of the corner of his eyes. Men on the water tower. With rifles.

One big hand closed around the butt of a .44. He hesitated. Were they railroad men, posted there in case of a robbery attempt? He didn't think so. But he wasn't going to shoot until he knew for sure.

He saw the brakeman coming up the side of the coaches and Smoke called to him softly just as he dropped to the shoulder. "My name's Jensen, brakeman. Smoke Jensen. There are armed men on the water tower."

The man's head jerked up. "They damn sure ain't railroad men, Smoke. And we're carryin' a lot of gold and cash money."

"That's all I need to know," Smoke said. He leveled a .44 and knocked a leg out from under one gunman crouching on the water tower. The man fell, screaming, to the rocky ground.

Another gunman, hidden in the rocks alongside the tracks, opened fire, the slugs howling off the sides of the cars.

Smoke yelled, "Get these pilgrims down on the floor, Sally." To the brakeman, who had hauled out a pistol and was trying to find a target, he called, "How far to the next water stop?"

"Too far," the man said. "We got to water and fuel here or we don't make it."

"We'll make it," Smoke told him, pulling out his second .44 and jacking back the hammer.

One outlaw tried to run from the darkness to the locomotive. Either the engineer or the fireman shot him dead.

"How far is this payroll going?" Smoke asked, crouching down.

"All the way to the end of the line, up in Montana."

He knew the end of the line, at that time, was near Gold Creek. They would change trains before then. Smoke plugged a running outlaw and knocked him sprawling; but it wasn't a killing shot. The man jumped up and limped off. "Why in the hell doesn't the railroad put guards on these payroll shipments?"

"Beats me, Smoke. But I'm damn sure glad you decided to ride my train for this trip."

The pounding of horses' hooves punctuated the night. The outlaws had decided to give it up.

17

"Let's see what we got," Smoke said, shoving out empties and reloading as he walked over to the man he'd knocked off the water tower.

The man was dead. He'd landed on his head and broken his neck. He walked over to the man the engineer had shot. He was also dead. The third man Smoke had dropped was gut-shot and in bad shape, the slug blowing out his left side, taking part of the kidney with it. He looked up at Smoke.

"You played hell, mister. What's your name? I'd like to know who done me in."

"Smoke Jensen."

The man cussed. "Val sure picked the wrong train this time."

"Val Singer?" Smoke asked.

"Yeah. You know him?"

"I know him. Me and him . . ." Smoke broke it off as he looked down at the man. He was dead, his eyes wide open, staring at the cloudy sky. He looked over at the brakeman. "I winged another. Let's see if we can find him."

But he was gone. Smoke tracked a blood trail to where the outlaws had tied their horses. "He made the saddle. But as bad as he's bleeding, he won't last long. I must have hit the big vein in his leg."

The fireman walked up, his face all dark with soot. "Lem, you wanna toss them bodies in the baggage car and keep on haulin'?"

"I ain't having that crud in with me," the guard to the gold shipment said, walking up. He had not taken part in the fight because in case of an attempted robbery, he was under orders not to open the doors to anyone. "Toss 'em in with the wood and tote 'em that way."

Smoke shrugged his shoulders and helped wrap the men in blankets and carry them to the wood car. Back in his seat, Sally asked, "You suppose we'll have any more trouble?"

Smoke pulled his hat brim down over his eyes and settled down for a nap. "Not from that bunch," he said.

They changed trains in southern Idaho, staying with the

Union Pacific line. This run would head straight north. End of track would put them about a hundred and fifty miles south of their destination.

The news had spread up and down the line that Smoke Jensen was on the train, and crowds gathered at every stop, hoping to get a glimpse of the West's most famous gunfighter. Smoke stayed in the car while the train was in station. He had never sought publicity and didn't want it now.

No more attempts were made to rob the train during the long pull north.

At end of track, Smoke off-loaded their horses while Sally changed from dress to jeans.

Packhorse loaded, they rode into the small town and purchased a side of bacon and some bread, a gaggle of kids and dogs right at their heels all the way.

"Right pleased to have you in town," the shopkeeper told them. "Sorry you can't stay longer. Things liven up quite a bit when you're around, I'd guess, Mr. Jensen. Be good for business."

"It usually is for the undertaker," Smoke told him, and that shut him up.

Smoke signed his name to a half-dozen penny dreadfuls, then he and Sally hit the trail, pointing their horses' noses north.

A young would-be tough, two guns tied down low, stepped out of the saloon and watched the Jensens ride out of town. He pulled his hat brim low, hitched at his guns, and said, "Huh! He don't look so tough to me. It's a good thing he didn't get in my way. I'd a called him out and left him in the street."

The town marshal looked at the kid, disgust in his eyes, then shoved the punk into a horse trough, guns and all, and walked away, leaving the big-mouth sputtering and cussing.

Smoke and Sally made their first camp alongside a fast-running and very clear and cold little creek. It didn't take either one of them very long to bathe. They knew it was time to exit the creek when they began turning blue.

They were up before dawn. After bacon and bread and

coffee, Sally strapped on her short-barreled .44, and then they were in the saddle and heading north.

They were both ready for a hot bath and food they didn't have to cook over a campfire when they topped a ridge and looked down on a little town just south of Flathead Lake.

"Well," Sally said, straightening her back. "It has a hotel."

"Yeah," Smoke said with a grin. "And I'll bet they change the sheets at least once a month."

She smiled sweetly at him. "I'll bet they change them for me."

"Oh, yes, ma'am!" the desk clerk said, paling slightly as he checked the names on the register. "The feather ticks was just aired out and we'll get fresh linen on your bed pronto. You bet we will, Mrs. Jensen."

"And make sure the facilities are clean," Sally told him.

"Oh, yes, ma'am. I sure will."

The room was clean and it faced the street. Smoke laid out clean clothes and shook out and hung up one of Sally's dresses while she bathed. He looked out the window and was not surprised to see a crowd gathering on the boardwalks below their room. Neither was he surprised to see the sheriff and two deputies among the gawking people. The desk clerk had not been slow in running his mouth.

He bathed and shaved while Sally got herself all fixed up, then dressed in a dark suit, white shirt, and string tie. He strapped on his .44's and they went down to the dining room for an early supper.

Smoke got a shot of whiskey from the bar for himself and a glass of wine for Sally, then rejoined his wife in the dining room. The sheriff approached them.

"Mind if I join you for a moment?" the lawman asked respectfully, his hat in his hand.

Smoke pushed out a chair with one boot.

"Coffee, Marie," the sheriff ordered.

"Nice little town, Sheriff," Sally said, taking a sip of wine.

"Thank you, ma'am. And it's peaceful, too."

Smoke knew his cue when he heard it. "It'll stay peaceful, too, Sheriff. We're here to rest for the night and then we'll be moving on."

20

"Nothin' is peaceful around you for very long, Jensen," the sheriff said. "You attract trouble like honey does flies."

"We don't have any trouble in the town near where I live," Smoke rebutted. "Hasn't been a shot fired in anger in a long, long time."

"How do you manage that?"

"We get rid of the troublemakers, Sheriff. It's really very simple."

"You run them out of town, eh?"

"We usually bury them," Sally said.

The sheriff cut his eyes to her. Strong-willed woman, he reckoned. Man would be hard-pressed to hold the reins on this one, he figured.

He'd of course seen them riding into town, her astride that mare and packing a pistol. Way she carried it, the sheriff figured she knew how to use it. And, more importantly, would use it.

"There's some pretty randy ol' boys in this town, Smoke. Some of them would like to make a reputation. I thought I'd warn you."

"The only way they're going to get to me, Sheriff, is if they come into the lobby of this hotel and call me out while I'm reading the newspaper, come in here while I'm eating and call me out, or try to backshoot me when I'm pulling out in the morning."

"And if they call you out? . . ."

"Then I guess the local undertaker is going to get some business, Sheriff."

"The one that'll more than likely try to crowd you is called Chub. He's a bad one, I'll give him that. He's killed a couple of men and wounded a couple more in face-downs. He's quick, Jensen."

'I'll bear that in mind, Sheriff."

The sheriff drank his coffee and eyeballed Smoke. Wrists as big as some men's forearms. And his upper arms; Lord have mercy! The man had muscle on top of muscle. The sheriff had heard of Smoke Jensen for years, but this was the first time he'd ever seen him. And as far as the sheriff was concerned, it was a sight that he'd not soon forget.

The sheriff pushed back his chair and stood up. "See you, Jensen. Ma'am."

"See you around, Sheriff," Smoke told him just as the waitress put their dinner in front of them.

"Smells good," Smoke said.

"Then you'd better enjoy it, mister," a small boy said, walking up to the table. " 'Cause Chub Morgan told me to tell you he was gonna kill you just as soon as you got done eatin'."

3

Smoke looked at the boy. "You go tell Chub I said to calm down. When I finish eating and have my brandy, I'll step outside to smoke my cigar on the boardwalk. I get testy when people interrupt my dinner."

"Yes, sir."

Smoke gave the boy a coin. "Now get off the streets, boy."

"Yes, sir."

But Smoke knew he wouldn't. The boy would gather up all his friends and they'd find them a spot to watch. A shooting wasn't nearly the social event a good hanging was, but it would do. Things just got boring in small western towns. Folks had been known to pack lunches and dinners and drive or ride a hundred miles for a good hanging. And a double hanging was even better.

"Who is Chub Morgan, honey?" Sally asked.

"I have no idea, Sally. But I'll tell you what he's going to be as soon as I finish my food."

She looked at him. "What?"

"Dead."

Smoke had his coffee and a glass of brandy, then bought a cigar and stepped outside. Sally took a seat in the lobby and read the local paper.

It was near dusk and the wide street was deserted. All horses had been taken from the hitchrails and dogs had been called home. Smoke lit his cigar and leaned against an awning support.

He had played out this scene many times in his life. and Smoke knew he was not immortal. He'd taken a lot of lead in his life. And he would rather talk his way out of a gunfight than drag iron. But he was realist enough to have learned early that with some men, talking was useless. It just prolonged the inevitable. Smoke also knew—and had argued the belief many times with so-called learned people—that some men were just born bad, with a seed of evil in them.

And there was only one way to deal with those types of people.

Kill them.

Smoke puffed on his cigar and waited.

A cowboy rode into town and reined up at the saloon. He dismounted, looked around him, and spotted Smoke Jensen, all dressed in a black suit with the coat brushed back, exposing those deadly .44's.

The cowboy put it all together in a hurry and swung back into the saddle, riding down to the stable. He wanted his horse to be out of the line of fire.

After stabling his horse, the cowboy ran up the alley to the rear of the saloon and slipped inside. Everybody in the place, including the barkeep, was lined up by the windows.

"What's goin' on?" the cowboy called.

"Chub Morgan's made his brags about killin' Smoke Jensen for years. He's about to get his chance. That there's Smoke Jensen over yonder in the black suit."

The cowboy pulled his own beer and walked to the window. "You don't say? Damn, but he's a big one, ain't he? What's he doin' in this hick town?"

"Him and his wife rode in a couple hours ago. She's a pretty little thing. Right elegant once she got out of them men's britches and put on a proper dress. Packs a .44 like she knows how to use it."

"Jensen doesn't seem too worried about facin' Chub," the cowboy remarked.

"Jensen's faced hundreds of men in his time," an old rummy said. "He's probably thinkin' more about what he's gonna have for breakfast in the mornin' than worried about a two-bit punk like Chub."

"Chub's quick," the cowboy said. "You got to give him that. But he's a fool to face Jensen."

"Yonder's Chub," the barkeep said.

Smoke, still leaning against the post, cut his eyes as a man began the walk down the street. As the man drew nearer, Smoke straightened up. He held his cigar in his left hand, the thumb of his right hand hooked under his belt buckle.

"He's gonna use that left hand .44," the cowboy said. "Folks say he's wicked with either gun."

"Reckon where his wife is?"

"Foster from the store said she was sitting in the lobby, readin' the newspaper," the barkeep said.

"My, my," the cowboy said. "Would you look at Chub. He's done went home and changed into his fancy duds."

Smoke noticed the fancy clothes the punk was wearing. He'd blacked his boots and shined his spurs. Big rowels on them; looked like California spurs. His britches had been recently pressed. Chub's shirt was a bright red; looked like satin. Had him a purple bandana tied around his neck. Even his hat was new, with a silver band.

Smoke waited. He knew where Sally was sitting; he'd told her where to sit, with a solid wood second-floor support to her back to stop any stray bullet. Not that Smoke expected any stray bullets from Chub's gun. He doubted that Chub would even clear leather. But one never really knew for sure.

Smoke watched the man approach him and, for another of the countless times, wondered why a man would risk his life for the dubious reputation of a gunfighter.

"Jensen!" Chub called.

"Right here," Smoke said calmly.

"Your wife's a real looker," Chub said, a nasty edge to the words. "After I kill you, I'll take her."

Smoke laughed at the man. Chub's face grew red at the laughter. He cursed Smoke.

Smoke was suddenly tired of it. He wanted a good night's sleep, lying next to Sally. He hadn't ridden into town looking for trouble, and he resented trouble being pushed upon him. He was just damned tired of it.

"Make your play, punk!" Smoke called.

Chub's hands hovered over his pearl-handled guns. "Draw, Jensen!" he shouted.

"I don't draw on fools," Smoke told him. "You called me out, Chub, remember? Now, if you don't have the stomach for it, turn around and go on back home. I'd rather you did that."

"Then you a coward!"

Smoke waited, his eyes unblinking.

"You a coward, damn you!" Chub hollered. "Draw, damnit, draw!"

Smoke's cold, unwavering eyes bored into the man's gaze.

"How's it feel to be about to die?" Chub called, trying to steel himself for the draw.

"I wouldn't know, Chub," Smoke's voice was calm. "Why don't you ask yourself that question?"

The sheriff and his two deputies watched from the small office and jail.

"Now!" Chub yelled, and his hands closed around the butts of his guns.

Smoke drew, cocked, and fired with one fluid motion. A draw so fast that it was only a blur. Blink, and you missed it.

The .44 slug took Chub in the center of the chest, knocking him off his boots and down to his knees in the dusty street. His hands were still on the butts of his guns. The guns were still in leather.

"Good God!" the cowboy said. "I never even seen him draw."

The sheriff and his deputies stepped out of the office just as the boardwalks on both sides of the street filled with people.

Smoke stepped off the porch and walked to the dying Chub. He held a cocked .44 in his right hand.

Sally had risen from her seat to stand at the window, watching her man.

Chub raised his head. Blood had gathered on his lips. His eyes were full of anguish. "I . . . never even seen you draw," he managed to gasp.

"That's the way it goes, Chub," Smoke told him just as the lawman reached the bloody scene.

Chub tried to pull a pistol from leather. The sheriff reached down and blocked the move.

"Bastard!" Chub said. It was unclear whom he was cursing, Smoke or the sheriff.

A local minister ran up. "Are you saved, Chub?"

"Hell with you!" Chub said, then toppled over on his side. He closed his eyes and died.

The sheriff looked at Smoke. "Now what?"

Smoke shrugged his shoulders as he punched out the empty and reloaded. "Bury him."

Smoke and Sally rode out before dawn. The hotel's dining room had not even opened. They would stop along the way and make breakfast.

"Why do they do it, Smoke?" Sally broke the silence of the gray-lifting morning.

Smoke knew what she meant. "I've never understood it, Sally. Men like Chub must be very unhappy men. And very shallow men. Let's get off the trail and follow this creek for a ways," he changed the subject. "See where it goes."

The creek wound around and lead them to the Swan River. There they stopped and cooked breakfast. "Fellow back at the hotel said the Swan would lead us right to Hell's Creek. We may as well stay with the river. There are two more little towns between here and Hell's Creek. He said it was right at a hundred miles."

"You've been in this country before?"

"Not right here. It's all new to me. But you can bet the news of the failed train robbery has reached Huggins by now."

"You think any of those men recognized you?"

"I doubt it. But the news of our heading north reached Huggins the day after we boarded the train in Denver. But I doubt he knows we're heading for Hell's Creek."

"I'm sorry I pushed this on you, Smoke."

"You didn't push anything on me, Sally. You want to visit an old friend who's in trouble. That's your right. And anybody who tries to prevent you from doing that is wrong.

If they try to stop you, they'll answer to me. It's as simple as that."

She leaned over and kissed him on the cheek. "Everything will always be black and white to you, won't it, honey? No gray in the middle."

"I know what's right, and I know what's wrong. Lawyers want to make it complicated when it isn't. We'll see your friend and her husband and help them work out their problems."

"Legally?"

Smoke munched on a piece of crisp bacon. "Depends on whether you interpret legal by using common sense or what a lawyer would think, I reckon."

Smoke and Sally followed the river north. Two days later they crossed the river and rode into a small village located on the east side of the Swan. There was no hotel in the village but there was a lady who took in boarders. Smoke and Sally got them a room and cleaned up.

The town marshal was waiting on the front porch of the boarding house when Smoke stepped out for some fresh air while supper was being cooked.

"Mr. Jensen," the marshal said respectfully.

"Afternoon," Smoke replied, then waited.

"I got to ask," the marshal finally said. "You in town trouble-huntin'?"

"No. You can relax. I don't hunt trouble. Me and my wife are just passing through."

The marshal sighed. "That's a relief. I thought maybe you was on the prod for Jake Lewis."

"Who is Jake Lewis?"

The marshal looked startled. "One of the men who survived that shoot-out you had some years ago. Over to that minin' camp on the Uncompahgre."

It was Smoke's turn to look startled. "I didn't know there were any survivors."

"Only one that I know of. Jake Lewis. And you shot him all to hell and gone. There was fifteen men in that camp. You killed fourteen of them. Jake lived. He hid in a privy 'til you rode out."

"It's news to me, Marshal. I know he wasn't one of the men who raped and killed my wife and killed our baby. I know that for a fact."

"No, sir. He sure wasn't. He joined up with Canning and Felter later. Jake's brother was known as Lefty. You killed him in the shoot-out."

"I have no quarrel with Jake, Marshal. You can tell him that."

"Why don't you tell him, Mr. Jensen? It would sure set his mind to ease."

"Where is he?"

"Down at the saloon."

Smoke stared hard at the marshal, wondering if he were being set up.

The marshal picked his thoughts out of the air. "I run a clean town, Mr. Jensen. I don't take no payoffs from nobody and never will. This ain't no setup. But I got to warn you that Jake is armed, and he ain't drinkin'."

"What you're telling me is that you don't know what he might do, right?"

The marshal exhaled slowly. "That's about it, Mr. Jensen. He may throw down on you. I just don't know."

"But you want it settled one way or the other?"

"Yes. Jake's been livin' with this for a long time. Lately, it's been eatin' at him. When he heard you was on the rails, comin' north, he about went out of his mind with worry."

"Does he know Big Max Huggins?"

"I got to tell you that he does. He spends some time up in Hell's Creek."

"So he hasn't changed his ways much, right?"

"He ain't never caused no trouble around here. You know how it is, Mr. Jensen. I ain't got no warrants on him."

The marshal's authority ended at the edge of town.

Sally had stepped out on the porch to listen. Smoke turned and met her eyes. "Be careful," she said. "I'll save a plate for you."

Smoke nodded and slipped the hammer thongs from his

.44's. He stepped off the porch and looked at the marshal. "You walk with me. If this is a setup, I'll take you out first."

"That's fair. If this is a trap, it ain't one of my doin'."

Smoke believed him, and he told him so as they walked up the street to the village's only saloon.

"Does Big Max ever get down this far south?"

"Not no more," the marshal said. "I killed one of his men several years ago and got lead in another one. I ain't the fastest man around with a gun, but I shoot straight."

"That's the most important thing. His men stay out of your town?"

"That's it. I allow any man one mistake. He leaves after the second one. Or he stays forever."

Smoke smiled, finding that he liked this blunt-talking marshal.

They stepped up onto the short boardwalk, walking past a dress shop, a gunsmith, and a large general store. The marshal pushed open the batwings and Smoke stepped into the saloon right behind him.

Jake Lewis stood alone at the bar. The other customers had taken tables. Smoke stared at the man, trying to place him. But the shoot-out at the old silver camp was years behind him, and he could not remember Jake Lewis.

Jake had brushed back his coat, exposing a pistol, the holster tied down. Smoke was curious about that. If the man wanted no trouble, why get set for it? Smoke concluded that Jake was wearing a hide-out gun. Maybe a sleeve gun. Shake his arm and the gun falls into his hand.

Smoke walked to the bar and ordered a beer. Jake turned mean little eyes on him. Jake was no lightweight. He'd hit a good two hundred pounds and looked to be in good shape. About forty years old, Smoke figured.

"You lookin' for me, Jensen?" Jake broke the silence.

"Nope."

"Just happened to ride into town and take a room, hey?"

"That's right."

"I wish I could believe that."

"Believe it. I got no quarrel with you, Jake."

"I wish I could believe that, too."

"You can. The silver camp was long ago. You weren't part of the bunch who killed Nicole and the baby. They're all dead. I know that for a fact."

"I damn near died, Jensen."

"That was your problem. You should have picked better company to run with."

"You sayin' my brother was no good?"

"You walk through a barnyard, you're going to get crap on your boots."

Someone in the seated crowd laughed at that.

Jake's face flushed. "Lefty was a good man."

"He wasn't good enough," Smoke told him.

Jake ordered a drink and sipped at the bourbon. He set the shot glass down and said, "I'm glad you showed up. We can settle this thing once and for all."

"There is nothing to settle, Jake. Nothing at all."

"I think there is. I sure do think that."

"I'm sorry to hear it."

Jake took another small sip of whiskey. "Momma took Lefty's dyin' pretty hard."

"I'm sorry for your mother. Not for Lefty. You keep walking around something, Jake. Get to it. I've got supper waiting at the boarding house."

"Don't crowd me, Jensen."

Smoke chuckled and Jake gave him a queer look. "I came in here to tell you that I wasn't trouble-hunting, and instead of being happy about it, you want to give me a bunch of lip. That shooting in the silver camp was ten years ago, Jake. I wouldn't have known you if you walked in my front door wearing pink tights and totin' a rose between your teeth."

All the men in the room had them a laugh at that. Jake's face tightened and flushed deeper.

"Big Max is waitin' for you up at Hell's Creek, Jensen," he said, grinding his teeth together in anger.

"Yeah? It figures that trash like you would end up rubbing elbows with trash like Huggins."

The crowd fell silent.

Jake slowly turned to face Smoke. "You know what I think, Jensen?"

31

"I'm not even sure you're capable of thinking, Jake. I think you're about as smart as a rock."

Jake curled one big hand around his glass and downed his whiskey. "You're a big man with them guns on, Jensen. What are you with them off? Can you bare-knuckle fight, gunfighter? Or do you have to let them .44's do your talkin' for you?"

"There's sure one way to find out, Jake. Providing you have the stomach for it." Smoke walked toward the man, stopping well within swinging distance.

"We take off our guns together?" Jake asked.

"Just as soon as you get rid of that hide-out pistol you're packing."

Jake grunted and nodded his head. "It's in my sleeve."

"I know it."

Jake shook his arm and the derringer fell out onto the bar. Together, they took off their gunbelts. They faced each other.

"I'm gonna stomp your face in, pretty-boy," Jake bragged.

"I doubt it," Smoke told him, pulling on a pair of leather gloves to protect his hands and to hit harder. He knocked the man down with a quick, hard right.

Smoke stepped back, took a sip of his beer, and said, "You going to lay on the floor all evening, Jake? Come on, hurry up. I have supper waiting for me."

With a roar of rage, Jake jumped to his boots and charged.

4

Jake swung a big fist and Smoke ducked it, at the same time driving his right fist into Jake's gut and stopping him with the blow. Jake backed up and caught his wind.

With a curse, Jake came at Smoke, swinging both fists. Jake was a brawler, Smoke knew then, relying mostly on brute strength with little finesse about him. But he could be dangerous, Smoke reminded himself, if he landed one of those powerful fists.

Smoke danced back, forcing the big man to come after him, using up his wind swinging wildly and cussing.

Smoke saw a chance and took it, popping Jake smack in the mouth with a combination left and right. The blows brought blood and one tooth was knocked out, to roll and bounce on the sawdust floor.

With a howl of rage, Jake charged, both fists flailing, the blows catching Smoke on his arms and shoulders and doing no damage. Smoke back-heeled Jake and sent the man tumbling to the floor. He could have ended the fight right then, by kicking Jake in the mouth. But Smoke stepped back. He felt no anger toward Jake; but, then, he didn't especiallly feel sorry for him, either. He proved that by knocking Jake down just as soon as the man got to his boots.

It was another combination, both blows connecting to the jaw of Jake Lewis this time and knocking him back against the bar. Jake grabbed a bottle of whiskey and hurled it at Smoke. Smoke grabbed the bottle, popped the cork and, with a grin at Jake, took him a sip.

"You son of a . . ." Jake choked back the obscenity. He leaned against the bar, catching his breath.

"You want to quit, Jake?" Smoke asked. "You say so, and we'll have a drink together and call the fight over, with no hard feelings."

"Take him up on it, Jake!" the marshal said. "The man's bein' more than fair."

"You stay out of this," Jake yelled at the marshal. He looked at Smoke. "To hell with you, Jensen!"

Smoke shrugged his shoulders. "Whatever you say, Jake." Then he threw the bottle of whiskey at Jake, the bottle striking the man in the face and busting, spewing whiskey all over Jake and momentarily blinding him.

Smoke stepped up to him and began hitting Jake in the face, his big work-hardened fists like huge hammers as they pounded the man again and again. Jake's nose was broken, one eye closing, his lips smashed to pulp, and his jaw swelling. Smoke pounded the man with more than a dozen blows, then stepped back.

Jake wiped the blood and whiskey out of his eyes and reached down, pulling up his pants leg and jerking a knife out of his boot. "Now, Jensen, you get your guts spread all over the room."

The marshal jerked iron and jacked back the hammer. "Drop the knife, Jake," he warned. "This is a fair fight and it's one that you wanted. You either drop the knife, or I'll kill you."

With a disgusted snarl, Jake tossed the knife to one side.

"Now you made me mad, Jake," Smoke told him. "Now you get what you've probably had coming to you for a long time." Smoke walked toward the man, his big hands clenched.

Jake lifted his fists and decided to use what boxing skills he had. He swung a roundhouse blow at Smoke, which would have knocked Jensen to the floor had it connected. Smoke grabbed the wrist with both hands, turned to one side, and Jake found himself flying through the air. He crashed through a front window and bounced off the boardwalk.

Smoke stepped out the batwings and was all over Jake.

Smoke hit the man twice in the belly, doubling him over. He grabbed Jake behind the head and brought his face down and his knee up. The knee connected squarely, and what was left of Jake's nose was now spread all over his face.

Smoke backhanded Jake, knocking him off the board-walk and into the horse-crap by the hitchrail. One startled horse kicked Jake in the butt and sent him rolling and squalling into the middle of the street.

Smoke didn't let up. He had given the man a chance to not fight at all. Jake turned it down. Then Jake had shown his true colors by pulling a knife. To hell with him!

Jake staggered to his feet and feebly raised his fists. Smoke looked at the beaten man with blood dripping from his face and lowered his fists. He turned his back to Jake Lewis and walked back into the saloon. Jake sank to his knees in the street and tried to get up. He could not.

"Couple of you boys go out there and toss him into a horse trough," the marshal ordered. "Then I'll tell him to get the hell gone from town and don't come back." He looked at Smoke. "You'll have to kill that man someday, Jensen. You know that, don't you?"

"I hope not," Smoke said, then ordered a mug of cool beer.

"You will," the marshal stated flatly. "You humiliated him, and men like Jake can't live with that. It eats on them like a cancer."

Smoke drank half his beer. "He'll have to come looking for me if he wants a killing. As far as I'm concerned, it's over."

Smoke drained his mug and walked back to the boarding house. He needed a hot bath.

The man and wife rode out of town before dawn the next morning and made camp at noon. Sally heated water for

Smoke to soak his hands in to keep down the swelling.

They stayed in camp for two days, relaxing, fishing, and behaving like a couple of kids. They walked through the woods, went skinny-dipping in a creek, and loved every minute of it. The swelling went down in Smoke's hands, and they packed up and pulled out, heading north toward Hell's Creek, following the Swan.

Two days later they rode into a small town at the south end of a lake. They were a couple of hours ride away from Hell's Creek. Their welcome in the town was slightly less than cordial. When they tried to check into the small hotel, they were told all the rooms were taken.

"Is there a boarding house?" Sally asked.

"It's full, too," the desk clerk at the hotel told them.

"Must be a convention in town," Smoke said dryly, looking around him at the deserted hotel lobby. "Sure are a lot of people stirring about."

Sally tugged at his sleeve. "Let's go, honey. We can camp outside of town."

"You don't know how the game is played, Sally," Smoke told her. "The word's gone out on us from Big Max. These people here are scared to death of him. I've seen a few western towns buffaloed before, but this one takes the prize for being full of cowards."

The desk clerk refused to meet Smoke's eyes.

Smoke spun the register book around and inspected it. The hotel was nearly empty.

Smoke dipped the pen and signed them in. He tossed money on the counter. "That's for your best room. Give me the damn key," he told the clerk.

The clerk hesitated, then with a slow exhalation of breath, he handed Smoke the room key.

"Thanks," Smoke told him. "Would you recommend the food in the dining room?"

"Yes, sir," the clerk said wearily. "I would. Dinner is served from five to eight."

"Thank you. You're a nice fellow."

Five minutes after checking in and finding their room, a knock came at the door. Two mean-eyed and unshaven men, both wearing deputy sheriff's badges, stood in the hall.

"You don't come into this town throwin' your weight around, Jensen," one told him. "You're goin' to jail."

"On what charge?"

"We'll think of something," the second deputy said. "And we'll see that your woman is taken care of, too."

Smoke hit him with a sneaky left. The blow snapped the man's head back and knocked him against the hall wall. Smoke backhanded the other deputy, spun, and knocked the second man down with a hard right to the mouth. He grabbed the stunned deputy he'd just slapped by the nape of the neck and the seat of his pants, propelled him down the hall, and threw him out the second-story window. The man landed on the awning, bounced once, and then rolled off, to land on the dusty street. He did not move. One leg was bent under him, broken.

Smoke ran back up the hall, jerked up the stunned and clearly frightened other so-called deputy sheriff, and gave him his exit-papers the same way. Smoke hurled him out the window, using all his strength, which was considerable. The man fell screaming, missing the awning and landing in the street on his belly, one arm bent under him. The sound of the arm breaking was nearly as loud as a pistol shot. Like his buddy, he did not move.

A crowd began gathering, looking at the two so-called lawmen and stealing glances up at Smoke, who was standing in the hall and glaring out the broken window.

"We do not wish to be disturbed," Smoke called down to the crowd. "I'll kill the next man who bothers us." He turned and walked back to the room. He smiled at Sally. "That's how you play the game, honey," he told her.

"My, my," she said with a grin. "The things I'm learning on this trip."

"Your education is just starting. It'll really get interesting in Hell's Creek. I'll order up some hot water and you can take your bath. You tell me which one, and I'll shake out and hang up your dress."

Smoke loaded up the usually empty cylinder he kept under the hammer and walked downstairs to the clerk. The lobby was filled with people.

"Send a boy upstairs with hot water," he told the room clerk. "Lots of it. My wife wishes to bathe. And she damn well better be left alone while she's doing it."

"Y . . . y . . . yes, sir," the clerk stammered.

"Who was that trash I threw out the window?"

"Big Max Huggins men," a portly man said, stepping up. "Duly appointed deputies. By me. I'm Judge Garrison. And you're in a lot of trouble here, young man. We don't like ruffians coming into our town stirring up trouble."

Smoke slapped him. The blow knocked the man back, one side of his face reddening and blood leaking out of one corner of his mouth. The judge stumbled on a couch and fell down, landing heavily on his butt.

"So Max bought you, too, huh?" Smoke said, looking down at the scared judge, the sarcasm thick in the words. "Looks like he's got the whole damn town in his pocket."

"Not all of us," another man spoke up.

"You sure could have fooled me."

"You've brought us a lot of trouble, Mr. Jensen," another man said. "Come the morning, Big Max will be riding in here to settle up. Not just with you, but with all of us."

"Poor scared little sheep," Smoke said, looking at the knot of men. "Do you have to ask Big Max's permission to go to the bathroom?"

"Smoke," the citizen who first spoke said, "Max has got a hundred men up yonder in Hell's Creek. They's maybe thirty-five of us in town who'd stand up to them. Them ain't very good odds."

"Thirty-six," Smoke told him. "Thirty-seven counting my wife. And she's got more guts than any of you have shown me. How'd all this buffaloing come about?"

"Huggins killed our marshal and put in his own law," the citizen said. "Then he burned out or beat up anyone who tried to stand up to him. We used to have a paper here in town. The editor was killed. The minister over to the church was taken out one night and horsewhipped and tarred and feathered. Two of our women was molested by Max's men. A few of us stayed; most left."

"We're not cowards, Mr. Jensen," yet another citizen said. "We've all fought Indians and outlaws and scum. But Max has threatened our children. He ain't never come right out and done it plain. But we all got the message."

"How do you mean?"

"My little girl come home with a sack of candy. Told her ma and me that a man give it to her. Said that next, if I didn't stop bad-mouthin' Max, they might take a little walk in the woods. We got the message."

Smoke said, "You all wait right here. I got an idea." He went back upstairs and peeked in the bathroom. Sally was up to her neck in suds. "Now there is a nice sight."

She made a face at him.

"You reckon Robert and Victoria have made it known that we're coming to see them?"

"Absolutely not. I told them not to say a word about it, and they won't."

"How about the letters you've sent them? The people at the post office will be on Max's payroll."

"They were sent to Kalispell. Robert goes there once a week to see patients."

Smoke winked at her. "Good girl."

"What's up, Smoke? I know that look in your eyes."

"We're going to stay here for a time. I got an idea."

"Suits me."

Smoke shut the door and let her finish her bath. He walked downstairs. He pointed to the judge, who was sitting on a couch, holding a wet cloth to his face. "Get up," he told him. The judge got up.

"One of you men go to the marshal's office and get me a marshal's badge."

Grinning, a man ran out the door and jogged across the street. The two deputies were still lying in the street, moaning and calling out for help.

Smoke faced the judge. "Are you a real judge? Commissioned by this territory?"

"I certainly am! And I'm going to swear out a warrant for your arrest . . . you hooligan!"

Smoke popped him again, staggering the man, rocking

39

him back on his feet. This time the judge was really scared and his expression showed it.

"Oh, you're going to be issuing arrest warrants, Garrison," Smoke told him. "But probably for the first time in a long time, they're going to be legal warrants." He turned to a man. "Go outside and get me one of those deputy sheriff's badges from that crud in the street."

"Yes, sir!" the citizen said, not able to hide his grin.

The judge began to put it all together then, and his face became shiny with fear-sweat. "You won't get away with this, Jensen," he said.

Smoke smiled at him. "You wanna bet?"

"He did what?" Big Max Huggins yelled, rising from his chair behind the desk.

"He's the marshal down at Barlow," the gunhand repeated. "And it was all done legal. Judge Garrison signed the order creating a special election and the citizens voted him in. And that ain't all. The judge also swore him in as a deputy sheriff. That was done after Jensen whupped the hell out of Bridy and Long. Tossed 'em both out of a second-story winder at the ho-tel. Bridy's got a busted leg and Long's right arm is broken. That's in addition to a bunch of bruises and cuts. They stove up for a long time."

Big Max Huggins nodded his big head, sat back down, and pondered these new events. Big Max did not get his name from the size of his feet, although they were large. He was large. Six six and two hundred eighty pounds. A handsome man, Max was also vain about his looks. He dressed carefully and neatly and never missed a day shaving. He was intelligent with a criminal's cunning. He was also a very cruel man.

And right now, he was a puzzled man. "What does Jensen want?" he mused aloud.

The gunhand who had brought him the news stood in silence and shook his head.

"Jensen's got him a big fine ranch down in Colorado. He married into old New England money; his wife's as rich as a

40

king. Or queen," he added. "Supposed to be a real looker, too. The way I hear it, the only time Jensen leaves the ranch is when he takes a notion to stick his nose into someone else's business. He ruined Dooley Hanks a couple of years back. Just like he did Jud Vale last year. Right here in this territory. Now he's ten miles away and packin' a badge. That means he's come after me. But why?"

The gunhand knew that no reply was expected. He stood quiet.

Max leaned back in his chair. "Somebody sent for him," he finally said. "But who? Had to be somebody down in Barlow."

Max stood up and reached for his guns. "Get the boys. We're riding."

The gunhand grinned. "Down to Barlow, boss?"

"Where else? I'm going to settle Smoke Jensen's hash once and for all."

5

Big Max rode into Barlow at the head of a small army. He had fifty men behind him, all heavily armed. They kicked up enough dust riding into town to put a thin cover of dirt on every storefront.

Max dismounted and walked to the boardwalk in front of the marshal's office. He turned to face his men, and the instant his back was to the office, he felt the twin barrels of a sawed-off shotgun pressing into his back.

"Move, and I'll scatter your guts all over the street, Huggins," the voice told him.

Max froze. He knew what an express gun could do. A sawed-off shotgun could literally blow a man in two. "I'm froze," he told the voice. "You Smoke Jensen?"

"That's me. Now tell your men to drop their guns in the street. Every gun they've got. In the dirt."

"And if I don't?"

The muzzle of the shotgun nudged his back. That was all it took.

Max gave the order.

Men began appearing out of stores, all of them armed with rifles or shotguns, all of them with pistols belted around their waists.

Women came out after them, holding buckets of water and rags.

"What the hell? . . ." Max said.

"Your men created all this dust in town," Smoke told him.

"So your men are going to clean it up. They're going to wash all the windows, sweep the boardwalks, and wipe down everything."

"I'll be goddamned if I will!" a gunny said, sitting his saddle.

Smoke stepped to one side and let one barrel of the express gun roar. It belched smoke and flame, and the mouthy gunhand was blown out of the saddle. He landed about ten feet behind his rearing and frightened horse, hitting the dirt in a bloody pile of torn flesh.

Holding the shotgun in his right hand, Smoke palmed one of his .44's and stuck the muzzle to Max's ear. "Give the order," Smoke told him, his voice very cold and deadly.

Max swallowed with an audible gulp. He was a hard man in a hard land and he'd known some salty ol' boys in his time. But none as hard as this man holding a .44 to his head. Smoke Jensen was death walking around.

"You boy's get to cleaning," he told his men. "I'm paying you and you take orders from me. Do it."

"And drag that trash out of the street and bury it," Smoke said. He looked at a citizen who'd introduced himself as Tom Johnson. "You get some boys and gather up their guns, Tom. All of them. And take their rifles from the saddle boots. Bring them to me at the jail." He lowered and holstered his .44 and jerked Max's guns from leather. "In my office, Max. Move."

Seated, Max studied Jensen. And he was impressed. Smoke was about four inches shorter than him and probably weighed sixty pounds less, but he was a hell of a man, Max concluded. No doubt about that.

"You won the first little skirmish, Smoke," Max told him. "But you can't win the war."

Smoke poured them both coffee and sat down behind the desk. "What war, Max?" he asked innocently. "I did what I did in this town because I don't like to see citizens bullied, and I especially don't like to hear about children being threatened."

Max grunted. "There . . . may have been some incidents where my men got a little heavy-handed. But as far as I know, no kids have been harmed."

"But if you continue, Max, they will be. The odds are tilted that way."

"And you intend to do what about that?" Max challenged the gunfighter.

"For the good of humanity, I ought to just stop it right now."

"How?" Max smiled the question.

"By killing you," Smoke said bluntly.

Max studied Smoke Jensen carefully. He concluded that Smoke meant what he'd just said. He also concluded that if he was to leave this town alive, he'd better play his cards close to the vest. Very close.

Max was a cold-blooded killer. But he was an intelligent one. He knew he was sitting very close to the grave. He also knew that like himself, Smoke Jensen had been born without that one tiny cog in his psyche that prevented man from killing without remorse. But unlike Max, Smoke Jensen had landed on the side of the law. He would always defend the underdog, the poor, the right and just causes.

"Are you?" Max asked softly.

"Am I what?"

"Going to kill me?"

"Probably."

Max felt the cold touch of fear grip his heart.

"Someday," Smoke added.

Max struggled with all his might to contain the emotion of relief that flooded him. He was not accustomed to the sensation of fear. It angered him that just by looking at Smoke Jensen such an emotion could be unleashed within him.

Big Max Huggins knew this, too: Smoke Jensen had to die. And soon.

"But for right now?" Max asked.

"I don't know," Smoke admitted. "But I wouldn't press it if I were you."

"I can't buy you off, can I?"

"No."

"Women?"

"I'm married to a beautiful woman. I have never been unfaithful to her and never will be."

"You're everything I am not, is that it?"

Smoke smiled. "Oh, we're somewhat alike, Max. We just took different paths, that's all."

And damned intelligent, too, Max thought. I'm not confronting some ignoramus. "What is it, specifically, that I do that offends you so?"

Smoke laughed softly. He turned his swivel chair and pecked on the window, pointing. "You missed a spot," he told the red-faced gunhand on the boardwalk with a wet rag in his hand. He turned his attention back to Max. "Everything about you, your type, offends me, Max. You're an intelligent man; could have been a success at anything you tried to do. But you chose to be an outlaw. You've probably been a bully and a thief all your life. You like to humiliate people. You like to grind them down under your boot heel. I'm going to play a game with you, Max. You like games?"

"I'm a gambler, you know that."

"But in my game, Max, if you cheat, you die."

Sweat broke out on Max's face. Goddamn this man! He's sitting there as cool as an icehouse and talking about my death. He glanced out the window. The body of Butch had been removed and another gunhand was sprinkling dirt over the blood-soaked spot on the street. He cut his eyes back to Smoke.

"You see, Max, I don't have to work. My ranch practically runs itself. My wife is very rich. And I have a lot of money personally. Do you have any idea how many thousands and thousands of dollars in reward money I've collected over the years just by shooting wanted men?"

Max personally knew of several dozen wanted men who had gone facedown in the dirt under Smoke's guns. And there were probably a hundred more that he didn't know about. "I know you're a wealthy man, Jensen," he said grudgingly. "What kind of game do you have in mind?"

"You're going to be a solid citizen, Max. You're going to run all the trash out of your town, build a new school, a new church, a new town hall, and be a credit to this territory."

46

"Are you out of your damned mind!" Max almost yelled the question. "If I ran all the scum out of Hell's Creek, there wouldn't be fifty people left."

"That is a fact," Smoke acknowledged.

"You're not going to shoot me now, are you, Jensen?"

"Not unless you push me to it."

"Don't worry, I'm not." The words were bitter on the big man's tongue. He had never kowtowed to anyone in his life. Until this moment. And he didn't like it one bit.

"You want to play the game or not, Max?"

"No." Max's courage was returning after standing on the edge of death. He stood up slowly. "If you shoot me, Jensen, you're going to have to shoot me in the back. And I don't think you'll do that. I'm going to walk outside, gunfighter. I'm going to sit on the bench just outside this office and smoke me a cigar. I'm not going to bother a soul. When my men have finished mopping and scrubbing this crappy little town, we're going to ride out. We won't bother this town again. I'll give my people orders to stay clear. But if you ever come to Hell's Creek, I can't guarantee your safety. Badge or not. That's my deal." He walked out the door and sat down, pulling a cigar out of a breast pocket of his suitcoat and lighting up.

Smoke stood up and stepped outside just as Tom Johnson and several others came walking up, carrying sacks of guns taken from the outlaws.

"Put the weapons in a cell and lock it," Smoke told them.

When that had been done, Smoke locked the front door to his office and walked up the boardwalk, leaving Big Max Huggins sitting quietly and smoking his stogie.

Smoke stopped to inspect the work of Larry Gayle, the New Mexico gunslinger. Gayle turned mean eyes to him.

"I guess I'll have to kill you before long, Larry," Smoke told him.

"You'll try," Larry growled the words at him.

Smoke chuckled and walked on a few yards, stopping at the side of a gunny he didn't know.

"You ain't gonna kill me, Smoke," the man said. " 'Cause just as soon as I get done with this spit-polishin', I'm gone like the wind."

Smoke patted him on the shoulder. "Good man. Find a job and settle down somewhere. Be a good citizen."

"I ain't promisin' that. But I will get gone from wherever you is."

Smoke walked on. He stopped when he spotted Pete Akins, a gunhand he had met down in Arizona about six months back. "You going to stay on Huggins's payroll, Pete?"

"Yep." Pete put the finishing touches on a windowpane. It was so clean it squeaked under the rag.

"There's going to be a lot of blood spilled before this is over, Pete."

"For shore."

"Sorry to hear you're staying. You've never done me a harm. But if you stay, you're my enemy. I just wanted you to know that, Pete."

"You could pull out, Jensen."

"Not likely. I never leave a job unfinished."

"Me neither. Now get on out of here and leave me alone. I got winders to wash."

Chuckling, Smoke walked on. He didn't really dislike Pete Akins. But that wouldn't prevent him from gunning Pete if push came to shove.

He crossed the wide street and stopped by the side of a young man probably still in his late teens. The boy still had a few pimples on his face.

"You better haul your ashes out of here, boy," Smoke told him. "Straighten up while you've got the time."

"I'll see you in hell, Jensen," the punk told him.

"You'll be there long before I pass by, son," Smoke replied, and walked on.

He stopped by Ben Webster, who had finished his windows and was sitting on the boardwalk, smoking a cigarette. "You hire your guns, Ben, but I never knew of you working for someone as low as Big Max Huggins."

"He pays good, Smoke. 'Sides, the man who finally drops you can write his own ticket."

48

"You intend to be that man?"

"Yep."

"Make your will out. Ben. 'Cause when you pull iron on me, I'm gonna kill you."

Ben looked up at him. "That's a risk we take in this business, ain't it, Smoke?"

Smoke stared at the man hard. Ben finally dropped his eyes. "I don't hire my gun, Ben. Not for money."

Ben looked up. "Why then, Smoke? Why do you do it?"

"Because I have a conscience, Ben. And I've got to live with myself."

Ben spat in the street. "I don't have a bit of trouble sleepin' at night. Or in the daytime, for that matter."

"That'll make it easier when you decide to brace me, Ben."

Ben tossed his cigarette into the street and looked away. Smoke walked on. "Sid," he spoke to Sid Yorke.

"Smoke. I ain't gonna forget this damn winder-washin'."

"Least it got your hands clean, Sid. That's probably the first time they've been clean since your mother stopped takin' a belt to your butt."

"There's always a day of reckonin', Jensen. My day's comin'."

Smoke crossed the street and sat on the bench beside Max. Now that he knew he'd live through this day, Max was beginning to see the humor in some of the toughest men in the territory washing windows and mopping up the boardwalk.

He saw Smoke watching him. "Yes, Jensen, I can see the humor in it. But have you thought about this: You've made some rough boys awfully angry at you. And they're going to be sore about this for a long time."

"They'll either get over it or come hunting me. If they come hunting me, they'll be over it permanently."

Max stared at him. "You're that sure of yourself, aren't you, Jensen?"

"I've put more than a hundred men in their graves, Max. I'm still standing."

"How many men have you killed, Jensen?"

49

"I honestly don't know. I would be very happy if I never had to kill another human being."

"Then quit."

"I can't."

"Why?"

"Because of people like you."

That stung the big man. His face darkened with color. He took several deep breaths, calming himself. "I never thought of myself as a bad person, Jensen. And that's the God's truth."

"You have any plans to change, Max?"

"No. And that's the truth, too. Why should I? You won't stay around here long. So I pull in my horns for a summer. So what? What have I lost? No, Jensen. Unless you kill me now, right now, in cold blood, I'll survive. Because you're going to have to come to my town to get me. And you won't last two minutes in Hell's Creek."

"You got it all figured out, huh, Max?"

"I believe so, yes."

"It promises to be an interesting summer, Max."

Max threw his smoked-down cigar into the street and rose from the bench. "I hope I don't see you again, Jensen," he said, with his back to Smoke.

"Oh, you will, Max. You will."

Smoke sat on the bench and watched as the sullen bunch of gunfighters rode slowly out of town, being very careful to kick up as little dust as possible. Only Pete Akins raised a hand in farewell.

With a grin on his face, he called, "See you around, Smoke."

"Take it easy, Pete."

The pimply-faced boy whose name Smoke had learned was Brewer, glared hate at him as he rode past.

"You bear in mind what I said, son," Smoke called to him.

The young man gave Smoke an obscene gesture.

Bringing up the rear of the procession was a wagon, the two bone-broken deputies lying on hay in the bed, groaning as the wagon lurched along.

Tom Johnson crossed the street, leading a group of men and women, Judge Garrison among them.

"Tom, did you send those wires like I asked?" Smoke said.

"Yes, sir. Folks should start arriving in about a week. What about those people in town loyal to Huggins?"

"Tell them to hit the trail, Tom. You're the newly elected mayor."

"How about me?" Judge Garrison asked.

"You're staying, Judge. You and me, we're going to see to it that justice prevails in this part of the county. Tom has arranged for a man to come in and reopen the newspaper. He's got people coming in that include a schoolteacher, a preacher, and some shopkeepers. Barlow is going to boom again, Judge. Nice and legal."

"Young man," the judge said, sitting down on the edge of the boardwalk, "have you given any thought as to what will happen when you decide to leave?"

"Oh, yes."

They waited, but Smoke did not elaborate.

The judge sighed. "I must admit, it's a good feeling to be free of Max Huggins." He cut his eyes to Smoke. "For as long as it lasts, that is."

"Trust me, Judge," Smoke told him, putting a finger to the side of his head. "I've got it all worked out up here." He pulled out his watch and clicked it open. "What times does the stage run?"

"It'll be here in about an hour," Tom told him.

"It turns around at Hell's Creek?"

"That's right."

Smoke smiled. "Well, then, I'll just make plans to meet the stage. Right now, I have to see about finding a deputy."

"That's not going to be easy, Smoke," the judge said. "I don't know of a single person who is qualified. Most of the ranches in this part of the county have only the hands they absolutely need to get by. There's about a dozen farmers in this area. Good people, but not gunslingers."

"Who is that prisoner in the jail? What's he being held for?"

The judge rolled his eyes. "His name is Dagonne. Jim Dagonne. He's not a bad sort; matter of fact, he's rather a likable fellow. He just likes to fight. The problem is, he never can win one. He's a good cowboy. Works hard. But when he starts drinking, he picks fights. And he always loses."

Smoke nodded his head, a smile on his face. "All right, folks, let's get to work. We've got a lot to do."

6

Smoke unlocked the cell door and dragged the sleeping Jim Dagonne out of the bunk. He looked to be in his mid-twenties and in good shape, although not a big man.

"What the hell!" Dagonne hollered as Smoke dragged him across the floor and out the back door.

"Shut up, Jim," Smoke told him. He shoved him in a tub of cold water and tossed him a bar of soap. "Strip and scrub pink. I'll have your clothes washed and dried. Then we'll talk."

"Who the hell are you?" Jim hollered. "You let me out of this tub and I'll whup you all over this backyard."

"Smoke Jensen."

Jim sank into the tub and covered his head with water.

Twenty minutes later, sober and clean, wrapped in a blanket, Jim Dagonne sat in front of Smoke's desk and waited. He did not have a clue as to what Smoke wanted of him.

Smoke stared at the young man. Maybe five feet seven. Not much meat on him, but wiry; rawhide tough. Hard to tell what he looked like, with his face all banged up and both eyes swollen nearly closed, but he appeared to be a rather nice-looking young man.

"You don't have a job, Jim," Smoke finally broke the silence. "The judge said you got fired from the Circle W."

"I probably did. Joe got tired of bailing me out of jail, I reckon."

"Joe who?"

"Joe Walsh. Owns the spread."

"Good man?"

"One of the best. Arrow straight. Are you really Smoke Jensen?"

"Yes." Smoke tapped the gunbelt on his desk. "This yours?"

"Yes, sir."

"Can you use it?"

"I'm not real fast, but I don't hardly ever miss."

"That's the most important thing. You wanted anywhere, Jim?"

"No, sir! I ain't never stole nothing in my life."

Smoke reached down on the floor and picked up a bulky package. He tossed it to Jim. "New jeans, shirts, socks, and drawers in there. Go get dressed. You're my new deputy."

Jim stared at him. "I'm a what?"

"My deputy. Your drinking days are over, Jim. You're now a full-fledged member of the temperance league. You take one drink, just one, and I'll stomp your guts into a greasy puddle in the middle of that street out there, and then I'll feed what's left to the hogs. You understand me?"

"Yes, sir!"

"Fine. Get dressed and go down to Judge Garrison's office. He'll swear you in as a deputy sheriff. Then you meet me back here." He looked at the clock. "Right now, I've got to meet a stage."

"Out," Smoke told the passengers before the stage had stopped rocking. Two hurdy-gurdy girls, a tin-horn gambler, one drummer selling corsets and assorted ladies' wear, and Al Martin, a gunfighter from down Utah way, stepped down.

"You stopping here or going on to Hell's Creek?" Smoke asked the drummer.

"Hell's Creek."

"Get back in the stage. The rest of you come with me."

"And if I don't?" the gambler challenged him.

Smoke laid the barrel of a .44 against the man's head, knocking him to the street. He handcuffed him to a hitchrail, then faced Al Martin.

"You got trouble in you, Al?"

"Probably. I know you, but I can't put a name to the face."

"Smoke Jensen."

Al eyeballed Smoke, his eyes flicking from the badge to his face. The hurdy-gurdy girls stood off to one side.

"Get moving," Smoke told the driver.

"Yes, sir. I'm gone!"

He hollered at the fresh team and rattled up the street.

"I'll just have me a drink and wait for the southbound stage," Al said.

"That's fine. Stay out of trouble." He looked at the saloon girls. "You ladies get you a room at the hotel and stay quiet. You're on the next stage south. It rolls through in the morning."

They wanted to protest. But the name Smoke Jensen shut their mouths. They twirled their parasols, picked up their baggage, shook their bustles, and sashayed down the boardwalk.

"Off the street, Al," Smoke told the gunfighter.

Al tipped his hat, got his grip, and walked into the saloon.

Smoke dragged the gambler to the jail and tossed him in a cell.

"What's the charge, marshal?" the gambler called.

"Disobeying an officer of the law and littering."

"Littering?"

"You were lying in the street, weren't you?"

"Hell, man. You put me there."

"Tell it to the judge. He'll have court sometime this month."

Smoke stepped outside and rolled one of the few cigarettes he smoked a day. He lit up and smiled. It was going to be an interesting summer. He was looking forward to it.

Jim walked up, all decked out in his new clothes and with a shiny badge pinned to his shirt.

"What'd I miss?"

"Not much." Smoke brought him up to date.

"Littering?" Jim laughed. "Now that's a new one on me."

"We'll see what the judge has to say about it."

"Al Martin's a bad one. He's one of Big Max Huggins's boys. He'll try you, Smoke. Bet on that."

"He won't do it but once. Come on. I'll introduce you to my wife and we'll get something to eat."

They were halfway across the street when a dozen men came riding into town from the south, kicking up a lot of dust.

"That's Red Malone and his crew," Jim said. "He likes to ride roughshod over everybody. Owns the Lightning brand. I never worked for him 'cause I don't like him and he don't like me."

Smoke stood in the middle of the street and refused to move, forcing the horsemen to come to a stop.

"Get out of the damn street, idiot!" the lead rider yelled.

"You Malone?" Smoke asked.

"Yeah. If it's any of your business."

"There's a new law on the books, Malone. No galloping horses within the city limits."

Red laughed, and it was an ugly laugh. "I'd like to see the two-bit deputy who's gonna stop me." Then his smile faded. "Hey, you're new here. Didn't your boss tell you that me and the boys are to be left alone?" His face mirrored further confusion when he saw Jim and the badge pinned to his shirt. "What the hell's goin' on around here? You got stomped in a fight a couple of nights ago and got tossed in jail. Where is Bridy and Long?"

"Max come and got them this morning," Jim said with a grin. "They was all stove up after Smoke Jensen here tossed both of 'em out of that window up yonder yesterday." He pointed to the boarded-up window of the hotel.

Red Malone and all his men looked . . . first at the window and then back at Smoke.

"You asked what two-bit deputy was going to stop you, Red?" Smoke said. "You're looking at him."

"Lemme take him, boss," a scar-faced man said. "I think I'm better than him."

Red Malone did not reply; he was studying Smoke

carefully. "Heard about you for years, Jensen. You're supposed to be the fastest gun around. So what are you doing in this hick town?"

"Helping out the people, Malone. They had some bad law enforcement here. They asked me to take over."

"What'd Max have to say about that?"

"Not a whole lot, actually. And his men were too busy washing windows and mopping up the boardwalk to say very much."

Malone silently chewed on that for a moment, not really sure what Smoke was talking about. For a fact, something big had gone down here in Barlow; something that had drastically changed the town.

And that something big and drastic had a name: Smoke Jensen.

"Come on, Red!" the scar-faced man insisted. "Lemme take him." He stepped out of the saddle, handing the reins to another man.

Malone looked at the man. He wasn't worth a tinker's damn as a cowboy, but he was fast with a gun. Malone nodded his head. "All right, Charlie. It's your show."

Red Malone and his crew lifted their reins and moved to the other side of the street.

"Watch my back, Jim," Smoke said.

"You got it."

"I been hearin' about you for fifteen years or more, Jensen," Charlie said. "I'm sick of hearin' about you. Makes me want to puke."

Red Malone cut his eyes to a rooftop. Tom Johnson stood there, a rifle in his hand. Marbly from the general store stepped out of his establishment, also with a rifle in his hands. Benson from the blacksmith shop appeared to Malone's right, a double-barrel shotgun in his hands. Toby from the hotel appeared on a rooftop, carrying a rifle.

The town was solidly behind Jensen, for sure.

Malone turned to his foreman. "John, we're out of this fight. Look around you. Pass the word."

John Steele looked. More townspeople had stepped out of their businesses and homes, all of them carrying weapons.

John softly passed the word: Whatever happens between Jensen and Charlie, we're out of it.

Smoke stood relaxed in the center of the street. He had not taken his eyes off of Charlie.

The scar-faced gunny stood with his legs apart, body tensed for the draw. "You ready to die, Jensen?" he called.

"Not today, friend," Smoke said. "You got anything you want me to pass along after you're gone?"

Charlie cursed him.

"As a legally appointed deputy sheriff of this county, I am ordering you to surrender your guns, Charlie. There will be no charges filed against you if you do that."

Charlie laughed at him.

"You were warned," Smoke said softly.

"Draw!" Charlie yelled, and his right hand dipped down, the fingers closing around the butt of his pistol.

He felt something heavy and hard strike him in the chest. Charlie was on his back in the street, the sun-warmed dirt hot through his shirt. A shadow fell over him. Through the mist that had suddenly covered his eyes, he could see Smoke Jensen standing over him, a pistol in his hand, held by his side, the hammer back.

Charlie fumbled for his gun. He was astonished to find it was still in leather.

"I never seen anybody that fast," John Steele said to his boss. "It was like the wind."

"Yeah," Red reluctantly agreed.

The rest of Malone's bunch, all hard cases in their own right, sat their saddles quietly. They were all brave men, loyal to the brand, and all good with a gun. But they wanted no part of Smoke Jensen. Not face to face, anyway.

"You should have stayed in the bunkhouse today, Charlie," Smoke told the dying man.

"You! . . ." Charlie gasped the word. Then he closed his eyes and died.

Smoke holstered his .44 and walked over to Red Malone. "No trouble in this town, Malone. No racing your horses and kicking up dust. No discharging of firearms. No foul language outside the saloon. Any of your crew gets drunk, you take them home, or me or Jim will put them in jail and the judge will fine them. Is all that understood?"

Hate leaped out of Red Malone's eyes. No one talked to him like that and got away with it.

He stepped out of the saddle without replying and turned his back to Smoke. A hard hand fell on his shoulder and spun him around, almost jerking him off his boots. Smoke Jensen stood staring at him, eyeball to eyeball.

"I asked you a question, Malone. I expect a reply."

Red noticed that Smoke had slipped on leather gloves. "I'll give you a reply, gunslinger," Red said. "and here it is."

Red swung a big fist. Had it connected, it would have knocked Smoke off his boots.

It didn't connect.

Smoke sidestepped and planted one big fist in Red's belly. The air whooshed out of the man as he stumbled back. Smoke stepped in and popped him on the jaw with a left, following that with a right. Red fell back against a hitchrail. He shook his big head and cussed Smoke.

"Anytime you've had enough, Red," Smoke told him, "you just holler quit and that's it."

"I run this end of the county, Jensen," he said, his lips peeled back in an animallike snarl.

Smoke answered him with a sneaky left that snapped Red's head back and bloodied his mouth. Smoke stepped back and waited.

A thin middle-aged cowboy sat his saddle and cut his eyes to John Steele. He whispered, "The boss better uncle, Steele. Jensen's givin' him a chance. If he don't, Jensen'll beat him half to death."

"I got twenty dollars that says you're wrong, Sal," John replied.

"You're on."

Red faked with a left and connected against Smoke's jaw with a right. The punch hurt. Smoke stepped back and shook his head. Red pursued him out into the street, grinning through the blood on his mouth.

Smoke ducked a punch and hammered a right over Red's kidney, following that with an uppercut to the man's mouth. Blood leaked from Red's lips.

Red backhanded Smoke in the face and charged, trying to grab him in a bear hug. Smoke danced to one side and hit Red twice in the face with a left and a right.

Red slipped a fist through and busted Smoke on the jaw, but the punch had lost a lot of steam. Smoke hit him with another combination, belly and jaw, then tripped the man, sending him sprawling to the dirt.

Red came up with a fistful of dirt and hurled it at Smoke, trying to momentarily blind the gunfighter. But Smoke had been raised by mountain men, and he knew all the tricks and then some. He ducked under the dust cloud and rammed Red in the belly with his head, both hands around the man's hard waist. Smoke drove him into a hitchrail. The hitchrail broke under the impact and Smoke released the man just in time to see Red fall into a horse trough.

Smoke stood on the outside of the trough and hammered Red's face into a bloody mask. Red lost consciousness and slipped down into the water, bubbling.

Smoke stepped back, found his hat, and put it on just as John Steele and several others were frantically pulling their boss out of the trough before he drowned.

"Drag him over to the jail and dump him in a cell," Smoke ordered.

"I'll be damned if I will!" Steele shouted at Smoke.

Jim walked up and laid his pistol across the back of the foreman's head, and it was Steele's turn to fall into the trough, face first.

"Drag both of them to jail," Smoke ordered. This time, no objections were forthcoming. The Lightning brand crew dragged the boss and the foreman across the street and into the jail, depositing both of them in a cell.

John Steele opened his eyes and glared hate at everybody. Red Malone snored and bubbled on his bunk.

"Gimme my twenty dollars," Sal said.

John dug in his damp pockets and threw a double eagle at

the man. "Here's your damn money. And here's something else: You're fired!"

"Suits me," Sal said, slipping the twenty-dollar gold piece into his vest pocket. "I'm tarred of listenin' to your big mouth a-flappin' anyways."

"The next time I see you, Sal, you better be ready to drag iron."

The thin bowlegged cowboy lifted his eyes and stared at the foreman. Smoke knew that look; he had worn it himself, many times: It was the look of a very dangerous and very confident man. Smoke smiled, thinking: I've found another deputy.

"You best think about that, John." Sal's words were softly spoken and ringed with tempered steel. "I've helped bury a lot better men than you."

John spat through the bars and cursed him.

Smoke caught Jim's eyes and tapped the star pinned to his shirt, pointing at Sal. Jim grinned and nodded his head in agreement.

Smoke stepped outside and faced the Lightning crew. "You boys can have your drinks at the saloon, buy your tobacco and needs, or whatever else legal you came to town to do. Make trouble, and you'll either join your bosses in there"—he jerked his thumb toward the jail—"or join Charlie in a pine box. The choice is yours."

"We're peaceful, Smoke," a hand said. "But this here is a friendly warnin' to you, and don't take it the wrong way. When you let Red outta there, he's gonna be on the prod for you. And right or wrong, we ride for the brand."

"That's your choice to make. Now, clear the street and drag Charlie off to the undertaker."

Jim and Sal stepped out onto the boardwalk. Smoke turned to the just-fired puncher and said, "You know anything about deputy sheriffing?"

"I've wore a badge a time or two."

"You want a job?"

"Might as well. Seein' as how I done been fired from cowboyin'."

"I have to warn you: It's going to get real interesting around here."

Sal hitched at his gunbelt. "I 'spect it will. Makes the time pass faster, though."

"Lemme out of here, you son of a bitch!" John Steele hollered.

7

"I've had your suit pressed," Sally told him. "We're going to a party tonight."

"Oh?"

"Yes. The ladies of the town are giving us a party. They're all quite taken with you and want to meet you up close."

Smoke rolled his eyes. "I can hardly wait."

Red Malone had woken up and had joined John Steele in bellowing from their cell.

"What are you going to do about that?" Sally asked.

"I can either shoot them, hang them, or cut them loose. What do you suggest?"

"They probably deserve the former. The latter would certainly quiet the town considerably."

"Lay out my suit. I'll go speak with Judge Garrison."

"Oh, let's bond them out," the judge said. "All that squalling is giving me a headache." He smiled. "We'll set the bond at a hundred dollars apiece."

"A hundred dollars!" John Steele recoiled from the bars and screamed like a wounded puma.

"Relax, John," Malone said. The man's face was horribly bruised, both eyes almost swollen shut, his lips puffy, and his nose looked like a big red beet that an elephant had stepped on. He took a wad of still-damp greenbacks from his pocket and carefully counted out two hundred dollars, passing the money through the bars.

Smoke took it and infuriated the man by counting it again.

"It's all there, you son of a . . ." He choked back the oath and stood gripping the bars, shaking with anger.

"Sure is," Smoke said cheerfully. He unlocked the door and waved the men out. "You boys take it easy now. And come back to Barlow anytime, now, you hear?"

The rancher and his foreman did not reply. They stomped out and slammed the door behind them. Smoke sat at his desk and chuckled.

Smoke suffered through the party given by the good ladies of Barlow. He answered the questions—from both men and women alike—as best he could, and ate fried chicken and potato salad until he felt that if he ate another piece, he'd start clacking and laying eggs.

Walking back to the hotel—they had now been moved to the best room in the place, the Presidential Suite, which included a private water closet—Sally said, "Max Huggins had pretty well beaten these people down, hadn't he, honey?"

"Yes. And that first day in town, I came down hard on them—probably too hard. It's easy for someone ruthless to cut the heart out of people. It's ridiculously easy. Max is a smart man as well as a ruthless one. He went after the children of the townspeople. That shows me right there how low he is."

"You'll have to kill him, won't you, honey?"

"Me, or somebody. Yes."

Sal walked up, making his rounds, rattling doorknobs and looking up dark alleyways.

"Quiet, Smoke," the small man said. "I figure it'll be that way for three, maybe five days. Until Red gets back on his feet. And then he'll come gunnin' for you."

"I expect he will, Sal. I doubt if the man has ever received so thorough a beating as he got today."

"Smoke, he ain't never even been whipped before this day. And that's the God's truth."

"Walk along with us, Sal. Tell me about him."

"I ain't from this part of the country, Smoke. I was born in Missouri and come west with my parents in '50, I think it was. They settled in Nebraska and I drifted when I was seventeen. Most of my time I spent in Colorado and Idaho. That's how come it was I knowed who you was. I didn't come to this area until last year. I was fixin' to drift come the end of the month anyways. I just don't cotton to men like Red Malone and John Steele. I'll tell you what I know about him and about Max Huggins. I was told that Malone come into this area right after the Civil War. He was just a youngster, maybe nineteen or so. He carved him out a place for his ranch and defended it against Injuns and outlaws. Built it up right good. But he's always been on the shady side. Lie, cheat, steal, womanize. I was told his wife was a decent person. She bore him one son and one daughter, and then she took off when it got so Red was flauntin' his other women in her face. He's got women all over the country."

Smoke stopped them and they sat down on a long bench in front of the barber shop.

Sal pulled out the makings and asked Sally, "You object, ma'am?"

"Oh, no. Go right ahead. I'll take a puff or two off of Smoke's cigarette."

Sal almost dropped the sack at that. He kept any comments he had to himself. Strong-willed woman, he thought. Probably wants the vote, too. Lord help us all.

Sal rolled, shaped, licked, and lit up. "Red's daughter is a right comely lass. But Tessie is spoiled rotten, has the manners of a hog, and the morals of a billy goat. Melvin is crazy. Plumb loco. He likes to hurt people. And he's fast, Smoke. Have mercy, but the boy is quick. And a dead shot. But he's nuts. His eyes will scare you, make you back up. He's killed maybe half-a-dozen men, and they weren't none of them pilgrims, neither. Red's good with a short gun, but Melvin is nearabouts as fast as you, Smoke. And I ain't kiddin'.

"Naturally, just as soon as Big Max come into the area, him and Red struck a deal. Max would own the law enforcement of the county—and it's a sorry bunch—and control the north end of the county, and Red would control the south end. Red didn't have no interest in runnin' this town. He just wanted his share of the crooked games up in Hell's Creek, and his share of the gold and greenbacks taken in robberies. In return, he'd see that no one come in here with reform on their mind. So that means, Smoke, that you got to go. There ain't no other way for Red and Max to keep on doin' what they're doin'.

"Big Max, now, that's another story. Bad through and through. He's run crooked games and killed and robbed folks and run red-light houses from San Francisco to Fort Worth and north into Canada. He's a sorry excuse for a human being. I'd be happy to kill him if for no other reason than to clear the air for other folks."

"I can see why Max settled here," Smoke said.

"Sure. Wild country. One road runnin' north and south, one road runnin' east and west. No trains yet. Proper law ain't reached this part of the territory yet." He smiled, then added, " 'Cepting in this little town, that is."

The next morning, Smoke escorted the gambler he'd jailed to the stagecoach office. Jim fetched the hurdy-gurdy girls from the hotel.

"You might eventually get to Hell's Creek," Smoke informed them all. "But it won't be by going through Barlow."

"This ain't legal," the gambler protested.

"Sue me," Smoke said, and shoved the tinhorn into the stage. He looked up at the driver. "Get them out of here."

"Yes, sir!" the driver grinned, and yelled at his team.

Smoke began his walk to the hotel to deal with Al Martin. The gunfighter had sent a boy to tell Smoke he wasn't about to be run out of town.

"How are you gonna deal with this guy?" Sal asked.

"He wants to stay in Barlow," Smoke replied. "So I'm going to let him stay."

"Huh?" Jim looked at Smoke.

66

"Forever," Smoke said tightly. "If that's the way he wants it."

Al Martin was lounging on the boardwalk in front of the hotel, having an after-breakfast cigar.

"He's quick," Sal told Smoke. "With either hand. I've seen him work."

Smoke had no comment about that.

Al Martin tossed his cigar into the dirt and stepped out into the street.

"You boys get out of the way," Smoke told his deputies.

Sal and Jim stepped to one side.

Al brushed back his coat, exposing the butts of his .45's.

"One more chance, Al," Smoke called, never breaking his stride. "You can rent a horse at the livery and ride south."

"I'm headin' north," Al returned the call.

"Not through this town," Smoke told him.

"You don't have the right to do that."

"I'm doing it, Al."

Joe Walsh, the owner of the Circle W, had left his ranch early with two of his men, to buy supplies in Barlow. The men stood in front of Bonnie's Cafe and watched. Joe had heard of Smoke Jensen for years, but he had never seen him until now.

He was very impressed by this first sighting. He'd heard of what had happened to Red, and that amused him. If any man had a beating coming to him, it was Red. And Max Huggins. But Joe wondered if Smoke was hoss enough to take the huge Max Huggins.

"Last chance, Al," Smoke called. "I am ordering you to leave this town immediately."

Smoke stopped about forty feet from Al.

"You know where you can stick that order, Jensen."

"Then make your play, Al," Smoke said calmly.

Al went for his guns. He got both barrels of the .45's halfway out of leather before Smoke drew. Smoke shot him twice, in the belly and the chest, the slugs turning the man around and sitting him down in the street, on his butt.

"Holy Mother of Jesus!" Joe Walsh whispered the words.

"He's so quick it was a blur."

His hands shook their heads in awe.

Smoke walked up to Al Martin. The gunfighter looked up at him. "Melvin's quicker, Jensen," he pushed the words past bloody lips. "You'll meet your match with the kid."

"Maybe. But you'll meet your Maker long before that happens."

Al fell over on his side. "Cold," he muttered. "Gimme a decent buryin'," he requested. "One fittin' a human being."

"I would," Smoke told him, his words carrying to both sides of the street, "if you were a decent human being."

"Bastard!" Al cursed him.

"That's a hard man yonder," Joe told his hands. "Probably the hardest man I ever seen."

Al Martin died cursing the name of Smoke Jensen.

Smoke punched out the empty brass and reloaded just as the combination barber/undertaker came walking up.

"What kind of funeral you want him to have, Sheriff?" he asked.

"Whatever his pockets will bear," Smoke told him. "Bring his guns and personal items to the office."

"Them's right nice boots he's wearin'," the man said. "Be a shame to waste that leather."

"Whatever," Smoke said. He walked over to the cafe and stepped up on the boardwalk.

The rancher stuck out his hand. "Joe Walsh," he introduced himself. "I own the Circle W."

Smoke took the hand.

"Good to have some decent law enforcement around here." He looked across the street at Jim Dagonne and grinned. "How'd you get him off the jug?"

"I told him I'd stomp his guts out and feed what was left to the hogs if he ever took another drink."

Joe laughed. "He's a good boy. I would have rehired him in a day or two, but I think he's better off in what you got him doing." He looked at Sal. "That's a good man, too."

"I think so."

"Watch your back when you ride out in the county. Red Malone don't forget or forgive. I'll tell the wife you're in

68

town. You and your missus come out to the ranch anytime for dinner. We'd love the company."

"I'll do it."

Smoke had sized up the rancher and thought him to be a good, hard-working man. And one who would fight if pushed. Probably the reason Red and Max had left him alone. His hands wore their guns like they knew how to use them . . . and would.

Sal walked over. "The undertaker said Al had quite a wad on him. He's gonna hire some wailers and trot out his black shiny wagon for this one. He said the weather bein' as cool as it is, Al can probably stand two days. Ought to be a new preacher in town by that time."

Smoke nodded. "You and Jim watch the town. I'm going to lay in some supplies and take a ride. I'll be gone for a couple of days, getting the lay of the land."

"Watch yourself, Smoke. Red's probably sent the word out for gunhands."

Again, Smoke nodded. "You and Jim start totin' sawed-off shotguns, Sal. Any gunslicks that come in, either move them on or bury them."

"You got it."

"I'll see you in two or three days."

Smoke rode out of the valley and into the high country. The high lonesome, Old Preacher had called it. It pulled at a man, always luring him back to its beauty. The valley was surrounded by high snowcapped peaks, with the lower ridges providing good summer graze for the cattle.

Smoke had checked out the boundaries of the Lightning spread at the surveyor's office, and he carefully avoided Malone's range. Keeping Mt. Evans to his right, Smoke rode toward Hell's Creek. He wasn't concerned about Sally's friends being worried about their not showing up. By now, everyone in the county knew Smoke was in Barlow. He only hoped the doctor and his wife had sense enough to keep their mouths shut about their being friends with Sally.

He rode up to a farmhouse and gave a shout. A man in bib

overalls came out of the barn and took a long look at Smoke. Then he went back in and returned carrying a rifle.

"If you be friendly, swing down and have some coffee," the farmer called. "If you've come to make trouble for us, my woman and my two boys have rifles on you from the house."

"I'm the new marshal at Barlow," Smoke called. "The name is Smoke Jensen."

"Lord have mercy!" the farmer said. "Come on in and put your boots under our table. The wife nearabouts got the noonin' ready to dish up."

"I'm obliged."

The fare was simple but well-cooked and plentiful, consisting of hearty stew made with beef and potatoes and carrots and onions, along with huge loaves of fresh-baked bread. Smoke did not have to be told twice to dive in.

Not much was said during the nooning, for in the West, eating was serious business. The farmer told Smoke his name was Brown, his wife was Ellie, and his boys were Ralph and Elias. And that was all he said during the meal.

After the meal, Ellie poured them all coffee and Smoke brought the family up to date on what had taken place in Barlow.

The farmer, his wife, and his sons sat bug-eyed and silent during the telling.

"Lord have mercy!" Brown finally exclaimed. "You whupped Red Malone. I'd give ten dollars to a seen that!"

Smoke imagined that ten dollars was a princely sum to Mr. Brown.

"I stopped going into Barlow because of the hoodlums and the trash, Mr. Jensen," Ellie said. "And I certainly wouldn't be caught dead in Hell's Creek."

"I can understand that, Mrs. Brown," Smoke said. "I surely can."

"I take the wagon and go into town about once every three months," Brown said. "We're pretty well set up here. I got me a mill down on the crick, and we grind our own corn and such. Haul my grain and taters into town come harvest, and we get by."

"You got neighbors?"

"Shore." He pointed out the back. "Right over the field yonder is Gatewood. Just south of him is Morrison. And beyond that is Cooter's place. Just north of me is Bolen and Carson. We done that deliberate when we come out. In twenty minutes of hard ridin', we can have twelve to fifteen guns at anybody's house."

"Smart," Smoke agreed. "Has Max Huggins given any of you any trouble?"

Man and wife cut their eyes to one another. The glance did not escape Smoke.

Ellie sighed and nodded her head.

"Yeah, he has, Mister Smoke," Brown said. "His damned ol' gunhands has ruint more than one garden and killed hogs and chickens. They killed the only milk cow Bolen had, and his baby girl needed that milk. His woman had dried up. The baby died."

Smoke drew one big hand into a huge fist. "Who led the gang that did it?"

"Vic, they called him."

"Vic Young," Smoke put the last name to it. "I know of him. He's poison mean. Rode into a farmyard down in Colorado and shot a girl's puppy dog for no reason. I haven't had any use for him since I heard that story."

"Man who would shoot a girl's puppy is low," Elias said.

"He's got him a widow woman he sees about five miles from here," Brown said softly.

Both boys grinned.

"Does he now?" Smoke said.

"Be fair and tell it all," his wife admonished him gently.

"You're right, mother," Brown said. "I'm not bein' fair to the woman." He looked at Smoke. "Martha Feckles—that's the wider's name—does sewin' for them painted ladies in Hell's Creek. She's a good woman; just got to make a livin' for her and her young'uns, that's all. This trash Vic, he come up to her place one night and—" he paused, "well, took advantage of her."

"He raped her, Mister Smoke," Ralph said.

"Hush your mouth," Ellie warned him.

"No, it's all right, ma," Brown said. "Let the boy tell it.

71

Mister Smoke needs to know, and these young folks know more about it than we do."

"He beat her up bad, Mister Smoke," Ralph said. "Miss Martha, she's got her a daughter who's thirteen—Elias is sweet on her—"

"I am not neither!" Elias turned red.

"Shut up," the father warned him. "You are, too. Ever time you get around her you fall all over your big feet and bleat like a sheep. Tell it, Ralph."

"This Vic, he told Miss Martha that if she didn't go on . . . seein' him, he'd do the same to Aggie."

"I ought to kill him!" Elias said, considerable heat in his voice.

"Hush that kind of talk!" his mother told him. "The man's a gunfighter."

"Listen to your ma," Smoke told the boy, whom he guessed to be about fifteen at the most. "You have a right to defend hearth and home and kith and kin. You leave the gunfighting to me. Is that understood, boy?"

"Yes, sir."

Smoke rose from the table and found his hat. "I'll be riding now. You all feel free to come shop in Barlow. We'll soon have us a newspaper and a schoolteacher and a preacher. I thank you for the meal." He reached into his pocket and pulled out a double eagle. Before Brown could protest, he said, "Buy some ammunition with that. It's going to get real salty in the valley before long."

8

Smoke rode over to the Widow Feckles's house and made a slow circle of the grounds around the neat little home before riding up to the gate and swinging down from the saddle. A girl opened the front door and stepped out onto the porch. She looked to be about thirteen or fourteen, and Smoke pegged her as Aggie.

"Good morning," Smoke said. "I'm the new marshal over at Barlow. Don't be afraid of me. I'm here to help, not hurt you or your mother."

The girl's eyes widened. "Are you really Smoke Jensen?"

"Yes, I am. Is your name Aggie?"

"How'd you know that?"

"I nooned over at the Brown farm. Thought I'd come over and say hello to you and your ma. Is she home?"

"I'll fetch her for you."

Smoke waited by the gate. A very pretty woman stepped out onto the porch and smiled at him. "Mr. Jensen?"

"Yes, ma'am."

"I'm Martha Feckles. You wanted to see me?"

"If I may, yes."

"Please come in. I've just made a fresh pot of coffee."

The sitting room was small but neat, the furniture old and worn, but clean.

"You go look after your brother, Aggie," Martha said. "And don't stray from the house."

"Yes, Momma."

When the girl had closed the door behind her, Smoke said, "Are you expecting Vic Young?"

That shook the woman. Her hands trembled as she poured the coffee. "Brown spoke out of turn, sir."

"I don't think so. I think they spoke because they're worried about you. You're in a bad situation—not of your doing—and they'd like to see you clear of it."

"I'll never be free of Vic," she said with bitterness in her voice.

"Oh, you'll be free of him, Martha. You can write that down in your diary. When do you expect him again?"

"This evening."

Smoke sipped his coffee—mostly chicory—and studied the woman. She was under a strain; he could see that in her eyes and on her face. And he could also see the remnants of a bruise on her jaw. "Did Vic strike you, Martha?"

Her laugh held no humor. "Many times. He likes to beat up women."

Smoke waited.

With a sigh, she said, "Vic's killed women before, Mr. Jensen. He brags about it. I have to protect Aggie. I have to do his bidding for her sake."

"No longer, Martha. You'll not see Vic Young again. That's a promise."

"If you put him in jail, he'll come back when he gets out and really make it difficult for us."

"I don't intend to put him in jail, Martha. I intend to kill him."

His words did not shock her. She lifted her eyes to his. "I'm no shrinking summer rose, Mr. Jensen. I was born in the West. I don't hold with eastern views about crime and punishment. Some people—men and women—are just no good. They were born bad. I'll be much beholden to you if you saw to it that Vic did not come around here again. I can mend your shirts, and I do washing and ironing. I—"

Smoke held up a hand. "Enough, Martha. Do you have friends who would take you in for the night?"

"Why . . . certainly."

"I'll hitch up your buggy, and you take the children and go

74

to your friends for the night. You come back in the morning. All right?"

"If you say so, Mr. Jensen."

After they had gone, Smoke put his horse up in the small barn, closed the door securely, and walked the grounds, getting the feel of the place. Back in the house, he read for a time. He dozed off and slept for half an hour, waking up refreshed. He made a pot of strong coffee and waited.

Just as dusk was settling around the high country, Smoke heard a horse approaching at a canter. He stood up and slipped the hammer-thong from his .44's. He worked the guns in and out of leather and walked softly to the front door.

"Git ready, baby," a man called from the outside. "And git that sweet little baby of yourn ready, too. It's time for her to git bred."

Smoke's face tightened. He felt rage well up inside him. He mentally calmed himself. Only his eyes showed what was boiling inside him.

"You hear me, you . . ." Vic spewed profanity, the filth rolling from his mouth like sewerage.

Smoke opened the door and stepped out onto the small porch. Vic crouched like a rabid animal when he spotted him.

"No more, Vic," Smoke told him. "You won't terrorize this good woman anymore."

"Who the hell are you?"

"The name is Jensen. Smoke Jensen."

Vic spat on the ground. "You rode a long ways to die, Jensen."

"You're trash, Vic. Pure crud. Just like the man you work for."

"No man calls me that and lives!"

"I just did, Vic. And I'm still living."

"Where's Martha and Aggie?"

"Safe. And I intend to see they remain safe."

"You got no call to come meddlin' in a man's personal business."

"I do when the man is trash like you."

"I'm tarred of all this jibber-jabber, Jensen. You tell me where my woman is at and then you hit the trail."

"You got any kin you want me to notify, Vic?"

"Notify about what?"

"Your death."

"Huh!" Vic looked puzzled for a moment. Then he laughed. "You may be a big shot where you come from, Jensen, but you don't spell horse crap to me."

"Then make your move, punk."

Vic was suddenly unsure of himself. He looked around him. "You alone, Jensen?"

"I don't need any help in dealing with scum like you, Vic."

"I'm warnin' you, Jensen, don't call me that no more."

"Or you'll do what, Vic? I'll tell you what you'll do. Nothing. You woman beaters are all alike. Cowards. Punks. Come on, Vic. Make your play."

All the bluster and brag left the man. His eyes began to jerk and the right side of his face developed a nervous tic. "I'll just ride on, Jensen."

"No, Vic. I won't allow that. You'd just find some other poor woman to terrorize. Some child to molest. It's over, Vic. You'll kill no more women."

"They had it comin' to them!" Vic shouted as the night began closing in. "All I wanted from them was what a woman was put on earth to give to a man."

Smoke waited.

Vic began cursing, working his courage back up to a fever. "Drag iron, Jensen!" he screamed.

"After you, punk."

Vic's hand dropped to his gun. Smoke drew, cocked, and fired as fast as a striking rattler, shooting him in the belly, the slug striking the child molester and rapist two inches above his belt buckle. Vic stumbled and went down on one knee. He managed to drag his pistol from leather and cock it. Smoke shot him again, the slug taking him in the side and blowing out the other side. Vic Young fell backward, cursing as life left him.

Smoke stood over him. Vic said, "You're dead, Jensen. Max has put money on your head. Big money. He . . ."

Vic jerked on the cooling ground and died staring at whatever faced him beyond the dark river.

Smoke took the man's gunbelt and tossed leather and pistol onto the porch. He fanned the man's pockets, finding a very respectable wad of greenbacks and about a hundred dollars in gold coins. Martha would put the money to good use. He put the money on the kitchen table, along with Vic's gun and gunbelt and the rifle taken from the saddle boot.

Smoke wrote a short note and left it on the table: HE WILL BOTHER YOU NO MORE.

He signed it Smoke.

He saddled up Star and rode around to the front of the house. Smoke tied Vic across the saddle of his suddenly skittish horse and locked up the house.

Leading the horse with its dead cargo, Smoke headed north, toward Big Max Huggins's town of Hell's Creek.

It was late when he arrived on the hill overlooking the bawdy town. Lights were blazing in nearly every building, wild laughter ripped the night, and rowdy songs could be heard coming from drunken throats.

Smoke slipped the lead rope and slapped the horse on the rump, sending it galloping into the town.

He sat his saddle and waited.

He didn't have to wait long.

"Vic's dead!" the faint shout came to him as the piano playing and singing and drunken laughter gradually fell away, leaving the town silent.

Smoke watched the shadowy figures untie the body of Vic Young and lower it to the ground. He couldn't hear what the men were saying, but he could make a good guess.

Every rowdy and punk and gun-handler in the town would have known that Vic was seeing Widow Feckles. And everyone would know that she was being forced into acts of passion with Vic. And since none of the sodbusters would have the nerve to face Vic—so the gunhandlers thought; whether that was true or not, only time would tell—it had to have been the Widow Feckles who did Vic in.

Smoke kneed Star forward, moving closer to the town.

"Let's burn her out!" the shout reached Smoke's ears.

"Yeah," another man yelled. "I'll get the kerosene."

Smoke swung onto the main street of Hell's Creek and reined up. Staying in the shadows, he shucked his Winchester from the saddle boot and eared back the hammer. He called, "Martha Feckles had nothing to do with killing Vic. I killed him."

"Well, who the hell are you?" came the shouted question.

"Smoke Jensen."

"Jensen! Let's get him, boys."

They came at a rush and it was like shooting clay ducks in a shooting gallery. Smoke leveled the Winchester and emptied it into the knot of men. A dozen of them fell to one side, hard hit and screaming. Smoke spun Star around and headed for the high country, leaving a trail a drunken city slicker could follow.

About five miles outside of town, Smoke found what he was looking for and reined up. He loosened the cinch strap and let the big horse blow. He took a drink of water from his canteen and filled up his hat, letting Star have a drink.

Smoke had reloaded his rifle on the run, and he took it and his saddlebags down to the rocks just below where he had tucked Star safely away in a narrow draw. He eared back the hammer when he heard the pounding of hooves. The men of Hell's Creek rounded a curve in the trail and Smoke knocked the first man out of the saddle. Shifting the muzzle, he got lead in two more before the scum started making a mad dash for safety.

Smoke deliberately held his fire, watching the men cautiously edge toward his position under a starry sky and moon-bright night. With a grin, he opened his saddlebags and took out a stick of dynamite. He had a dozen sticks in the bag. He capped the stick of giant powder and set a very short fuse. Striking a match, he lit the fuse and let it fly, sputtering and sparking through the air.

The dynamite blew and shook the ground as it exploded. Smoke saw one man blown away from behind a rock, half of an arm missing. Another man staggered to his boots and

Smoke drilled him through the brisket. A third man tried to crawl away, dragging a broken leg. Smoke put him out of his misery.

Smoke put away the dynamite. Taking it along had been Sally's idea, and it had been a good one.

The trash below him cursed Smoke, calling him all sorts of names. But Smoke held his fire and eased away to a new position, which was some fifty feet higher than the old one. He now was able to see half-a-dozen men crouched behind whatever cover they could find in the night, some of that cover being mighty thin indeed.

Smoke dusted one man through and through. The man grunted once, then slowly rolled down the hill, dead. He shifted the muzzle and plugged another of Max's men through the throat. The man made a lot of horrible noises before he had the good grace to expire. Smoke had been aiming for the chest, but downhill shooting is tricky enough; couple that with night, and it gets doubly difficult.

The men of Hell's Creek decided they had had enough for this night. Smoke let them make their retreat, even though he could have easily dropped another two or three. He tightened the cinch strap, swung into the saddle, and headed south. He found a good place to camp and picketed Star. With his saddle for a pillow, he rolled into his blankets and went to sleep.

Two hours after dawn, he rode into the front yard of Martha Feckles. An idea had formed in his mind over coffee and bacon that morning, and he wanted to see how the widow received it.

"I think it's a grand idea!" she said.

Barlow had another resident.

Big Max Huggins sat in his office and stared at the wall. His thoughts were dark and violent. At this very moment, that drunken old preacher—he was all that passed for religion in Hell's Creek—was praying for the lost souls of three of those Jensen had shot in the main street of town last night. Those that had pursued him came back into town, dragging their butts in defeat. They had left six dead on the mountain. One of those had bled to death after the bomb Jensen had thrown tore off half of the man's arm.

"Goddamn you, Jensen!" Max cursed.

He leaned back in his chair—specially made due to his height and weight. He hated Smoke Jensen, but had to respect him—grudgingly—for his cold nerve. It would take either a crazy person or one with nerves of steel to ride smack into the middle of the enemy. And Smoke Jensen was no crazy person.

What to do about him?

Big Max didn't have the foggiest idea.

Smoke had put steel into the backbones of those in Barlow. A raid against the town now would be suicide. His men would be shot to pieces. There was no need to send for any outside gunfighters. He had some of the best guns in the West, either on his payroll or working out of the town on a percentage basis of their robberies.

Max's earlier boast that he would just wait Smoke out was proving to be a hollow brag. Jensen was bringing the fight to him.

Of course, Max mused, he could just pick up and move on. He'd done it many times in the past when things had gotten too hot for him.

But just the thought of that irritated him. In the past, dozens of cops or sheriffs and their deputies had been on his trail. Jensen was just one man. One man!

Max sighed, thinking: But, Jesus, what a man.

It was a good thing he'd invited those friends of his from Europe. A damn good thing. They would be arriving just in time.

The good ladies of Barlow welcomed Martha Feckles and her children with open arms. The mayor gave her a small building to use for her sewing. And Judge Garrison, now that he was free of the heavy hand of Max Huggins, was proving to be a decent sort of fellow. He staked Martha for a dress shop.

The preacher and schoolteacher had arrived in town. The newspaper man was due in at any time. Some of those who had left when Max first put on the pressure were returning. Barlow now had a population of nearly four hundred. And growing.

The jail was nearly full. Each time the stage ran north, Smoke jerked out any gamblers, gunfighters, and whores who might be on it and turned them around. If they kicked up a fuss, they were tossed in the clink, fined, and were usually more than happy to catch the next stage out—south.

A depty U.S. Marshal, on his way up to British Columbia to bring back a prisoner, was on the stage the morning a gunslick objected to being turned around.

"There ain't no warrants out on me, Jensen," the man protested. "You ain't got no right to turn me around. I can go anywheres I damn well please to go."

"That's right," Smoke told him. "Anywhere except Hell's Creek."

Amused, the U. S. Marshal leaned against a post and rolled himself a cigarette, listening to the exchange. He knew all about Hell's Creek and Big Max Huggins. But until somebody complained to the government, there was little they could do. He knew the sheriff, the city marshal, and all the deputies in Hell's Creek were crooked as a snake. But the outlaws working out of there never bothered anyone with a federal badge, and as far as he knew, there were no federal warrants on anyone in the town—at least not under the names they were going by now.

"Git out of my way, Jensen!" the gunny warned Smoke.

"Don't be a fool, man," Smoke told him. "You're in violation of the law by bracing me. I don't have any papers on you. So why don't you just go to the hotel, get you a room, and catch the next stage out?"

"South?"

"That's it."

"I'll rent me a horse and go to Hell's Creek."

"Sorry, friend," Smoke told him. "No one in this town will rent you a horse."

"Then I think I'll get back on the stage and ride up yonder

like my ticket says."

Smoke hit him. The punch came out of the blue and caught the gunny on the side of the jaw. When he hit the ground, he was out cold.

Jim and Sal dragged him across the street to the jail.

"Slick," the U.S. Marshal said. "Against the law, but slick."

"You going to report what I'm doing?" Smoke asked.

"Hell, no, man! But I can tell you that the word's gone out up and down the line: You're a marked man. Huggins has put big money on your head. And I'm talkin' enough money to bring in some mercenaries from Europe."

"Are they in the country?"

"As near as the Secret Service can tell, yes. Two long-distance shooters, Henri Dubois and Paul Mittermaier, are on their way west right now. Our office has sent out flyers to you. Oh, yes. We know what you're doing here. We can't give you our blessings, but we can close our eyes."

"Thanks. Dubois and Mittermaier—Frenchman and a German?"

"Yep. And they're good."

"I don't like back-shooters. I'll tell you now, Marshal: If I see them, I'm going to kill them."

"Suits me, Smoke. Good hunting." He climbed back on board the stage and was gone.

Smoke turned to Jim and Sal, who had just returned from the jail. "You hear that?"

They had heard it.

"Pass the word to all the farmers and ranchers. Any strangers, especially those speaking with an accent, I want to know about. You boys watch your backs."

Sal spat on the ground. "I hate a damned back-shooter," he said. "These boys are gonna be totin' some fancy custom-made rifles. I see one, I'm gonna plug him on the spot and apologize later if I'm wrong."

"You know what this tells me?" Smoke asked. "It tells me that Max is in a bind. What we're doing is working. We can't legally stop and permanently block freight shipments to Hell's Creek. But we can hold them up and make them open up every box and crate for search. And I mean a very long and tedious search. It won't take long for freight companies to stop accepting orders from Hell's Creek."

Jim and Sal grinned. "Oh, you got a sneaky mind, Smoke," Sal said. "I like it!"

"The last freight wagons rolled through a week ago," Jim said. "There ought to be another convoy tomorrow, I figure."

"OK," Smoke said. He looked at Sal. "You get a couple of town boys. Give them a dollar apiece to stand watch about two miles south of town. As soon as they hear the wagons, one of them can come fogging back to town for us. Everything going north has got to pass through here." Smoke smiled. "This is going to give Max fits!"

The men grinned at each other. One sure way to kill a town was to dry up its supply line. Big Max was not going to like this.

Not one little bit.

9

"Some of the boys is grumblin' about you puttin' up money on Jensen's head and then lettin' them foreigners come over here," one of Max's gunhands complained.

Max spread his hands. "I put up the money, Lew. Anybody who nails Jensen gets it. As far as Dubois and Mittermaier are concerned, they're old friends of mine. I sent for them long before Jensen entered the picture. Besides, they are much more subtle in their approach than most of those out there." He waved his hand. "You and I, of course, could handle it easily. I'm not too sure about the others."

The outlaw knew he was getting a line of buffalo chips fed him, but the flattery felt good anyway. "Right, Big Max. Sure. I understand. What do I tell the boys?"

"Tell them . . ." Max was thinking hard. "Tell them that we must be careful in disposing of Jensen. If we draw too much attention to us, the government might send troops in here and put us all out of business."

"Yeah," Lew said. "Yeah, you're right. They'll understand that, Max. I'll pass the word."

After Lew had left, Max leaned back in his chair. What next? he thought. What is Jensen going to do next?

"What are y'all lookin' for?" the teamster asked.

"Contraband," Smoke told him. "Unload your wagons."

The teamster paled under his stubble of beard and tanned

skin. "All the wagons? Everything in them?"

"All the wagons, everything in them."

Griping and muttering under their breaths, the men unloaded the wagons, and Smoke and Jim and Sal went to work with pry-bars. With his back to the teamsters, Smoke pulled a small packet from under his shirt and dropped it in a box. "Check this box, Sal," he said. "I'll be opening some others."

"Right, Smoke."

After a moment, Sal called out, "Marshal, I got something that looks funny."

Smoke walked over. "The box says it's supposed to have whiskey in it. What's that in your hand?"

"Durned if I know." He handed the packet to Smoke.

Smoke had found the contents way in the back of the safe in the marshal's office. It was several thousand dollars of badly printed counterfeit greenbacks.

Smoke opened the packet. "Hey!" he said, holding one of the greenbacks up to the sunlight. "This looks phony to me."

A teamster walked over. "What is that?"

"Counterfeit money," Smoke told him. "This is real serious. You could be in a lot of trouble."

"Me!" the teamster shouted. "I ain't done nothin'."

"You're hauling this funny money," Smoke reminded him.

"Well, that's true. But that phony money sure as hell ain't mine."

"Oh, I believe you," Smoke eased his fears. "But this entire shipment is going to have to be seized and held for evidence."

"Marshal, you can have it all. Me and my boys work for a living. We're not printing no government money."

"Is this shipment prepaid?"

"Yes, sir. Everything sent to Hell's Creek is paid for in advance. That's the only way the boss would agree to do business with them thugs up yonder."

"So you and your men would prefer not to do business with those in Hell's Creek?"

"That's the gospel truth, Mr. Jensen. There ain't a one of us like the run past Barlow."

"All right, boys. You're free to turn around and head on back. We're sorry to have inconvenienced you."

After the wagons had gone, the men nearly broke up laughing as they stood amid the mounds of boxed supplies. Wiping his eyes, Smoke said, "Sal, go get some wagons and men from town. We've got to store all this stuff."

"Bit Max is gonna toss himself a royal fit when he hears about this," Sal said. "This here is food and supplies for a month."

"Yeah. I figure they have probably a month's supplies left on the shelves. After that, things are going to get desperate in Hell's Creek."

Sal headed back to town and Jim said, "You know, Smoke, Max can't let you get away with this. His men would lose all respect for him."

"Yeah, I know. This may be the fuel to pop the lid off. What's the latest on Red Malone; have you heard?"

"Not a peep. I 'spect he's still recovering from that beatin' you gave him."

"He's got to have a meeting with Max. They'll get together and try to plan some way to get rid of me."

"No way to cover all the trails up to Hell's Creek. There must be a dozen, and probably a few more that I don't know about."

"Oh, I wouldn't try to do that. But I was thinking: Red has to buy supplies and he buys them in Barlow. It would be too time-consuming and costly to go anywhere else. Marbly hates Red. He never did knuckle under to him. He told me himself he still has the right to refuse service to anyone."

Jim smiled. "Oh, now that would tick Red off. He'd go right through the ceiling."

Smoke chuckled. "I'm counting on it, Jim. I am really counting on it."

"He did what?" Big Max roared, jumping up from his chair and pounding a fist on his desk.

The outlaw Val Singer repeated what he had heard.

"That's why the damn supplies didn't arrive yesterday," Max said, sitting down and doing his best to calm himself. "Jensen . . . that low-life, no-good, lousy . . ." He spent the next few moments calling Smoke every filthy name he could think of. And he thought of a lot of them.

Big Max shook himself like a bear with fleas and took several deep breaths. What to do? was the next thought that sprang into his angry mind.

Thing about it was, he didn't know.

"Burn the damn town down," Val suggested.

"They'd rebuild it," Max said glumly.

"Grab some of their kids, then."

"I have been giving that some thought, for a fact. But we'd have to be very careful doing it, Val. Very subtle."

Val smiled, a nasty glint in his eyes. "That daughter of Martha Feckles is prime. She could pleasure a lot of us."

Big Max had thought of Aggie a time or two. For a fact. Something ugly and archaic reared up within him when he thought of Aggie.

He could envision all sorts of perversions, all with Aggie in the lead role . . . with him.

"I'll think about it," Max said, his voice husky.

Days passed and there was no retaliation from either Big Max or Red Malone. And that worried Smoke. To his mind, it meant that Max and Red were planning something very ugly and very sneaky. He warned everybody in town to keep a careful eye on their kids, to know where they were at all times. He warned the women to never walk alone, to plan shopping trips in groups. He visited everyone who lived just outside of town and warned them to be very, very careful.

He rode out into the county, visiting the small ranchers and farmers, repeating his message of caution at every stop.

"What do you think they're gonna do, Mr. Jensen?" Brown asked. Smoke had stopped in for coffee.

"I don't know, Brown. I wish I did so I could head it off. Whatever Max does, and probably Red Malone, too, is going to be dirty. Bet on that."

"Would the army come in if we was to ask them?"

"No. This is a civilian matter. I can't tell you who told me this, but I was told that the government is going to turn its back and let us handle it the way we see fit."

"That seems odd. I mean, why would they?"

"I've worn a U.S. Marshal's badge a time or two, Brown."

Smoke had worn a marshal's badge before, but that didn't mean the government owed him any favors. He hoped Brown wouldn't push the matter, and the farmer didn't.

"If we got to go clean out that bunch at Hell's Creek, or if we got to ride agin' Malone and his bunch of trash, you can count me and all my neighbors in, Smoke."

Smoke smiled. "The word I got is that you farmers won't fight. That you're scared."

"You believe that?"

"Not for one second, Brown. I got a hunch you're all Civil War veterans."

"We are. Gatewood and Cooter fought on the side of the South, rest of us wore blue. But that's behind us now. We seldom ever talk about it no more. And when we do, it ain't with no rancor. Funny thing is, we never knowed each other during the war. We just met up on the trail and become friends. But don't never think we won't fight, Smoke. Some hoodlums along the trail thought that. We buried them."

They chatted for a while longer and then Smoke pulled out, heading back to Barlow. He had him a hunch that Max Huggins had already sounded out Brown and Cooter and the other farmers in that area. Max was no fool, far from it, and he had guessed—and guessed accurately—that tackling that bunch would be foolhardy. Like most men of his ilk, Max preferred the easy way over the hard.

He pulled up in front of his office and swung down, curious about the horses tied to the hitchrail. He did not recognize the brand.

He looped the reins around the rail and stepped up on the boardwalk. The door to his office opened and several men filed out, one of them wearing the badge of sheriff of the county.

"You Jensen?" the man asked, a hard edge to his voice.

"That's right."

The man held out his hand. "I'll take your badge, Jensen. I name my deputies."

"This badge is legal, partner. Judge Garrison swore me in and he has the power to do it. So that means that you can go right straight to hell."

The sheriff shook a finger in Smoke's face. "Now let me tell you something. . . ."

Smoke slapped the finger away and his hand returned a lot harder. He backhanded the crooked sheriff a blow that jarred the man and stepped him to one side.

"Don't you ever stick your finger in my face again," Smoke warned him. "The next time you do it, I'll break it off at the elbow and put it in a place that'll have you riding sidesaddle for a long time."

Sal and Jim had stepped out of the office, both of them carrying sawed-off shotguns. It made the sleazebag sheriff's deputies awfully nervous.

"Come on, Cart," one of his men said. "I told you this wouldn't work."

Smoke laughed. "You have to be Paul Cartwright. Sure. I remember reading about you. You served time in California for stealing while you were a lawman out there. Get out of this town, Cartwright."

"Come on, Cart," one of his men pulled at his sleeve.

"I'll be damned if I will!" Cart blustered. "I'm the sheriff of this county. And no two-bit gunslinger tells me what to do."

He took a swing at Smoke, who in turn grabbed him by the arm and tossed him off the boardwalk and into the street. Smoke jumped down just as Cart was grabbing for his gun. He kicked the .45 out of his hand and jerked the man to his boots.

Then he proceeded to beat the hell out of him.

Every time Cart would get up, Smoke would knock him down again. The editor of the paper had grabbed his brand-new, up-to-date camera and rushed out of his office in time to see Smoke knock Cart down for the second time. He quickly set up and began taking action shots.

Cart was out of shape, and Smoke really didn't want to inflict any permanent injuries on the man. He just wanted to leave a lasting impression as to who was running things in Barlow and the south end of the county.

The editor, Henry Draper, got some great shots of Cart being busted in the mouth and landing in the dirt on his butt. Jim and Sal thought it very amusing. Cart's deputies failed to see the humor in it. But they stayed out of it mainly because of Jim and Sal and the express guns they carried.

Joe Walsh and several of his hands rode into town just as Smoke was knocking Cart down for about the seventh time. The rancher sat his saddle and watched, amusement on his face and in his eyes.

The county sheriff staggered to his boots, lifted his fists, and Smoke decked him for the final count. Cart hit the dirt and didn't move.

Smoke washed his face and hands in a horse trough, picked up his hat, and settled it on his head. He looked up at Cart's deputies and pointed to the sheriff. "Get that trash off the streets and out of this town. And don't come back. You understand all that?"

"Yes, sir," they echoed.

Smoke jerked a thumb. "Move!"

The deputies grunted Cart across his saddle, tied him in place, and rode out.

"You do have a way of making friends, Smoke," Joe said, walking his horse over to the hitchrail and dismounting.

"Let's just say I leave lasting impressions," Smoke smiled the reply, shaking the rancher's hand.

"What a headline this will make!" Henry said. The editor of the *Barlow Bugle* grabbed up all his photographic equipment and hustled back to his office to develop the pictures and write the story.

"Stick around," Smoke told Joe. "We'll have some coffee in a minute." He looked at Sal. "When did Cart get here?"

"'Bout an hour ago. He was full of it, too. He had me and Jim plumb shakin' in our boots."

"I'm sure he did," Smoke said, noticing the wicked glint in the man's eyes. "I can tell that you haven't recovered yet."

"Right," Jim said, grinning along with Sal. "They're runnin' scared, Smoke. All of them up at Hell's Creek. Cart said that Big Max can't get a freight company to haul goods up to them. He's tryin' to get goods pulled in from that new settlement to the west of him . . . Kalispell; but the marshal over there told him to go take a dump in his hat. Or words similar to that."

Joe Walsh and his men laughed out loud, one of the hands saying, "Me and the rest of the boys talked it over, Smoke. When you need us, just give a holler. We'll ride with you and you call the shots."

"I appreciate it. Max won't stand still and get pushed around much longer. I expect some retaliation from Hell's Creek at any moment. Unfortunately, I don't have any idea in what form it might be." He told them all what he'd been doing that day, riding and warning those in the south end of the county . . . or as many as he could find.

"A man who would harm a kid is scum," Joe said. "I suggest we keep a rope handy."

A crowd had gathered around and they heatedly agreed.

Smoke let them talk it out until they fell silent. "You watch your children, people. Tell them not to leave the town limits. Not for any reason. Always bear in mind that we're dealing with scum. And these people have no morals, no values, no regard for human life. Adult or child. The farmers in this part of the county are breaking ground and planting. And they're doing it with guns strapped on. I don't want to see a man in this town walking around without a gunbelt on or a pistol stuck behind his belt. It's entirely conceivable that Max and Malone may even try to tree this town. If they do that, we want to be ready. Any woman here who doesn't know how to shoot, my wife will be conducting classes." He smiled. "She doesn't know that yet, but I'm sure she'll be more than willing to teach a class."

"You better watch out, Tom," a good-natured shout came out of the crowd. "Ella Mae learns to shoot, she's liable to fill your butt full of birdshot the next time you come home tipsy."

Tom Johnson grinned out of his suddenly red face. Tom liked his evening whiskey at the saloon.

"You're a fine one to talk, Matthew," the blacksmith yelled. "I 'member the time your woman tossed you out of the house with nothin' but your long-handles on."

The crowd burst out laughing and went their way. It was good laughter, the kind of laughter from men and women who had decided to make a stand of it. To not be pushed around and taken advantage of by thugs like Big Max Huggins.

"That laughter is good to hear," Joe said. "These folks have been down for a long time. I'm glad to see them back on their feet and standing tall." He paused to finish rolling his cigarette and light up. "And you're responsible for straightening their backbone, Smoke."

Smoke had been curious about something, and he figured now was the time to ask it. "Why didn't you do it, Joe?" he asked softly.

"Wondered when you'd get around to asking that. It's a fair question. Me and the wife left right after roundup three years ago. Took us a trip to see San Francisco. Spent all summer in California. Up and down the coast. The kids is all growed up and in college back east. We left right around the first day of May and didn't come back until late September. Hell, Smoke, it was all over by then. Big Max had built Hell's Creek, him and Red Malone was in cahoots around here, and Big Max's outlaws had cut the heart right out of this town."

He dropped the cigarette butt into the street and toed it dead. "I spent the next year just protecting my herds and my land. Red tried his damndest to run me out. But I wouldn't go. I lost . . ." He looked at one of his hands. "How many men, Chuck?"

"Four, boss. Skinny Jim, Davis, Don Morris, and John."

"Four men," Joe said quietly. "Good men who died for the brand. When Red finally got it through his head that I wasn't gonna be run out—and I can't prove it was Red doing it—he backed off and let me be."

"No way you can prove it was Red?"

"No. Not a chance. And I tried. That's on record at the territorial capitol. I raised some hell about it, and that, and with me and the boys fighting the night riders brought an end to it. They all wore hoods. Don't all cowards wear hoods or masks? I never was able to get a look at any of them." He smiled. "But I did recognize their horses. Unfortunately, that won't cut it in court." His eyes darted toward Sally as she stepped out of the hotel. "My wife is looking forward to you and your missus coming out. But I told her let's get this situation with Red and Max taken care of first, then we'll socialize."

"Yeah. My leaving town now, for any length of time, would not be wise. Hey! I got an idea. How about a community dance and box supper?"

Sally walked up. "You took those thoughts right out of my head, honey. Hi, Joe."

"Ma'am," the rancher touched the brim of his hat. "I think that's a good idea."

Smoke's grin turned into a frown.

"What's the matter with you?" Sally asked.

"It's not a good idea."

"Why not?" she asked.

"It would mean too many people would be leaving their homes unguarded. That might be all it would take for Max or Red to burn someone out."

"Oh, pooh!" Sally said, stamping her foot.

"Smoke's right. I didn't think about that. Must be getting old. Max and Red wouldn't pass up an opportunity like that. And we couldn't keep it quiet. It'd be sure to leak out."

Smoke began smiling again.

"Now what?" Sally asked.

"I know how to have the dance and avoid trouble—at least for the farmers and ranchers."

"How?" Joe asked. "What about Red and Max?"

"That's just it. We'll invite them."

10

Joe Walsh rode back to the ranch, chuckling as he went. Smoke Jensen was not only the slickest gunhandler he'd ever seen, but the man was damn smart, too.

There was no way a western man was going to turn down an invitation for a box supper and a dance with some really nice ladies. And both Max and Red would know that if anyone's place was torched that night, the fires could be seen for miles and there was no way either of them would leave Barlow alive.

"Slick," the rancher said. "Just damn slick."

"I had my mind all made up to not like Smoke Jensen," one of his hands said. "But I sure changed my mind. He's a right nice fellow."

"Yes, he is, Curly. I had my mind all made up to dislike the man. I figured he'd be a cocky son. Shows how wrong a man can be."

"I can't wait for this shindig," another hand said. "Been a long time since we had a good box supper and dance."

"Be a damn good time to put lead in Max Huggins and Red Malone, too," Curly said. Curly and Skinny Jim had been close friends.

"Be none of that, Curly," Joe cautioned his hand. "Not unless they open the ball. Too much a chance that women and kids would get hit."

"I hate both them men," Curly replied. "With Jensen leadin' the pack, we could ride into Hell's Creek and wipe it out. I don't see why we don't do that."

"It might come to that, Curly," Joe said. "For sure, a lot of blood is going to be spilled before this is over."

"Just as long as the blood spilled comes out of Max Huggins and Red Malone and them that ride for them," Curly said. "I don't wanna die, but I'll go out happy if I know I got lead in Max or Malone."

Joe cut his eyes to the puncher. I'm going to have to watch him, the rancher thought. He's let his hate bubble very nearly out of control.

Sally and the ladies of Barlow met with the editor of the paper and designed and had printed dozens of invitations. Smoke made certain that Max Huggins and Red Malone received an invite.

Max stared at his invitation for a long time, being careful not to smudge the creamy bond paper. "What's Jensen doing this time?" he questioned the empty office. "He's got to have something up his sleeve." Then it came to him: If he attended this shindig and there was any trouble caused by his men, Max and Red would be gunned down on the spot; shot down like rabid skunks.

The big man was filled with grudging admiration for Jensen. Slick. Very, very slick. If he and Red didn't attend, Jensen and the others would be put on alert that something was going to happen out in the county, and it would be open season for any Lightning rider or gunhand from Hell's Creek caught out after dark.

He sent one of his bodyguards to fetch Val Singer, Warner Frigo, Dave Poe, and Alex Bell to his office.

"Me and Red will be attending this shindig," he informed the outlaw leaders. "And there better not be any trouble out in the county. You hold the reins tight on your boys . . . and I mean tight."

"It might be a trap," Val pointed out.

Max shook his head. "No. I don't think so. The people of Barlow are going to let off a little steam, that's all." He waved the invite. "This is their way of insuring that they can do so

96

without fear of any trouble." He eyeballed them all. "And, by God, there isn't going to be any trouble. Those are my orders. See that they are carried out."

Red Malone had recovered from his beating at the hands—or fists—of Smoke Jensen. He stared hard and long at the invitation. He laid it on his desk and stared at it some more.

Was it a trap? He didn't think so. But he had a week to nose around and find out for sure.

"We goin', ain't we, Daddy?" Tessie asked, looking and reading over his shoulder.

Red turned his head and stared at his daughter, all blond and pretty and pouty and as worthless as her brother, Melvin. He loved them both—as much as Red Malone could love anything—but realized he had sired a whore and a nut.

"I don't know," he told her.

She pouted.

"Stop that, girl. You look like a fish suckin' in air."

Tessie plopped down in a chair and glared at him. "I got me a brand-new dress I got outta that catalog from New York, and I ain't had no chance to wear it. Now I got a chance to wear it and you tell me we might not go."

Red sighed. "Where's Melvin?"

"Same place he always is: shootin' at targets."

The boy was good with a gun, Red thought. Fast as a snake. But was he as fast as Jensen? Maybe. Just maybe the boy might do one thing in his life that was worthwhile: killing Smoke Jensen.

"Come on, Daddy!" Tessie said. "Let's go to the dance and have some fun."

Red stared at her, wondering whom she was bedding down with this time around.

The girl had more beaus than a dog had fleas.

"Pooh!" Tessie said. "I never get to do anything."

Except sneak out at night and behave like a trollop, Red thought. "I said I'd think about it," he told her. "Now go tell the cook to get dinner on the table. I'm hungry."

She sat in her chair and pouted.

"Move!" Red yelled.

She got up and left the room, shaking her butt like a hurdy-gurdy girl.

Red sighed and shook his big head. The only thing he regretted about his wife leaving him was that she didn't take those damn kids with her.

"Max has accepted," Sally told Smoke, holding out the note from Hell's Creek. "This came on the southbound stage a few minutes ago."

Smoke read the note and smiled. "One down and one to go. No word from Red yet?"

"No. Nothing."

"Smoke!" Jim's sharp call came from the outside. "Melvin Malone ridin' in. You watch yourself around this one. He's crazy as a skunk."

Smoke walked to the door and stepped out, after removing the hammer thongs from his .44's. He'd heard too much about Melvin to be careless around him. He watched the young man swing down from the saddle, being careful to keep the horse between himself and Smoke.

Smart, Smoke thought. He's no amateur.

Melvin stepped up on the boardwalk, studying Smoke as hard as Smoke was studying him. Melvin was about six feet tall and well built, heavily muscled. He was handsome in a cruel sort of way. He wore two guns, the holsters tied down. The spurs he wore were big roweled ones, the kind that would hurt a horse, and Melvin looked the type who would enjoy doing that.

"Jensen," the young man said, stopping a few feet away. "I'm Mel Malone."

"Nice to see you, Mel. What's on your mind?"

Killing you, was the thought in Mel's head. He kept it silent. Big bastard, Mel thought. Big as them books made him out to be. "My pa said to give you a message. We'll be coming to the dance and box supper."

"Well, I'm glad to hear that, Mel. Yes, sir. Sure am. You

be sure and tell Red I'm looking forward to seeing him again. He is feeling all right, now, isn't he?"

The young man stared at Smoke for a moment. Was Jensen trying to be smart-mouthed? He couldn't tell. "Uh, yeah. He feels just fine."

"That's good. Your sister Tessie makes a pretty good box supper, does she?"

"My sister couldn't fry an egg if the hen told her how," Mel replied. "But the cook can fry chicken that'll make you wanna slap your granny." Why the hell was he standing here talking about fried chicken with a man he was going to kill? He stared hard at Smoke. Fella seemed sort of likable.

Smoke chuckled. "Well, some women just never get the knack of cooking, Mel. Tell Red to take it easy now." Smoke turned and walked across the street, leaving Melvin alone on the boardwalk.

Feeling sort of stupid standing on the boardwalk all by himself, the young man wandered over to the saloon for a drink.

Sally watched it all from the window and she smiled.

"Smoke handled that just right," Jim said. "There wasn't nothing else to be said, so he just walked off leavin' Melvin standing there lookin' stupid. Which ain't hard to do, 'cause he is."

"But good with a gun," Sally remarked, watching the young man push open the batwings to the saloon. "I can tell by the way he carries himself. He walks a lot like Smoke."

"He's almost as fast as Smoke, ma'am. But not quite as good. But he's a dead shot, I'll give him that."

Sally felt just a twinge of worry that she quickly pushed aside. She had known what Smoke was when she met and later married him. She had long ago accepted that wherever he went, there would be men who would call him out. The West was slowly changing, but it would be years before gunfighting was finally banned.

When Melvin left town, Smoke was leaning up against an awning support watching him go. Smoke raised a hand in farewell. Melvin looked at him, then cut his eyes away, refusing to acknowledge the friendly gesture.

Smoke walked back to the office. Sally had just finished cleaning and straightening it up. "What do you think of Red's son, Smoke?"

Smoke poured a cup of coffee and sat down at his desk. He sipped and said, "He's crazy and he's cruel. I'll have to kill him someday."

Little by little, in small groups, Red's hands began drifting back into town for a drink or a meal or to buy this or that. So far, Red had not tried to buy any supplies from Marbly. The rancher was going to be in for a rude shock when he did.

Red's hands caused no trouble when in town. They had all noticed that every man in town was packing iron: the bartender, the editor of the *Bugle*, the store clerks . . . everybody. And they promptly took that news back to Red.

Red digested that bit of information with a sigh. "Then that's it, John," he told his foreman. "We've got to make a move and do it quick, before the town really gets together and runs our butts out of the country. And they'll do it eventually. Believe me."

"Before the dance, Red?"

Red shook his head. "No. After it. Maybe a week after it. Max has got some long-distance shooters comin' in from Europe. They was invited to come in here for a hunt long before Smoke Jensen showed up. They should be here this week. Early next week at the latest. We'll get things firmed up with Max after the party."

"Take Jensen out first?"

"I don't know. I think it'd be better to start working on the townspeople. I just don't know. Whatever Max decides to do, we got to back him up. That's the deal we made and I always keep my word." He looked around him and sniffed, a look of distaste crossing his face. "What in the name of God is that horrible smell?"

"The cook is tryin' to teach Tessie how to cook. Tessie is fixin' supper, so I'm told."

"Oh, my Lord. I'll eat with you boys tonight. What the Sam Hill is she cookin', skunk?"

"Fried chicken."

"She must have left the feathers on."

Henri Dubois and Paul Mittermaier were blissfully unaware of what was taking place in Barlow and Hell's Creek. They had seen the sights of St. Louis and were now ready to board the train west.

What they did not know was that they were under surveillance by agents of the U.S. Federal Marshal's office. They knew of the situation building in Barlow and Hell's Creek, and they also knew that with just a little help, Smoke Jensen would handle it and they would not have to get directly involved. The marshals sent a wire to the nearest town to Barlow, and the message was forwarded to Smoke Jensen by stage.

Smoke opened the envelope and read: Mercenaries left St. Louis this a.m. No charges against Dubois or Mittermaier. They are unaware of what is taking place in your area. Watch your back and handle situation as you see fit.

It was unsigned, but Smoke had a pretty good idea what federal office had sent it.

He showed the message to Jim and Sal. Neither man could understand why Smoke was smiling. Jim asked him.

"They have to come right through here, boys." He walked to a wall map and put his finger on a town south of them. "This is rail's end. From here to Barlow is either by horseback or stage, and I'm betting they take the stage."

"And you got what in mind?" Sal asked.

"Any trouble that happens out in the county, you boys handle it. Starting day after tomorrow, I've got to meet the stage."

"I wonder what he's got in mind?" Jim asked Sal after Smoke left the office.

"Be fun to watch, whatever it is."

"You reckon the Frenchman and the German will see the humor in it?" Jim asked with a grin.

"Somehow I doubt it. I really do."

"The saloons are runnin' out of whiskey," Max was

informed. "And the boys is gettin' right testy."

Max took a long pull on his stogie. "Yeah, and I had me five boxes of cigars on that shipment Jensen seized, too. So what else is new? I can't find any freight haulers to handle our orders. The only option we have is some outfit out of Canada, and by the time all the red tape is over with, it'll be six months before we get any supplies."

Alex Bell shifted in the chair. "Max, the boys ain't gonna stand still for this very much longer. They all got cash money to spend and nothin' to buy. The women is raisin' holy hell 'cause the boys is unhappy. Somethin' has got to pop, and damn soon."

Max Huggins's little empire was crumbling at the edges and he didn't know what to do about it. For the umpteenth time since Jensen entered the picture, the thought that he should pull out entered his brain. And for the same number of times, the thought galled him; but with each revival of the thought, the intensity of the sourness was somewhat lessened as common sense fought to prevail.

"I'll talk to the boys," he finally said to Alex. "Damnit!" he cursed, pounding a fist on the desk and scattering papers. "He's just one man. Just one man! He's not a god, not invincible. There has to be a way."

"There is," Alex said. "Me and Val and the others been talkin'."

Max waited, staring hard at the outlaw gang leader.

"Wipe the town out. Kill every man, woman, and child. It can be done, and you know it."

"Damnit, Alex," Max said, struggling to maintain his patience with the gang leader. "This is 1883, man. The country is connected by telegraph wires and railroads. Ten years ago, I would have said yes to your proposal. But not now. I think the press would pick it up, and the public would be up in arms and all over us. We'd have federal marshals and troops in here before you could blink."

"Fires happen all the time, Max," Alex pointed out. "We pick a night with a good strong wind and that town would go up like a tinderbox. You think about that."

"The people would still remain, Alex."

"Maybe not. Maybe not enough of them to do any good. Lots of folks die in town fires. And charred skin don't show no bullet holes. By the time the newspapers got 'hold of it, them folks would be rottin' in the ground and nobody could do nothin' about it."

Max jabbed out his cigar in an ashtray. With a slow expelling of breath, he said, "We may have to do that, Alex. It's a good plan, I'm thinking, but very risky." He stared hard at the outlaw. "Have you ever killed a child, Alex?"

"Yeah. I gut-shot a kid durin' a bank stickup; sqalled like a hog at butcherin' time. I shot him in the head to shut him up. I shot half a dozen or more ridin' with Bloody Bill Anderson. All the boys has. It ain't no big deal."

Max nodded his head in agreement. He had killed several children—accidentally and deliberately—during his bloody life. And as Alex had stated: It was no big deal. He had no nightmares about it. They got in the way, they were disposed of. It was all a matter of one's personal survival.

The plan that Alex was proposing would have to be very carefully worked out. There could be no room for error or miscalculation. And the men involved would have to be chosen carefully, for if word ever leaked out, nationwide condemnation would be certain to follow—quickly. It was a good plan, but very chancy. Very chancy.

"What do you think, Max?"

"It would take a lot of planning, Alex. And the men would have to be chosen carefully. The ones who don't ride on the raid must never know what took place. Now, then, is that possible?"

The outlaw and murderer thought about that. Slowly, he shook his head affirmatively. "Yeah. Forty men could pull it off. Any more than that would be too many. Most of the men here would keep their mouths shut about it. Out of whole bunch, maybe ten might blab later on."

"Dispose of them now, Alex," Max gave the killing orders. "Once that is done, we start planning on destroying the town."

Alex rose with a grin on his face. "My pleasure, boss."

11

Something nagged at Smoke as he walked through the town. He walked up and down the streets, on the boardwalks wherever they were, on the dusty paths where they had not yet been built.

Something was wrong, and Smoke could not pull it out of his brain. Then it came to him. The town lacked adequate water barrels for bucket brigades in case of fire.

Swiftly, he walked back to his office and sent Jim out to round up Tom Johnson, Judge Garrison, and several others in the town.

"What's the drill in case of fire?" he asked bluntly, as was his way.

"Why . . ." Tom looked puzzled. "There isn't any."

"There will be by dark. Judge, alert the people. I want water barrels by every store and every house; buckets placed nearby. And I want those barrels to stay full at all times. We have an old pumper down at the livery stable. See that it's checked out and the hoses inspected for leaks. Benson," he looked at the blacksmith, "you're in charge of the fire brigade."

The blacksmith nodded his head. "You're thinkin' Max might try burning us out?"

"That's exactly what I'm thinking. I'll start rounding up volunteers to clear out the brush and other cover that surrounds the town. I'll ride out to Joe's place and see if he'll lend us some hands to help. Check out and destroy any place where sharpshooters could hide and pick us off. Get on it now, Sal."

The man quietly left the room.

"Max would do it, too," Judge Garrison said. "He told me when he first confronted me that if I didn't do exactly as he said, he'd pick out a child and kill her in front of me. I didn't like what I was doing, but I figured it was the only way to save some children's lives."

"I understand, Judge." Smoke leaned back in his chair. "If we can get most of this done by the dance night and keep a close eye on Max to check his reaction, we can know pretty well that he had burning us out in mind. Then he'll have to come up with another plan."

"He will," Judge Garrison said. "The man is totally and utterly ruthless."

"What are you gonna do with them mercenaries when they step off the stage, Smoke?" Jim asked.

"Oh, welcome them to town, Jim," Smoke said with a smile. "Roll out the red carpet."

That afternoon, Smoke met the southbound stage and was pleased to see it was full, with several men riding on top. The driver handed the mailbag to Marbly's wife—who was the town's postmistress—and seeing there were no passengers departing Barlow, he hollered his team forward.

Those men perched precariously on top gave Smoke some extremely dirty looks as the stagecoach pulled out. Its next stop would be a way station some fifty miles south, where it would change teams, another stop near Salmon Lake for food and a fresh team, and then on into Missoula, some one hundred twenty-five miles from Barlow.

"Stage was full today," Mrs. Marbly noted, handing Smoke a letter posted from Kalispell, addressed to Sally Jensen, the Grand Hotel, Barlow, Montana Territory. "That means some are giving up on Hell's Creek."

"That it does, ma'am," Smoke said. "Those were all gamblers riding on top. The inside was filled with saloon girls. When the gamblers and the wilted roses start leaving a town, it's like they say about rats leaving a ship. It's about to sink."

"Good riddance to bad rubbish, I say," Mrs. Marbly said. "I'm not an evil-hearted person, Marshal Jensen. My motto is if you can't say something good about a person, don't say anything at all. But that motto has been sorely put to the test by those holligans and trash up at Hell's Creek. If God were to strike them all dead, I would dance on their graves, Lord forgive me."

She walked back into the store. A good, decent woman who had been pushed just too far, one time too often. Smoke knew she carried a Smith & Wesson pocket .38 in her purse. And he had no doubts but that she would use it.

He took the letter back to the hotel, gave it to Sally, and waited until she had read it.

"You guessed, of course, that it was from Victoria?"

He nodded his head.

"This was posted yesterday in Kalispell—that's only thirty miles away from Hell's Creek—but it's still fast service. There have been a rash of killings in Hell's Creek. Outlaws killing outlaws. One of them managed to escape from the town and came to Robert for treatment. He told Robert that Big Max had ordered the killings. He didn't know why, but that something big was up. Then the man died. Robert—he's no fool—took the body back into Hell's Creek and told Big Max he had found the body on the road and thought it should be reported to the authorities. Big Max thanked him for being such a civic-minded person and told Robert he'd take care of it. Max knows that Robert is scared to try to leave because of the threats made against Lisa. What does it mean, Smoke?"

"Probably that Val Singer and Warner Frigo and the other gang leaders are getting rid of those they feel might not be able to keep their mouths shut once this something big goes down. So much for honor among thieves."

"And this something big is? . . ."

"Probably a raid against the town. A raid that includes killing everyone here. Sally, have the hotel pack me a bait of food. I'm going to take a little trip. I should be back by late tomorrow afternoon. I'll arrange for Jim and Sal to meet the stage in case Dubois and Mittermaier should arrive; but I think it's still a couple of days early for that."

"Where are you going, honey?"

"To get the one thing this town needs, Sally." He grinned. "A doctor."

Smoke had checked the land office and knew where the Turner spread was located. He spared his horse, resting often, and rode into Big Max Huggins's country well after dark. He avoided the town by several miles and pulled up at what he hoped was the Turner spread about ten o'clock.

He circled the house to see if they kept a dog and was relieved to find they did not. Smoke picketed Star and slipped up toward the house. He flattened himself against the woodshed when the front door opened and a man stepped out. The man closed the door behind him and stood in the front yard, breathing in the cool night air.

"Dr. Turner?" Smoke called softly.

The man spun around, startled.

"Take it easy, Doctor," Smoke said. "I'm friendly. I'm going to walk toward you, both my hands in plain sight. OK?"

"Who are you?" the doctor demanded.

"The name is Jensen. Smoke Jensen." Smoke walked closer.

"Hold it right there!" the doctor warned. "I have a gun."

"No, you don't," Smoke replied, stepping closer. "And even if you did, it's doubtful you'd know how to use it."

Smoke stopped a few feet from the man and stared at him.

"If you're Smoke Jensen, tell me about yourself."

"My wife's name is Sally. We live in Colorado on a spread we named the Sugarloaf. My wife went to college back east with your wife, Victoria. Sally calls her Vicky. Vicky lost her parents while she was in school and had to work very hard to get through. You have one child that lived, Lisa. Your wife can't have any more children. Sally got a letter from Vicky today, telling us about the recent killings in Hell's Creek and the outlaw who staggered up to this ranch and told you about it. You got this ranch by befriending an old man who was visiting back east. You . . ."

"Enough." The doctor held up a hand, visible in the faint light of a quarter moon. He smiled and stuck out the hand for Smoke to shake it. "Welcome to our home, Mr. Jensen."

Smoke shook the hand. "We don't have much time, Doctor. Things are going to blow wide open around here very soon, and you and your family have got to get clear. Let's go in the house and talk."

Lisa was in bed, asleep. Vicky was introduced to Smoke. She stepped back and inspected him, good humor in her eyes. Smoke liked her immediately. He would reserve judgment on the doctor.

"Sally always could pick them," Vicky said. "You are one hell of a man, Smoke Jensen."

"Vicky," her husband said in a long-suffering tone.

Smoke laughed. "Relax, Robert. Sally can occasionally let the words fly herself. I can see why these two were friends at school."

"How about some coffee and something to eat, Smoke?" Vicky asked.

"That would be nice. While I'm eating, you two can pack."

That stopped them both in their tracks. Robert asked, "Pack? Where are we going?"

"Getting out of here." Smoke found the cups and poured his own coffee. Very quickly, he explained what was going on. "As far as your ranch goes, if Max burns the buildings down, you've still got the land. You don't have any cattle or any hands. You can always rebuild. You can't do anything from the grave. So pack. We're pulling out."

Smoke drank his coffee and ate a sandwich. Then he went outside and hitched up the teams to a wagon and a buggy. He helped the doctor load his medical equipment onto the wagon, then their luggage and a few possessions from the house. Lisa was awake and wide-eyed as she solemnly stared at the most famous gunfighter in the West.

"I'm surprised Lisa doesn't have a dog," Smoke said.

"I did," the little girl said, sadness in her voice. "Patches was his name. A man killed it a few months ago."

"A rather unsavory character named Warner Frigo rode

109

up into the yard and shot him," Robert said. "It was another one of Max Huggins's little not-too-subtle warnings."

Smoke knelt down and, with a gentleness in his voice that surprised Robert and Vicky, said to Lisa, "We'll get you another dog, Lisa. It won't take the place of Patches, I know that. You'll always remember him. But you can love your new puppy, too. How about it?"

"I'd like that, Mister Smoke. I really would."

Smoke picked her up with no more effort than picking up a feather pillow and smiled. "First thing after we get you all settled is a new puppy, Lisa."

"Frigo is a bad man," the girl said. "He's awful. Only cruel people kill dogs who aren't doing them any harm."

"That's right, Lisa. That's exactly right. Don't you worry about Frigo. I'll take care of him." He set her back down and said, "Let's go, people. We've got a long haul ahead of us."

Vicky walked through the house once more, and there was sadness in her eyes. "I've grown to love this old house, this land with the mountains and the eagles and all its vastness." She blew out a lamp, plunging the room into darkness. "I pray that Max and his hooligans will let the house stand." She sighed and squared her shoulders. "But if they don't . . . we'll rebuild."

"That's the spirit," Smoke told her. "But you might decide to relocate down in Barlow."

"Why would we do that?" Robert asked.

"Because I intend to destroy Hell's Creek, that's why."

Because with the wagons they would have to come within a half mile of Hell's Creek, Smoke wrapped the horses' hooves in sacking when they got close. Out of habit, he checked his guns, loading them up full. The action did not escape the eyes of the doctor and his wife. Lisa had fallen asleep in the back of the wagon, lying on a soft comforter and wrapped up in a blanket, for the night was cool.

"Rumor has it you've killed twenty-five men, Smoke," Robert said.

"Closer to two hundred, I reckon," Smoke corrected.

"Two hundred!" the doctor blurted out. "Two hundred men?"

"Killed twenty-five when I was about nineteen or twenty, I think I was. They raped my wife and then killed her and our son. I tracked them down to a silver camp on the Uncompahgre and read to them from the Scriptures, so to speak."

"You were only nineteen?" Vicky breathed the question.

"Maybe twenty. I don't remember."

"So young," Robert muttered.

"Oh, I dropped my first man when I was about seventeen, I think I was. After Pa died an old mountain man named Preacher took me in and raised me. It was a shooting just west of the Needle Mountains. They call the place Rico now. Two men braced me in the trading post. Pike and another man. Never did know his name. I killed them both."

Robert and Victoria listened in silence, their mouths open in shock and fascination, their expressions much like one would wear while gazing at a rattlesnake.

"Me and Preacher, we rode over to what's now called Pagosa Springs—that's Indian for healing water. Two men called me out over there. Man named Haywood and another fellow who was Pike's brother." Smoke tied another piece of sacking in place. "I dropped Haywood and let Pike's brother live. I only shot him twice, in the leg and the arm.

"Me and Preacher rode on over to La Plaza de los Leones; that's on the Cuchara River. It's now called Walsenburg. You see, I was looking for the men who killed my brother and my pa. Killed seven that day and hung one. Casey was his name.

"We drifted on over to Canon City, looking for a man named Ackerman. He found us, him and five of his gang. Killed five, left one alive."

"Lord Jesus," Robert said softly. "That's thirty-three men."

"Oh, I haven't even gotten started yet," Smoke said. "Me and Preacher, we spent the winter back at Brown's Hole, then come spring we drifted out again. That summer I met Nicole and we got married. Sort of. Within a year it all fell to

111

pieces. Bounty hunters got lead in Preacher and I thought they'd killed him. They did kill Nicole and the baby. That's when I rode up to the silver camp with hate in my heart."

"And there have been many more dead men since then?" Robert asked.

"More than I can count, Robert. They just keep coming at me. It was early spring in . . . oh, '74 I think it was. I rode over into Idaho looking for the rest of the men who killed my pa and my brother. Town called Bury. I was going by the name of Buck West."

The horses' hooves muffled, the small party moved out.

"A man called Big Jack braced me at a trading post. His partner buried him out back. I rode on. I had ten thousand dollars on my head at that time, and a lot of bounty hunters were hard after me.

"It was in Challis that two gunhands called me out in the street. I think their names were Carson and Phillips. After I killed them, the marshal asked me to leave. I don't blame him, and I left.

"I rode into Bury with no one knowing who I really was. I was looking to kill the last of the three men who killed my pa and brother: Josh Richards, Wiley Potter, and Keith Stratton. Sally was teaching school there. I saw my sister Janey for the first time in ten years. She was Richard's mistress. She didn't recognize me right off.

"I was walking Sally back to her home when two gunhandlers braced me on the street. Dickerson and Russell. I dropped them both.

"Things turned both tragic and funny after that. Sally lost her job school-teaching and went to live in a whorehouse."

"A whorehouse!" Victoria almost shouted the word. "Sally in a whorehouse?"

Smoke chuckled. "Yep. Oh, she didn't work there. She just lived there."

"My heavens!" Robert muttered.

"Ol' boy on the SRP payroll braced me. I don't remember his name. I had to kill him. It was that day that Janey recognized me as her brother." Smoke cut his eyes and turned his head. He held up a hand for the wagons to stop.

"What's the matter?" Robert asked.

"Something out there," Smoke said.

"How do you know that?"

"Star's ears just came up. A horse is a good as a dog about warning you."

They all heard the clop of horses' hooves and watched as two men rode out of the darkness and up to their wagon.

Both of the men had guns in their hands, the hammers jacked back.

"Well, now," one said. "Ain't this a sight? The doctor and his pretty wife tryin' to slip out, and Smoke Jensen leadin' them. Look here, Jensen. Look down the barrel of the gun that's gonna kill you!"

12

All Robert or Vicky would remember in the retelling of the event was a series of roaring gunshots. What they did not know was that at the sound of the horses' hooves, Smoke had wrapped the reins around the saddle horn and filled both his hands with .44's.

And neither Robert nor Vicky had seen the third man; but Smoke had.

It was all over in two heartbeats. Three men lay dead or dying on the ground. Robert started to climb down from the wagon.

"Sit down!" Smoke's words were sharp. "Pick up those reins and whap those horses on the butt. We've got to move and do it fast."

"But those men . . ." Robert protested.

Smoke knee-reined Star up to the wagon. When he spoke, his words were low and savage. "Mister, do you want to see your wife and little girl spread-eagled on the ground, being raped, over and over again, until dawn?"

"No. Of course not! But . . ."

"Then shut up and drive this wagon." Smoke slapped one horse on the butt and the team jumped forward, the doctor hanging onto the reins. "Go, Vicky!" Smoke shouted. "Stay on this road south. Don't get off of it. I'll catch up in about an hour. Move!"

Smoke jumped off Star and grabbed the outlaws' rifles from the saddle boots. He jerked off their gunbelts and swiftly loaded the two Winchesters and the Henry up full.

"You gotta help me!" one gut-shot outlaw moaned. "I'm hard-hit."

"That's your problem," Smoke told him. "You were going to kill me, remember?"

"You're a heartless bastard, ain't you, Jensen?"

"No," Smoke replied, levering a round in each chamber of the rifles. "Just a realist, that's all. Now either shut up or die; one or the other."

He left the man moaning in the road and, leading Star, got himself into position in the rocks above the road, in the center of the curve, several sticks of capped and fused dynamite beside him. He made him a little smoldering pocket of punk to light the fuses and waited. He could hear the pounding of hooves, the riders coming hard.

He lit a fuse and judged his toss, placing the charge about fifty feet in front of the laboring horses. The dynamite blew and the horses panicked, throwing riders in all directions. Most of them landed, rolled, and came up on their boots, running for cover. Several lay still, badly hurt and unconscious.

Smoke worked the lever on the Henry as fast as he could and knocked down half-a-dozen riders. He grinned when he saw where many of the gunhands had taken shelter. He poured dirt over the smoldering punk to kill it and left his position, working his way back and then up to about a hundred yards above the road.

He lit another stick of dynamite and tossed it in the middle of a rock pile above the men, then another stick. The explosions jarred the rocks loose and sent them bouncing and crashing onto the men below.

Smoke ran for Star, jumped into the saddle, and was gone into the night. It would take the outlaws anywhere from thirty minutes to two hours to round up their horses.

When he caught up with Robert and Vicky, he halted the parade.

"What did you do back there?" Robert asked, his eyes wide. "We heard explosions and shots."

"I showed them the error of their evil ways and put them

on the path of righteousness."

Vicky laughed out loud.

"In other words, you killed them?"

"Lord knows, I sure tried. We'll go on for a few miles and then stop and make camp."

"But those men of Hell's Creek . . . they'll be after us, won't they?"

"Not that bunch," Smoke assured the doctor. "I took the guts right out of them back yonder."

Five miles farther, off the road and camped in a little draw, Smoke drank his coffee and ate a cold sandwich. Lisa had tried to stay awake but finally closed her eyes and was sound asleep.

"Tell us the rest of the story," Victoria urged.

"Where was I?" Smoke asked.

"Killing people," Robert muttered.

Smoke suppressed a chuckle. He had a hunch the doctor was made of stronger stuff than he appeared. "Well, on the day in Bury that my real identity got known, I was trapped in the town. I'd just left the whorehouse talking with Sally and was coming up an alley when I was braced. That ol' boy let it be known that he was gonna collect that thirty thousand dollars that Potter and Richards and Stratton had put on my head. After I shot that fella, I told him to be sure and tell Saint Peter that none of this was my idea."

Robert was shaking his head but listening intently.

"Before I got out of that alley, another gunny braced me. I left him on the ground and got back to my horse. I put the reins in my teeth and charged the mob that was comin' up the street, led by a crooked sheriff name of Reese.

"Drifter—that was my horse—killed one with his hooves and I shot another gunhand name of Jerry. Me and Drifter scattered gunhands all over the main street of Bury, left that town, and linked up with Preacher and a bunch of old mountain men that was camped up in the mountains outside of town. Let me see . . . there was Preacher, Tennysee, Audie—he was a midget—Beartooth, Dupre, Greybull, Nighthawk—he was an Indian . . . a Crow—Phew, Deadlead, Powder Pete, Matt—he was a Negro. Matt was the

117

youngest of the bunch and he was about seventy.

"We blew the roadbank in and trapped those in the town. Wasn't but two ways in or out, and we closed them both. We gave the citizens a chance to leave and a lot of them did. In the days that followed, before I met a bunch in a ghost town, we got Sally and the wilted flowers out and then I went head-hunting."

"How many men did you kill during those days?" Victoria asked.

"Any who tried to kill me, Vicky. A half a dozen or so, I imagine. On that day we burned down Bury and I met Richards and his bunch in that ghost town, the first man to brace me was a man called Davis. Then Williams and Cross. Then a hired gun name of Simpson faced me. Then there was Martin and a man I didn't know. Rogers and Sheriff Reese came after me. I plugged Rogers and Reese's horse crushed him. I shot Turkel off a rooftop and Britt shot off part of my ear." He lifted one hand. "This part. I dropped three more. Britt, Harris, and Smith. Then Williams got lead in me and I blew Rogers to hell with a shotgun. Brown come up and I dropped him.

"I used my knife to pick the lead out of my leg and wrapped a bandana around it. I believe there were three more left. I plugged two and used a rifle to blow a hired gun name of Fenerty out of it."

Smoke's voice softened as memories filled him, taking him back years. Robert and Victoria could practically feel the pain of those years as they strained to hear him.

"All right, you bastards!" Smoke yelled, tall and bloody in the smoky main street of the ghost town. "Richards, Potter, Stratton. Face me, if you've got the nerve."

The sharp odor of sweat mingled with blood and gunsmoke filled the still summer air as four men stepped out into the bloody, dusty street.

Richards, Potter, and Stratton stood at one end of the street. A tall bloody figure stood at the other. All their guns were in leather.

"You son of a bitch!" Stratton screamed, his voice as high-pitched as a woman's. "You ruined it all. Damn you!" He clawed for his pistol.

Smoke drew, cocked, and fired before Stratton could clear leather.

Potter grabbed for his gun. Smoke shot him dead, holstered his pistol, and waited for Richards to make his play.

Richards was sure he could beat Smoke. He had not moved. He stood with a faint smile on his lips, staring at Smoke.

"You ready to die?" Smoke asked the man.

"As ready as I'll ever be, I suppose." Richards's hands were steady. There was no fear in his voice. "Janey gone?"

"Yeah. She took your money and pulled out."

Richards smiled. "That's one tough babe, Jensen."

"Among other things."

"Been a long run, hasn't it, Jensen?"

"It's just about over."

"What happens to all my holdings?"

"I don't care what happens to the mines. The miners can have them. I'm giving all your stock and the lands they gaze on to decent, honest punchers and homesteaders."

A puzzled look spread over Richards's face. He waved his hand at the carnage that lay all around them. "You did . . . all this for nothing?"

Someone moaned, the sound painfully inching up the dusty street.

"I did it for my pa, my brother, my wife, and our baby son."

"But killing me won't bring them back!"

"No. But it will insure that you never do anything like that again."

"I can truthfully say that I wish I had never heard the name Jensen."

"You'll never hear it again after this day, Richards."

"One way to find out, Jensen." He drew and fired. Richards was snake-quick but he hurried his shot, the lead digging up dirt at Smoke's boots.

Smoke's shot hit the man in the right shoulder, spinning him around. Richards grabbed for his left-hand gun and

Smoke fired again, the slug striking the man in the chest. He struggled to level his pistol. Smoke shot him again, the slug hitting Richards in the belly. Richards sat down hard in the street.

Smoke walked up the street to stand over the man. Richards reached out for the pistol that had fallen from his numb hand. Smoke kicked it away.

Blood filled the man's mouth. The light began to fade around him. Richards said, "You'll . . . meet . . ."

Smoke never found out whom he was supposed to meet. Richards toppled over on his face and died.

Robert and Vicky were silent for a few moments after Smoke had finished his story.

Vicky said, "And after that?"

"I got Sally and we took off, heading for Colorado. We've been there ever since." Smoke tossed the dregs of his coffee into the night. "We best get some sleep. We still got a pull ahead of us come morning."

Smoke led the wagon and buggy into Barlow. The group was met with cheers from the onlookers. Draper was there with his camera, taking pictures.

"I must admit," Robert said, "I rather like the welcoming committee."

Sally rushed out of the hotel and the two women hugged each other. With Lisa in tow, the ladies disappeared into the hotel. They had a lot of catching up to do.

"I'm teaching the women of the town who don't know much about guns to shoot," Sally told her friend. "Classes are this afternoon. Do you have any jeans?"

"Britches?" Vicky looked horrified.

"Sure. It's a changing world, Victoria. We'll get you some at Marbly's."

"Everything's been quiet, Smoke," Sal said, walking up. He shook hands with the doctor, his eyes sizing the man up. He took note that the doctor did not wear a gun.

"Do I pass inspection?" Robert asked with a smile.

"Won't know that until the shootin' starts."

"I've done more than my share of hunting, I assure you," Robert replied stiffly.

"Deer don't shoot back," Sal said, then walked off.

Robert looked around him. The people standing around them were all friendly-looking and he had shook a lot of hands. He also had noticed that every man was armed. Every man. Including the editor of the *Bugle*. No doubt about it, the doctor thought. This town is braced for trouble.

"Mrs. Jensen told us what you were doing yesterday, Smoke," Tom Johnson said. "We fixed up an office for Dr. Turner. It's right next to his house."

Smoke grasped the doctor by the shoulder. "You and Victoria get settled in, Robert. Big doings come Saturday night." He smiled. "The town is throwing a party."

Forty-eight hours before the dance and box supper, Smoke met the northbound stage and knew he'd hit pay dirt when two nattily-dressed men stepped off to stretch their legs. They were the only two passengers on the stage. Northbound business had dwindled since Smoke had arrived in Barlow and pinned on a badge. The two men were dressed like dandies but their eyes, cold and emotionless, gave them away.

Henri Dubois and Paul Mittermaier.

Smoke had talked with the driver several days before, setting things up, and the driver nodded his head at Smoke's glance. "It's gonna be about an hour 'fore we pull out, boys," he called. "I got to change this cracked brake lever and one of the pads. Yonder's the saloon. I'll give a hoot and a holler when I'm ready to go."

The team was led away, team and coach heading for the barn.

Henri and Paul headed for the saloon. One of the Circle W hands, Wesson, had agreed to his part in the action. He walked toward the men and slammed a shoulder into the big German.

"Watch where you're goin', stupid!" Wesson said.

"Get out of my way, you ignorant lout!" the German replied.

"What the hell did you call me?" the hand faced him.

"Back off, Paul," Henri said softly.

"What's the matter?" Wesson said with a sneer. "Your buddy have to do your fightin' for you?"

Paul drew back a fist and Wesson popped him on the nose. Henri gave Wesson a blow to the jaw just as the saloon cleared, all of Joe's hands pouring out. The Circle W crew then proceeded to kick the snot out of the pair of assassins, leaving them unconscious on the street.

"Clear out," Smoke told them. "I'll see you all come Saturday night. Thanks, boys."

"Our pleasure, Smoke," Curly grinned around the words. He looked down at the unconscious and badly battered men. "Them ol' boys won't be doin' much of anything for a week or two. Maybe longer."

The Circle W crew rode out of town.

"Now what?" Jim asked.

Smoke grinned and reached into his coat pocket, pulling out a bottle of opium-based elixir. "I bought a full case of this from a drummer last week. By the time these two wake up, they're going to be on a train, heading back east. Come on, help me drag them off the street."

They dragged the unconscious men into an alley and stripped them of their duded-up clothes, dressing them in filthy, ragged shirts and jeans. Henri moaned and tried to sit up. Smoke popped him on the noggin with a cosh he'd taken to carrying and the Frenchman laid back down.

With the two men now dressed like bums, Smoke poured a half bottle of knock-out medicine down each of their throats and placed them in the back of a freight wagon.

"Keep them unconscious," Smoke told the grinning freighters who had been more than willing to participate in the game. Anything to get rid of Max Huggins and his gang of outlaws. "When you get down to Helena, pour a bottle of the elixer down them and toss them in an empty eastbound railcar. They'll be somewhere in Nebraska when they wake up."

"Will do, Smoke," the freighter told him. "Don't worry about a thing. Man, this is more fun than I thought it'd be. We was lookin' forward to seeing a shoot-out; but, hell, this is better." Laughing, the freighters pulled out, joining other empty freight wagons on the pull back south.

"Now what do you have in the back of that devious mind of yourn?" Sal asked, unable to wipe the grin off his face.

"Let's go inspect their luggage. I want to see these fancy guns that were going to be used to kill me."

Sal whistled when Smoke opened the gun cases. Both men had seen rifles of this type before, but neither had seen one so duded-up. They were Winchester high-wall, falling block rifles. Single shot.

Smoke hefted one. The rifle had been reworked and the balance was perfect. The telescope was about two feet long, and the shells looked like either the German or the Frenchman or both had carefully and painstakingly loaded their own.

"That bullet would travel about three miles before it knocked you down," Sal said, inspecting one cartridge.

"You know," Smoke said, "most guns are tools. A man uses one snake-killing, or varmint-killing, or to protect himself or his loved ones. I've driven tacks and nails in horseshoes with the butt of my pistols. But these rifles are meant for only one thing."

"Yeah," Sal agreed, closing the lid to the gun case. "Man-killin'."

13

The people started coming into town for the dance and box supper during the middle of the day on a beautiful Saturday afternoon.

Most would spend the night camped under their wagons, or in the wagon bed under canvas if it was raining. A few took rooms at the Grand Hotel.

Just before dusk, Smoke had taken his bath and dressed in a black suit, white shirt with string tie, and slipped into his just-polished boots. He strapped on his guns and looked in on Sally. She had dressed in a simple gingham outfit; but with Sally, she could make a flour sack look good.

She gave her hair a final pat and turned to Smoke. "Are you expecting trouble tonight, honey?"

"Yes, I am. When Joe Walsh's crew meet up with Red Malone's Lightning crew, anything is apt to happen."

"All the crews coming in?"

"As far as I know. Joe really stripped his herds this spring, keeping mostly young stuff. So night-herding is not that essential."

"Shooting trouble?"

"No. We've taken care of that. All guns will be checked upon entering the dance area. If any object to that, they can carry their butts back home. If any trouble starts, it will be fists."

"But you and Sal and Jim will be armed?"

Smoke smiled. "Oh, yes, honey."

"This promises to be quite an interesting night."

"That . . . is one way of putting it, yes."

They walked down the stairs and were a head-turning couple, Sally a beautiful woman and Smoke a strikingly handsome man in a rugged sort of way.

They joined Dr. and Mrs. Turner in the hotel dining room for coffee.

"I will say this, Smoke," Robert said. "I find the people of Barlow a refreshing change from the hoodlums and rowdies of Hell's Creek. We both like it here."

"I'm glad you do. And I hope you decide to stay. It's going to be a growing little town."

"But you and Sally will eventually move on?"

"Oh, yes. Back to the Sugarloaf. It's home. We'll get this situation straightened out here and be back home in early fall."

"Will there be trouble tonight?" Vicky asked.

"Probably," Smoke gave her an honest reply. "But it won't be gunplay."

"Anyone from Hell's Creek made an appearance yet?" Robert asked.

"Not to my knowledge. But they'll be along. They can't afford not to show up."

They looked up, and Tom Walsh and his Circle W crew rode in and dismounted. Tom drove the buggy, sitting beside his wife. Mrs. Walsh joined the ladies in the dining room, while Smoke and Dr. Turner stepped outside to join Joe and his crew.

"All right, boys," Smoke spoke to the Circle W hands. "This is the way it's going to be this night. When you enter the dance and box supper area, you check your guns with Mrs. Marbly. The only people who will be armed will be me and my deputies. And I've appointed several special deputies for this night. Anyone who doesn't think they can abide by that rule, haul your ashes out of town."

"Suits me," Curly was the first to speak. "But it's gonna be interestin' to see you take Melvin Malone's guns offen him."

"I'll take them," Smoke replied. "Or tomorrow his dad will be burying him."

Tom Johnson, one of the special deputies, rode in from the north, just as Benson, another of the special deputies, rode up from the south end of town. Johnson said, "Big Max and half a dozen of his gunslicks coming in."

"Red Malone and his crew are just outside of town," Benson added.

"Get your shotguns, boys," Smoke said. "Line up with me on the boardwalk."

Johnson, Marbly, Benson, and Toby got sawed-off shotguns and lined up in front of the hotel, two on each side of Smoke. Jim and Sal stood a dozen yards off, one on each side of the five. They too were armed with Greeners.

Smoke knew some of the men who rode in with Max: Alex Bell, Dave Poe, Val Singer. He did not know the others with them. But he knew the breed: hired guns.

"I don't like this," Val muttered, eyeballing the shotgun-armed men on the boardwalk.

"Relax," Max told him. "It's just a show of force."

"Hell of a welcoming committee, boss," John Steele said.

"Don't nobody do nothin' stupid," Red Malone said to his men. "Them express guns would kill everybody in the whole damn street. Let's find out what's going on."

One of Red's hands was driving the buggy with the elegantly gowned Tessie. She took one look at Smoke and said, "Oohhh, I think I'm in love!"

In heat would be more like it, the hand thought. But he kept that to himself.

Tessie's exploits were known throughout the entire county—and several adjacent counties.

The crews of Max and Red swung their horses and faced Smoke and his deputies.

"Good evening, gentlemen, Miss Tessie," Smoke said. "Welcome to Barlow."

"What's the idea of all this force?" Red demanded in a loud voice.

Smoke ignored him. "It's a beautiful night, people, so we decided to move everything outdoors. The dance area is roped off, as is the box supper area. We have plenty of chairs and benches for your comfort if you didn't bring blankets to sit on. That tent set up just before you enter the entertainment area is where you will check your guns."

Smoke had stepped off the boardwalk as he was speaking, moving close to Mel Malone.

"I'll be damned if I'll check my guns!" the young man said.

Smoke jerked him off his horse, slapped him twice, ripped the gunbelt from him, and tossed guns and belt into a horse trough. He did it so quickly no one had a chance to interfere.

Smoke faced the young man as he spoke to his deputies. "Anybody who makes a grab for a gun, start killing the whole bunch of them."

Hammers were eared back on the sawed-off shotguns and the muzzles leveled at the mounted men.

"Now, hold on!" Red bellowed. Sawed-off shotguns at this range would tear them all apart.

Smoke grabbed Melvin by his fancy shirt and jerked him close. "You say one more word to me about what you're not going to do, sonny-boy, and I'll break both your goddamn arms so you'll never be able to pick up a gun again. You understand me?"

For the first time in his life, Melvin Malone knew real fear. It clutched at him, souring his stomach. He looked into the eyes of Smoke Jensen and saw death staring back at him. Death rode a fiery horse and the grim reaper wore the face of Smoke Jensen.

"Yes, sir," he said quietly. "I understand." Then rage overrode fear and the young man made up his mind. He carried a hide-out gun behind his belt buckle.

Smoke released him. He was expecting a sneak-play from the young man and was ready for it.

Mel grabbed for his Remington over-and-under .41 derringer and Smoke hit him. Smoke's big fist smashed into the young man's face, flattening his nose and knocking him flat on his butt in the street. Before Mel could shake the birds and bells and buzzing bees out of his head, Smoke had rolled him over and clamped handcuffs tight around his wrists.

Smoke straightened up. "Take him to jail, Jim. The charge is disorderly conduct, disturbing the peace, and attempted murder of a peace officer. Bond, if any, will be set by Judge

Garrison in the morning. That's it, people. Check your guns with Mrs. Marbly and have fun."

Smoke walked back onto the boardwalk, turned, and faced the mounted men.

Red cut his eyes to the south. A dozen men, all armed with rifles, stood in the street, blocking any escape. Max followed the glance, grunted, and then looked toward the north. Another dozen men, all heavily armed, blocked the north end of the street.

"I think," Alex Bell said with unusual restraint, "that we'uns better check our guns and get ready for the dance."

"We'll do that," Red said, swinging his gaze back to Smoke. "and there'll be no trouble in this town tonight. Not by any of my people. But you'll not try my boy on them charges, Jensen."

"He'll be tried, Red. And if convicted, he'd do his time in the territorial prison. Now hear me well, all of you. The days of lawlessness are over in this town. The days of any of you riding roughshod over decent, law-abiding people have ended. Pull in your horns and act right, or die. That's the only choice I'm going to give any of you. If any of you cause trouble at tonight's festivities, I'll kill you. I'll shoot you down like a rabid skunk and drag your carcass off and stick it in the first hole I come to. And if it's the lime pit of an old privy, that'll do just fine. Now stable your horses and check your guns."

Max was the first to move. He backed his horse and rode to the livery stable, Red and the others following. And it was a silent following. Not one of them doubted that Smoke Jensen meant every word they'd just heard him say.

In the stable, Val Singer said, "I'd hate to think I had to spend eternity in a shit-pit."

"And Jensen would do it, too," Alex Bell said.

"We got to do something about Jensen, Max," Dave Poe said. "And we got to do it damn quick."

"I know. Did you boys notice anything riding into town?"
No one had.

"Then open your damn eyes!" Max snapped at them "Look around you. You're supposed to be gunfighters, men who live by your wits. Hell, boys, there are water barrels everywhere. Full barrels. With buckets close by. This very stable is where the town used to keep their pumper. It's gone. That means that Jensen outguessed us . . . again. He guessed we might try to burn him out, and they're prepared for it.

"Did any of you see the clearing of brush that's been done around the town? And up on the ridges where a sharpshooter might hide? There is no place. Not anymore. The town is ready for an attack."

"Where is them high-priced sharpshooters from Europe that was comin' in?" Val asked.

"I don't know," Max admitted. "They should have been here by now. Unless . . ." he mused aloud. Then he shook his head. "No. Jensen had no way of knowing they were coming in. And neither one of them carries a sidearm . . . where it can be seen. He'd have no reason to pull them off the stage. I can but assume they are on their way in."

One of the gunslingers unbuckled his gunbelt and draped it over his shoulder. "Well," he drawled. "Let's go be good little boys and check our guns and dance with some real ladies, and then we'll eat some home cookin' for a change."

Smoke stood on the edge of the lantern-lighted perimeter and let Curly from the Circle W and a redheaded hand from the Lightning brand slug it out. He had no idea what had started the fracas, but as long as no guns were involved, he had told his deputies to let the men fight, but to just keep it away from the ladies.

"Anybody that would work for Red Malone would eat road apples," Curly told the puncher.

Red flattened him.

Curly jumped up, butted Red in the stomach with his head, and both of them went rolling across the dirt. Curly came up on top and proceeded to rearrange Red's face for him.

Smoke finally pulled the man off the Lightning puncher. "That's enough, Curly. He's out of it. Kill him and the matter becomes something other than a fistfight."

The blacksmith, Benson, grabbed Curly and led him off to a horse trough. Benson, strong as a grizzly bear, picked Curly up and dunked him headfirst into the trough several times.

"Now cool down, man," Benson told him. "Your sweetie's box is gonna be comin' up soon. You miss the bid on it and she'll never speak to you again." Benson was holding him by his boots, upside down.

"You do have a point," Curly sputtered. "Now turn me a-loose."

"You sure?" Benson asked.

"Damn right, I'm sure."

Benson turned him loose and Curly dropped headfirst into the horse trough.

Everybody gathered around, including Max and Red, had a good laugh at that.

Curly came up for air, sputtering and cussing.

Smoke walked to where Dr. Turner was kneeling down beside the moaning cowboy.

"He'll be all right," the doctor said. "His nose is broken and he's lost some teeth, but I can't find any broken ribs. He'll be sore for a few days. Barbaric method of settling arguments," he added.

"Beats the hell out of guns," Smoke told him.

"You have a point," the doctor conceded.

The rest of the evening went smoothly, with no more trouble. The bidding on the boxes was fast and sometimes heavy, depending on whether two young men were courting the same young lady. Smoke bid on Mrs. Walsh's box and Joe bid on Sally's, and everybody seemed to have a good time. Even Max got into the spirit of things and was laughing and telling jokes to the ladies . . . clean jokes.

After everyone had eaten and the dancing began, Max walked over to Smoke, standing in the shadows.

"You really think you've got the bull by the horns, now, don't you, Jensen?"

"Or riding a tiger."

Max chuckled. "Yes. The old East Indian proverb. I know it. And you surely must know, Smoke, that we of Hell's

Creek are not simply going to give up and desert the town."

"You'd be smart if you did."

"No way, Jensen. You've backed us into a corner. We have to fight."

"If you say so."

"Innocent people will be hurt . . . killed."

"That's usually the way it goes." He turned slightly to face Max. "Take some advice, Max: Pull out. Break up your gangs and leave the country. If you stay, I'm going to have to kill you. You must know that."

"Or I'll kill you."

"A lot of men have tried that, Max. I've soaked up a lot of lead in my day. I'm still here."

"Oh, I think Melvin is as good as you are. And you'll never bring that boy to trial, Smoke."

"Maybe not. We'll have to see, won't we?"

"And maybe I have a couple of aces in the hole, Smoke."

"By the names of Henri Dubois and Paul Mittermaier?"

Max's smile was not in the least pleasant to look at. The big man sighed in disgust. He had been counting on the back-shooting pair.

"I've got their fancy rifles locked up in my office. Those two are halfway back to New York City by now. They're so doped up it'll be days before they even know who they are, much less where they are."

Max chuckled. Outlaw, killer, thief, he nevertheless had a sense of humor. And while he did not like being bested, he could still appreciate—however reluctantly—the method that was used in doing so.

"Slick, Jensen. I keep underestimating you. I've got to stop doing that. Jensen, what is the point of your interference? Is this what you're going to do for the rest of your life, stick your damn nose in other peoples' affairs?"

"I hope not, Max. To tell the truth, my wife and I came up here to visit friends. Nothing else."

"Dr. Turner and his wife," Max put it together. "I should have guessed. Sure. Who else in Hell's Creek would your wife want to associate with? So, now Barlow has a doctor and we don't. What's next, Jensen?"

"Your packing up and pulling out."

"That is something I will never do, Jensen."

Smoke shrugged his heavy shoulders. "You've noticed the cleanup around the town, the new water barrels." It was not put as a question. "You've seen where we've fixed up our pumper. And you've seen how the people are all armed and willing to stand shoulder to shoulder to fight you and Red Malone. Don't you feel it in your guts, Max? Can't you see you're not going to win this one?"

Max felt it, all right. He'd been sensing it for several days. riding into Barlow had been depressing. The town was clean and neat, with swept boardwalks and washed windows and shrubs and flowers planted around the homes. Not like Hell's Creek, where litter was ankle-deep in some spots and the gunhands lived in shacks and tents and squalor. The stench of unwashed bodies was something one grew accustomed to in Hell's Creek. The people here took pride in their town. Here, in Barlow, there was a better class of people and good water.

Of course, that's all Hell needed.

Max's eyes flickered to the lush little body of Tessie, doing a reel with that pig-farmer's boy, Elias. His blood grew hot with perversion.

The quick glance did not escape the eyes of Smoke, who filed it away.

"I'll go down with my town," Max said, his voice husky with sudden desire. "If indeed we are to go down at all. And that certainly remains to be seen."

"Men like you never learn, Max. Civilization is fast spreading throughout the West. The people aren't going to tolerate men like us much longer."

"Us?" The statement confused Max. "Us!"

"Sure, Max. Us. I'm tolerated because I'm bringing a change to this town. When you and Red are either dead or run out of the territory, the people won't want me around. I'm a gunfighter, Max. The smell of gunsmoke lingers around me like some sort of invisible shroud. Just like the smell of perversion lingers around you."

Max's head jerked up. "What the hell do you mean by

133

that, Jensen? Perversion?"

"You touch that Feckles girl and I'll kill you, Max. I'll ride right into Hell's Creek and shoot you. As God is my witness, I'll do it."

"She's a woman, Jensen. She might be a child in mind, but she's got the body of a woman." Max knew he ought to shut his big mouth, but arrogance worked his tongue.

"You're pure crud, Max. I know that you lusted after both Victoria and Lisa. Tell you what, Max. I'm going to start sending out wires to a lot of law enforcement offices; I'm going to blanket your back trail and see what I can come up with. And I'm going to start with telegrams concerning child molestation and rape over . . . say, the past ten years or so. How does that grab you, partner?"

Max was thinking hard. He'd left a trail behind him, for sure.

If Jensen started digging, he'd soon put two and two together and Max would be forced to run. No question about that.

Max forced a laugh. "You do that, Jensen. My back trail is clean."

"We'll soon know," Smoke spoke the words softly. "It'll take me about a week to find out."

Max could scarcely control his wildly raging temper. He stared at Smoke for a moment and then spun on his boot heels, hollering for his men to get their gear and mount up. They were leaving.

"What's with Big Max?" Joe Walsh asked, walking up.

"I touched a festering boil," Smoke told him. "And it's just about ready to explode."

14

Over coffee the next morning in his office, Smoke told Jim and Sal and Judge Garrison what had brought on Max Huggins's sudden departure the night before.

"Let me start canvasing various law enforcement agencies, Smoke," Judge Garrison said. "I have many more contacts than you. I should have something within a week, probably in less time than that."

"Good, Judge. Get right on it, will you?"

"Immediately." The judge left the room and walked over to the telegraph office. He would be very busy for the next several days. Judge Garrison did not set a bond for Melvin Malone. He said the attempted murder charge meant he did not have to set a bond. Melvin would stay in jail.

"You're dead, Jensen," Melvin hollered from his cell. He rattled the barred door. "You're a dead man walking around and you're just too stupid to know that."

"Shut up, boy," Smoke called. "You're only making things more difficult for yourself."

"Son of a bitch!" Melvin yelled. "That's you, Jensen. Low-life, no-good . . ."

Smoke tuned him out.

"You know Red is gonna try to bust him out," Sal said.

"Sure. Once he hears no bond was set, he'll try force. Maybe as soon as tonight."

"You want us to set up cots and sleep here?" Jim asked.

"No." Smoke's reply was quick. "Red, so I'm told, likes to use dynamite. That's how he drove all those small farmers out that were settling around his holdings. He might decide to use explosives here. Too risky for us to sleep in."

"Hell, Smoke!" Sal said. "He uses dynamite, he might blow up Melvin tryin' to get him out."

Smoke shook his head. "We won't be that lucky, Sal." Smoke cut his eyes to the window in time to see John Steele riding up, the point man for several wagons, coming into town for supplies. They pulled up in front of Marbly's General Store.

"Oh, boy," Jim said. "Here it comes."

Smoke stood up and reached for his hat. "Yep," he said, heading for the door. "Storm clouds are gathering and it's about to rain trouble all over us. Let's go, boys. I wouldn't want to miss this."

The three men crossed the street just as John Steele was entering Marbly's store. They stepped up onto the boardwalk in time to hear John's shout of disbelief.

"What the hell do you mean, you little worm?" John roared. "My money is no good? My money is as good as anybody's, and by the Lord, you're going to sell me what I want."

"Get out of my store," Marbly stood his ground. "I don't want you or any of your scummy crew in my place of business. Get out, I say!"

John reached across the counter and grabbed Marbly by the shirtfront. Mrs. Marbly jerked an axe handle out of a barrel and bonked it across the top of John's Stetson-covered head. John's eyes rolled back in his head and he sank to the floor, out cold. One of the Lightning hands jerked out a gun and aimed it at the woman. Smoke dusted him through and through with a .44 slug. The force of the slug knocked the cowboy to one side and into a showcase. He died among women's underthings, his head on a corset.

The townspeople reacted immediately to the shooting. The street filled with armed men. The remaining Lightning crew held up their hands in a hurry, not wanting to get plugged from every angle.

Smoke holstered his .44 and pointed to John Steele. "Drag him to jail." He looked at Marbly. "You going to press charges?"

"Damn right!" the shopkeeper said, considerable heat in

his voice.

"Charge him with assault and battery," Smoke said to Sal. "Jim, get the undertaker."

Smoke stepped outside and faced the Lightning crew. "This town is off-limits to you and to anyone who works for Red Malone—including Red. I am officially banning any and all of you from Barlow. Take the word back to Red."

"Big talk, Jensen," the hand sneered at him. "I'll see your hide nailed to the wall afore this is over."

Smoke reached up and took off his badge, handing it to Marbly. "You want to try it now, cowboy? Guns or fists, it makes no difference to me."

The cowboy, who was going by the name of Dan since he was wanted in several states for cattle rustling and armed robbery, among other things, hesitated.

Smoke smiled, knowing he was giving the man no way out. It was the way of the West that when challenged, you had but two options: fight or be branded a coward. Smoke did not like the code but, in this case, felt he was justified in invoking it.

Dan took off his gunbelt and handed it to a Lightning puncher. He flexed his arms and looked back at Smoke. "You mind if I warm up a little first?"

"I don't care if you do the Virginia reel," Smoke told him, and that got a laugh from the gathering crowd, both men and women. "You probably can't dance any better than you can fight."

The crowd roared with laughter and Dan flushed in anger.

"I think I'll just clean your clock," Dan said.

"Then come on, cowboy."

Dan tried a sucker punch that brought no response from Smoke. He hooked a left that Smoke blocked and tried to follow through with a right that Smoke flicked away.

Smoke jumped lightly off the boardwalk and waved Dan down to join him.

"Stand still and fight, damn you!" Dan yelled.

"Oh!" Smoke said. "I see. That's what you want. I thought you were still warming up."

The crowd loved it and roared their approval.

Dan didn't think it was a bit funny and stepped in close.

Smoke rattled his teeth with a left and put a knot on his head with a right. Dan backed up, shaking his head and spitting out blood.

"I'm waiting to fight," Smoke taunted him.

Dan charged him with a shout of defiance, and Smoke stuck out a boot and tripped the man, sending him sprawling into the dirt of the street.

The Lightning cook sat his seat on the wagon and shook his head. Dan was gonna get the crap beat out of him for sure, and just as soon as that was over and done with and they got back to the ranch, Cookie was packin' up his kit and gettin' the hell gone from the Lightning brand. His oldest boy had been forever trying to get him over into Idaho to help on his horse ranch. This time, by God, he was going. Hadn't oughtta a stayed this long with this pack of screwballs.

That thought had just crossed his mind when Dan got up from the dirt and went charging and yelling toward Smoke Jensen. The cook grimaced as Smoke poleaxed the puncher with a solid right fist that turned Dan around and sent him stumbling out into the street.

As a matter of fact, the cook thought, there ain't no reason to go back to the ranch. I just got paid, I got my best clothes on, I'm wearin' my gun, and I ain't got nothin' back there no good for anything no how.

The dull smack of Smoke Jensen's fist again connecting with Dan's jaw prompted Cookie to climb down from the wagon seat and walk up toward the stage office. He had more than enough money in his pockets to get a room at the Grand and buy his ticket over to Idaho. Hell with Red Malone and his foolish boy and the whole damn crazy bunch out at Lightning.

Cookie turned in time to see Dan whip out a knife. "Stupid, Dan," he muttered. "Now Smoke's gonna kill you."

"I'll gut you, Jensen," Dan screamed his rage and frustration. He stepped closer.

Smoke reached behind his right hand .44 and pulled out a long-bladed Bowie knife. "You sure this is the way you want it?" Smoke asked him.

Dan moved closer, working the blade from side to side. He

tried to fake Smoke but Jensen wasn't falling for it.

"Don't do this, Dan!" one of the Lightning crew yelled. "It ain't worth it."

Dan pressed on, curses rolling off his tongue. He swung the blade and Smoke parried it, the metal clanking as the razor-sharp knives met.

Smoke stepped in and cut Dan from earlobe to point of jaw. "Drop the knife," he warned the puncher. "Mountain men raised me. I've been knife-fighting since I was sixteen."

"Hell with you!" Dan said as the blood dripped from the cut on his face.

"I don't want to kill you, boy," Smoke told him. "Give this up."

Dan moved in and Smoke cut his knife arm, opening him up from elbow down to hand. Dan screamed as the knife dropped from his numbed and useless hand.

"Get Dr. Turner," Smoke said to the crowd. "See what he can do with this fool."

Smoke wiped the blood from his blade and sheathed it. Turning to the Lightning punchers, he said, "You have one minute to get clear of this town. And don't ever come back."

Cookie watched from the boardwalk as the bleeding Dan was led to the doctor's office. "Told you so, boy," he muttered. "I learned fifty years ago to give mountain men a wide berth."

Cookie turned and walked into the ticket office. Idaho sure looked good to him.

Red Malone received the news of being banned from Barlow stoically. He had been expecting something like this, so it didn't surprise him.

But he was shook down to his boots at the news of John Steele being jailed. "How is Dan?" he finally asked.

"He ain't never gonna use his right arm again. Tendons was cut."

Red grunted. "Cookie?"

"He quit."

"Get my horse. I'm riding to Barlow."

"You want me to get the boys together?"

"No. I'm riding alone. Do it, Jake. I don't want to hear any arguments."

Red rode to the town limits and sat his saddle in the middle of the road. Malone was many things, but a fool was not one of them. Someone would soon spot him and take the news to Jensen. Smoke would ride out to see what he wanted.

In a couple of minutes, Jensen rode up and faced him. "Something I do for you, Red?"

"Has bond been set for John Steele?"

"Fifty dollars. He's out, saddling his horse. He'll be along shortly."

"He hurt?"

"He's got a knot on his noggin and his pride is bruised, that's all."

Red nodded his head. "You'd a done Dan a favor if you'd gone on and killed him. A one-armed puncher ain't good for much, Jensen."

"That's his problem, Red."

John Steele came riding out, wheeled his horse up beside Red, and faced Smoke. The man was killing mad and it showed on his face, which was chalk-white with anger. Smoke knew that was the sign of a very dangerous man. A red-faced man usually meant all bluff and bluster, but one whose face was chalk-white meant he was cold inside.

"I want to see my boy, Jensen. He ain't much, I'll give you that, but he's still mine. You can have my gun and search me. Have a deputy there with us. But I want to see him."

"All right, Red. I wouldn't have kicked up any fuss at that. A father has a right to see his own. John, you ride on to the spread. Don't come back to town. I mean it. Your high-handed, roughshod ways of dealing with the people of Barlow are over."

"You and me, Jensen," the foreman said tightly. "Someday, just you and me."

"Shut your mouth and clear out, John. Don't dig your own grave."

John wheeled his horse and rode away.

"Did this . . . incident with John go down the way my hand said it did?"

"What'd your hand say about it?" After listening to a brief

rundown, Smoke nodded his head. "That's about it, Red."

It was obvious that Red had more on his mind than seeing his son. Smoke got the impression Malone didn't even like the boy. He might love him, but he sure didn't like him.

"Where am I supposed to buy supplies, Jensen?"

"I don't know, Red. But if Marbly doesn't want you in his store, that's his right."

"You've pushed me up against a wall just like you're pushin' Max. Don't you think we'll push back, Jensen?"

"We're ready anytime you boys want to start the tug-of-war, Red."

"Damnit, man!" Red stirred in the saddle. "My boys will have to drive teams way the hell south of here for supplies."

"There's a way you can prevent that, Red, and you know it."

"There's two ways, Jensen. And you know the other way I'm talkin' about."

"You want to try it now, Red?" Smoke calmly laid down the challenge.

Red grudgingly smiled at the man's calmness and courage. He took a deep breath and shook his head. "I reckon not, Jensen. But you can't stick around here forever. You got to leave sometime. I'll wait."

"I'm betting you won't, Red. Oh, you might; I'll give you that. But sooner or later, your daughter is going to want some pretties from the dress shop or the general store, and she'll agitate you or someone else until you drive her in. One of your hands is going to get drunk and come rip-snorting in here. You or some of your crew or your kid will get sick and have to see the doctor or the man at the apothecary shop. Any of those things could blow the lid off. And one of them more than likely will."

"You'd stop me from bringing my girl or one of my men in to see the doctor?"

"That's right, Red."

"You're a heartless bastard, Jensen!"

"Oh, I wouldn't prevent the doctor from going out to your spread. Or you could bring them to this town limit and he could treat them. But after today, unless it's for a court appearance, neither you nor any of your family or crew sets a foot in Barlow."

Red curtly nodded his head. "I got a packet in my saddlebags for Mel. It's some readin' material and money so's he can buy himself some food from the cafe. Is that all right?"

"Suits me, Red."

Red unbuckled the straps and handed Smoke a small packet.

"You know I'll have to inspect it?"

"I know. It's a Bible, Jensen. That's the only book I could find in the house. Maybe he'll read it, maybe he won't. I reckon I should have."

"You think it's too late for that, Red?"

The rancher thought about that for a moment. "Yeah, I think it is, Jensen." He shook his head. "That don't make no never-mind. I'll deal with the devil when I meet him. Jensen, either I'm gonna kill you, John Steele is gonna kill you, Max Huggins is gonna kill you, or somebody is gonna kill you for that bounty on your head . . . and you know there is one."

"So I've heard."

"And there you sit, just as calm and unconcerned as a hog in slop."

"That's me, Red. I don't worry about things I have no control over. I don't fret about too little or too much rain. That's in God's hands. And I don't worry about what you or Max and your scummy crews are going to do. Oh, I could take control of that, Red, by blowing you out of the saddle right now. But even though I've killed lots of men, I'm not a murderer and I don't force gunplay on people who haven't pushed me. So I just wait."

"Lemme see if I can get through to you, Jensen. The people in this town are little people. You and me and Max, we're big people. Big people have always had little people under their thumb. That's what makes the world go round, Jensen. Do you understand that?"

"I hear your words, Red, and you're wrong. But you'll never see that, though. If you lived in a big city, you'd be running a sweatshop, forcing decent people to work long hours under miserable conditions for little pay. That's just the way you are, I reckon. Lots of folks are like you and

Max, Red. You're born that way. I call it the bad seed theory."

"Goddamn you, Jensen," Red flared. "I came out here in late '65 when this country was wild, man, wild! I built my spread with sweat and blood, a lot of it my blood. I fought Injuns and homesteaders and hog-farmers and white trash. I scratched and clawed and chewed my way to what I got. And I'll not see it tore apart in front of my eyes. I demand respect."

"You left out a lot of things, Red. You left out that you probably came out here running from the law back east. . . ."

Smoke knew he'd hit pay dirt from the expression on Red's face. The man looked like he'd been hit with a club. He ground his teeth together so hard Smoke could hear the gnashing. Red's face turned white and he fought to maintain control.

"You always were a liar and a cheat and a thief and a womanizer. I'm told you beat your wife so often and so savagely she finally had enough and quit you. Now I add all that up, Red, and do you know what the total is?"

Red stared at Smoke. He was killing mad but smart enough to know if he dragged iron, Jensen would beat him. Red was good with a gun, but no match for Smoke Jensen.

"So add it up and tell me what you come up with, gunfighter," Red spat the words.

"Scum," Smoke said softly. "One hundred percent stinking scum."

"I'll spit on your grave, Jensen."

"I doubt it."

"Goddamn you, Jensen!" Red flared. "Who gives you the right to pass judgment on me? You're nothin' but a gunhandler. You made your money killin' people. What in the hell gives you the right to think you're better than me?"

"Oh, I don't think I'm better than you in the Biblical sense, Red. We're all going to have to stand before our Maker and be judged."

Red's face had regained much of its normal color. He wore a puzzled look as he spread his hands wide. "Then? . . ."

"Red, I could stand here and try to explain the differences between us until I fell off my horse from exhaustion. No matter what I said, I'd never get through to you. So I'll tell you this: If you're not going to change your murdering, thieving ways and try to live a decent life, if you're not going to fire the scum from your payroll and run them out of this country, I suggest you go make your peace with God. Go make out your will and leave your ill-gotten holdings to Tessie."

"Tessie! Hell's fire, man. She'd go through my money like a whirlwind. I'll leave my holdings to my son."

"He won't be around very much longer, Red."

"Huh?"

"If he beats the charges—and he probably will; Judge Garrison says the attempted murder charge is pretty flimsy—he'll come after me. And I'll kill him. Then you'll go on the prod, and I'll put you down. The way I see it, Red, any way it goes, you're looking at a grave." Smoke glanced at the packet in his left hand. "I thought you wanted to see your boy?"

"I changed my mind. I got some ruminatin' to do, Jensen. I got to think on what all you've said this day. I don't know whether you're the bravest man I ever met or just damn crazy. But if you wanted another enemy, Jensen, you just made one with me."

"See you around, Red."

"You set foot outside this town, Jensen, you better be wearin' a gun."

Smoke smiled. "I'm wearin' one now, Red."

Red shook his head and wheeled his horse, heading back to his ranch.

Smoke rode back to the jail and inspected the contents of the packet. Exactly what Red had said. He rifled through the pages of the Bible to check for a derringer or a knife, then tossed money and Bible to Melvin.

"Your dad brought you some reading material, kid."

Melvin began tearing out the pages.

"What are you doing, boy?" Smoke asked. "That's the holy Bible."

"Damn heathen," Sal muttered.

Melvin grinned. "Tell my pa thanks, Jensen. I needed something to wipe my butt with."

15

Melvin Malone was released from jail, the attempted murder charge dropped. Sal picked up the torn pages from the Bible and carefully disposed of them, muttering about heathens and those doomed to the pits of hell.

A week passed, with no retaliation from either Max Huggins or Red Malone. But the townspeople did not relax; they knew an attack was coming. They just didn't know when or how.

Smoke received an unsigned telegram telling about the further misadventures of Paul Mittermaier and Henri Dubois. It seems the pair had been arrested and jailed in Kansas City for strong-arm robbery. They told some wild tale about being beaten and drugged in a small town out west, and then waking up in an empty railroad car. They claimed they were really foreign tourists, over here to do some buffalo hunting.

The judge laughed at them and sent them off to prison for a couple of years.

Smoke sent the wire to Max Huggins.

On a warm and bright summer's day, Aggie Feckles walked into a field on the outskirts of town to pick flowers for the kitchen table.

Several hours later, Martha showed up at the marshal's office, nearly hysterical.

Smoke didn't need a crystal ball to know what had taken place. He sent a boy over to the hotel for Sally, so she could look after Martha, and began stuffing his saddlebags with items he might need when he declared war on Hell's Creek.

"We'll get a posse together," Judge Garrison said.

"No, we won't," Smoke nixed that idea. "That's what Max wants. They want a posse chasing after shadows and leaving the town undefended." He looked around him. Sally and Martha had gone over to Mrs. Marbly's. "If Aggie is still alive, I'll bring her back."

"If she's still alive?" The blacksmith, Benson, questioned.

"The lawyers have a phrase for it," Smoke replied. He glanced at Judge Garrison.

"Corpus delicti," the judge told the crowded room. "It means the facts to prove a crime. In a case this heinous—and we might as well say the word: rape—Max, if it is Max, would probably dispose of the body after the viciousness was done. He'd be a total fool to keep her alive. And Max is not a fool. Let's all hope and pray he's savoring the anticipation and has not completed the act."

Smoke walked out of the office and stepped into the saddle.

Judge Garrison followed him out. "Smoke, I've received some confirmation about Max Huggins's back trail. I was on my way over to tell you when I heard about Aggie. He's wanted back east. Mostly for rape of young girls. He then killed them. In several states."

"Do you have the warrants?"

"That'll take some time. Probably a month or better. It's a time-consuming process, Smoke."

Smoke shook his head and grimaced as he picked up the reins. "Aggie doesn't have a month, Judge. Looks like this is going to be western justice. See you."

He rode out of town, heading north.

Smoke stopped at the Brown farm and pulled the farmer off to one side, briefing him.

Brown's face tightened. "I'll try to keep this from Elias. The boy is sure sweet on that girl; no tellin' what he'd try to do. Damnit!" the man cursed. "What kind of filth would do something like this?"

Ellie brought them coffee and her husband told her what

146

had happened.

"That poor child. How much hope do you hold out for her, Mr. Jensen?"

"Not much. Max will probably do the deed and then kill her. It's a pattern of his."

She frowned and said, "I'm a God-fearing woman, Mr. Jensen. But I have to ask this: Why doesn't society hang men like Max Huggins and others who do these terrible things? Why are they allowed to live?"

"I don't know, ma'am. It has something to do with a movement started back east. Something about the worth of a criminal's life or some such drivel as that. God help us all if it spreads out here."

They all turned at the sounds of a horse approaching. Pete Akins was coming up the road. He saw Smoke standing in the farmer's yard and turned in, closing the gate behind him. The gunfighter dismounted and walked over to the group.

"I'm out of it, Smoke," he said, taking off his hat in the presence of Mrs. Brown. "Bell and Frigo and some others grabbed the little Feckles girl and hauled her to Max Huggins. My gun may be for hire, but I'll be damned—'cuse the word, ma'am—if I'll have a part in abusin' a child or botherin' a good woman. If you want another deputy, you got one, Smoke."

"I had a hunch you'd come around, Pete. Where is Aggie being held?"

"She ain't bein' held nowhere, Smoke. She's dead. Max done his evil and give her to the men. Made me sick to my stomach. I'd ridden over to Kalispell for supplies; came back right in the middle of it. I just got out of Hell's Creek with my hide on."

"Are they planning on attacking the town, Pete?"

"If a big enough posse rides out, yeah. They got men on the ridges with signal mirrors to tell yea or nay. I figured I'd ride in and warn the townspeople."

Smoke scribbed a short note and handed it to Pete. "This will keep someone in the town from shooting you, Pete. I'm going to go show the citizens of Hell's Creek what hell is really like."

"You want some company?"

Smoke shook his head. "This is something I want to do myself. How many people pulled out with you?"

"No one, Smoke. There ain't nothin' but trash left up there. Men and women. There ain't no kids in the town. Not a one. Even that so'called minister up yonder took his turn with that poor child. When she went crazy-actin' after all the horribleness, Frigo shot her."

"You keep an eye on Elias, Brown. Hog-tie the boy if you have to."

Smoke stepped into the saddle and was gone.

The outlaw and gunslinger experienced the chill of a cold sweat as the muzzle of the .44 was pressed against his head. He'd just stepped out of the privy and was slipping into his galluses when the muzzle touched his head.

"If I think you're lying to me," Smoke's voice was as cold as the invisible grip of death that touched the hired gun, "I'll stake you out and skin you alive. Do you understand?"

"Yes, sir. Jensen?"

"That's right, punk. Did you take part in the rape of Aggie?"

"Yes, sir."

"How many more?"

"Jesus, Smoke . . . ever'body in the whole damn town. Includin' some of the women. She screamed and hollered until she couldn't holler no more. Went on all day. Then she went nuts in the head and Frigo shot her."

Smoke cursed under his breath. "How did you feel raping that child, punk?"

"I . . . liked it, damn you!"

"Yeah, scum like you would. They waiting for me down in town?"

"Yeah. They damn sure are. So go on down and git killed, Jensen. You . . ."

He never got to finish it. Smoke buried the big blade of his Bowie into the man's back and twisted it upward with all his considerable strength. Smoke slammed the man's face first onto the ground to stifle the scream building in his throat. He wiped the blade clean on the man's shirttail and sheathed the weapon. Smoke checked his guns, loading them full, then took the dead gunny's two Remington Frontier .44's, looping gunbelt and all over one shoulder. He made his way back to his horse and circled the town, keeping to the timber until he found a good spot to picket the animal.

He changed into moccasins, slung his saddlebags over his other shoulder, picked up his rifle, and began working his way toward the town. He knew they were waiting for him because of the silence of the usually raucous place. Lights were burning, but there was no laughter coming from any of the saloons.

And Smoke was determined that before he left that night, there would be no cause for joy in the town for a long, long time. If he could, he was going to destroy as much of Hell's Creek as possible.

He paused for a moment, listening. The old mountain man, Preacher, his mentor, had taught him many things, including patience. Smoke heard the faint jingle of spurs coming up the weed-grown alleyway. He pressed against the building. When the man drew close, Smoke hit him in the face with the butt of the rifle. The man dropped like a stone, faint moonlight glistening off his bloody and broken face.

Smoke walked on to a corral. He didn't want to hurt any animal; they could not choose their owners. He silently slid open the bars. When the action started, the horses would find the opening and bolt. He did the same at two other corrals. He glanced at the huge livery stable and decided to leave it alone. Men were probably lying in wait for him in there.

He slipped around to the back of a saloon, dug in a pocket of his saddlebags, and came out with six sticks of dynamite, taped together, already capped with a long fuse.

He softly entered through the back door. Now he could hear voices and the tinkle of glasses and beer mugs. But the conversation was low and the drinking was probably light.

Smoke thumbnailed a match into flame and lit the long fuse, placing the charge against the storeroom wall. With a smile on his face, he slipped back into the night.

Smoke planted two more charges on that side of the street before he was spotted by a man who'd stepped out of a back door to relieve himself.

"Hey!" the man shouted, turning and still spewing water.

Smoke shot him about five inches below the belt buckle. The man fell to the earth, screaming in agony.

"You'll not rape another girl," Smoke muttered, then dashed across the street, at the far end of town.

The saloon charge blew. Smoke saw one man thrown from the building, crashing through glass. He hit the street and did not move. Another man fell through the floor and onto the dusty walkway in front as the rear part of the poorly constructed building collapsed under the heavy weight of the charge.

The second and third charges blew, and chaos reigned for a few minutes as men and women poured into the street.

Smoke emptied the Remingtons into a knot of men, knocking them sprawling. He lit another charge, tossed that through a side window of a building, and dashed away. He collided with a man, recovered first, and pointed a pistol at the man's head.

"The body of the girl Aggie, where is it?" He jacked back the hammer. "And I'm only going to ask it one time."

"Sid tossed it into a backwater just off the river yonder. I swear to you I ain't lyin'."

Smoke jerked him to his feet. "Show me, you weasel. And you'd better be right the first time."

Keeping low, as the flames began licking at the dry timber of the destroyed buildings, the man led Smoke to a dry wash and from there to the slough. The naked body of Aggie was clearly visible.

"Get her, you crud," Smoke ordered, the menace in his voice chilling the man.

The man waded into the dark waters and pulled the girl to the shore.

"Pick her up and walk toward the timber," he ordered.

"But she ain't got nothin' on! That ain't decent!"

One look from Smoke's cold eyes convinced the man that

he'd better shut his mouth and do as ordered.

"Where is the bastard?" Smoke heard the voice of Max Huggins plain in the night. "Find him, you fools. Find him and kill him!"

At his horse, Smoke had the man wrap Aggie's body in a blanket.

"What are you gonna do with me?" the man asked.

"Did you take a part in raping this girl? And don't lie to me."

"Yeah, I did. Ever'body did."

Smoke hit him with one big gloved fist. The man dropped like a rock.

The flames in the town were slowly being contained by a bucket brigade and one small pumper.

Smoke knew there was no point in taking the man back to Barlow for trial. Once away from Smoke Jensen's gun, the man would lie, denying any part of the rape. If a deal could be worked out, everybody in Hell's Creek would alibi for the other and nothing would be accomplished there.

Smoke left the man on the ground and picked up the slender, blanket-covered body of Aggie Feckles. Star didn't like the idea of carrying the dead, but Smoke managed to get into the saddle. He headed back for Barlow, taking a route first west, then cutting south, to throw off any pursuers. He doubted there would be many; they were too busy fighting the fires.

At a farmer's house, he borrowed a horse and tied Aggie across the saddle. He rode into Barlow just as dawn was breaking fair in the eastern skies. People began lining the streets, silently watching as he rode in, leading the horse with the body of Aggie across the saddle.

Dr. Turner came out of the hotel, where he had just given Martha a sedative, and walked over to Smoke. Smoke stepped wearily out of the saddle and gave the reins to Jim. The deputy led the animal to the stable.

A crowd began to slowly gather around.

"After they abused her," Smoke said, his words soft, "Warner Frigo shot her in the head and dumped her body in a slough."

"Pete Akins told us the rest of it," Judge Garrison said. A little bit of soap was still on his face. He had been shaving when the news of Smoke riding in reached him. "This is absolutely the most dastardly act I have seen in all my years on the bench."

"How much damage did you do in Hell's Creek, Marshal?" a citizen asked.

"Burned down about a half-dozen buildings. Got lead in maybe a dozen people. I used some dynamite, and the explosions probably killed another six or seven and put that many out of commission for a time. How is Martha?"

"She's sleeping," Turner said. "Victoria and Sally are with her now. I just gave her a sedative about fifteen minutes ago. She'll be groggy when she wakes up."

"The girl was shot at close range," Smoke told him. "the slug took off about half her face. Have the undertaker do his work and then nail the coffin lid shut. Let's spare Martha that."

The doctor nodded his agreement.

"I've got to get some rest. I'll see you all this afternoon." Smoke wearily climbed the steps to their suite after asking Toby to have a boy get water for a bath.

He hung up his guns, pulled off his boots, waited in his long-handles until the tub was filled, and then took a bath. Sally came into the WC and scrubbed his back.

Smoke slipped under the cool, fresh sheets and closed his eyes. He slept deeply and soundly and dreamlessly. He awakened just after noon and was finishing shaving when the sounds of gunshots and women screaming sent him running down the hotel steps.

16

Max had not waited long to retaliate. The gunhands on his payroll and those who lived in Hell's Creek had hit the town hard from the north and were now preparing to strike again, from the south end. Several had thrown torches and two buildings were on fire; but the bucket brigades were working and the fires were being snuffed out before much damage could be done.

"Get into position!" Smoke yelled. "Just like we practiced. Move!"

The men and women of the town responded, quickly getting into battle positions on the roofs and behind shelter. The outlaws saw what was taking place and broke off the second attack before it could get started. They galloped south.

Smoke didn't need a fortune-teller to know where they were heading: to Red Malone's spread.

"Do we follow them?" Toby asked, coming out of the hotel carrying a rifle.

"Not a whole bunch of us. That's what they want. They'd set up an ambush point and nail us. Jim," he called, "saddle me a horse. Not Star. He needs a rest."

Smoke looked around. "Judge, deputize Pete Akins. Pete and Jim will stay here. Sal, come on. Let's do some head-hunting."

Sally pressed a couple of biscuits and salt meat in his hand while the hotel cook made a poke of food for the men to take with them. Smoke gulped down a cup of coffee and then was in the saddle, riding a long-legged buckskin with a mean look in his eyes.

"I know that horse," Sal said. "That's the stableman's personal ride. He's a good one."

Smoke nodded and the men were off, leaving the road just outside of town and cutting across country. From their tracks, it was clear that the outlaws had arrogantly elected to stay with the road, daring Smoke and any others to chase them.

The short cut that Smoke chose was one pointed out to him by Jim; and Sal knew it as well or better. It would cut off miles getting to the Lightning spread. It was rough country; high-up country.

The men rode the mountain trails and passes in silence. A great gray wolf watched them from a ridge. Smoke spoke to the wolf in Cheyenne, one of several Indian languages that Old Preacher had taught him. Preacher had taught him that for man to fear the wolf was downright ignorant. Preacher had said that he'd never known of a man being attacked by a wolf unless that man was threatening the wolf or got too close to a fresh kill. Either way, according to Preacher, it was the man's fault, not the wolf's.

"Magnificent animals," Sal said, looking at the timber wolf. "But they don't make good pets worth a damn."

"They're not meant to be pets," Smoke agreed. "God didn't put them here for that. Damn stupid hunters keep killing them, and the deer and elk population suffers because of it. They're part of the balance of nature. I wish the white man would understand that. Indians understood it."

The wolf stood on the ridge and watched the men pass. Then it turned and went back to its den, where it was watching over the cubs while its mate hunted for food, which is a lot more than can be said for a great many so-called superior humans.

"There they are," Sal pointed out.

Smoke looked to his right and slightly behind him. A group of riders, tiny from this distance, rode far below them. About twenty-five of them.

"We'll be a good fifteen minutes ahead of them after we cut off up yonder," Sal said. "I know a place that'll be dandy for an ambush."

"Take the lead, Sal. I'll follow you."

The men rode down from the high country, the temperature warming as they descended from the high-up into a valley. Wildflowers had burst forth, coloring the landscape with brilliant summer hues.

Smoke was going to add some more color to the scenery: blood-red.

The two men left their horses safe within boulders and timber and, with their rifles, got into place. They were about fifty yards above the road. This was not the stage road, but an offshoot that led to and stopped at Malone's ranch, some miles farther on. They were on Lightning range.

Sal pointed that out.

"Good," Smoke replied. "Maybe they'll hear the shots and come to lend their buddies a hand. We'll lessen the odds against the town if they do."

Sal took that time to point out that should that occur, the two of them would be outnumbered something like forty to one.

Smoke grinned and patted the bulging saddlebags he'd taken from behind his saddle. "Have faith, Sal. If worse comes to worse, we'll blast our way out."

"There ain't a nerve in your body, is there, Smoke?"

"Oh, I've known fear, Sal." Smoke thought for a moment, then smiled. "Back in '69, I think it was."

Both men laughed, then sobered as the outlaws came into view, riding around a curve in the road, still too far away for accurate shooting.

"Wish we had brung one of them fancy rifles you took from them foreigners," Sal said. "We'd a sure tried it out."

Smoke eared back the hammer on his Winchester. "They'll be in range in about a minute. I'll take the left side, you take the right."

"Good," Sal said flatly. "I can recognize Ernie's horse from here. Ain't neither one of them worth a damn for anything."

155

"Here we go, Sal."

The men lifted the rifles to their shoulders, sighted in, took up slack on the triggers, and emptied two saddles.

The outlaws appeared confused as their horses reared and bucked at the gunfire and the sudden smell of blood. Instead of turning left or right, or retreating, the outlaws put the spur to the animals' flanks and came forward.

"Like shootin' clay pigeons standin' still," Sal muttered, and emptied another saddle.

Smoke grabbed several taped-together sticks of dynamite from the open saddlebag, lit the fuse, and tossed it down the hill. The charge landed just above the road and blew, sending small rocks hurling through the air like deadly missiles.

Through the cloud of dust raised by the dynamite, Smoke and Sal could see a half-dozen more riderless horses, the outlaws on the ground, some of them writhing in agony with hideous head wounds and broken limbs, the others lying very still, their skulls crushed by the flying rocks.

Smoke and Sal started tossing the lead around. The dozen or so outlaws left in the saddle decided it was way past time to clear out. They put the spurs to their horses and were gone, fogging it to Red's ranch.

Smoke and Sal mounted up and rode down into the carnage, to see if anything could be salvaged. Sal rounded up the outlaws' horses while Smoke stood among the dead and wounded, making certain no one summoned up the courage to try a shot at either one of them.

They had just finished tying the dead across their saddles and securing the wounded on their horses when Red Malone and his crew thundered up, raising an unnecessary cloud of dust.

"What the hell are you doin' on my range, Jensen?" the man yelled.

"I'm a deputy sheriff of this county, Red," Smoke calmly told him. "And I'm carrying out my duties as such. You interfere and I'll put your butt in jail."

Sal had worked around; he now faced Red, a rifle pointed at the rancher's chest. The action did not escape Red, and he knew if trouble started, he would be the first one dead.

But he wouldn't, couldn't, leave it alone. "You got a warrant for the arrest of these men, Jensen?"

"I saw them attack the town of Barlow, Red. Me and several hundred other people. Those alive are going back to stand trial. Now back off."

All looked up as the sound of hooves pounding against the earth reached them. Twenty men from the town reined up, heavily armed, among them Joe Walsh and a half dozen of his hands.

"The town's secure, Smoke," Benson said. "We thought we'd ride out and give you a hand."

"It's appreciated. You men start escorting these bums back to town." Smoke and Sal swung into the saddle. Smoke looked at Red. "Their trial will begin in a couple of days. You and your men are still banned from the town. Keep that in mind, Red."

"Someday, Jensen," Red warned, his voice thick with anger. "Someday."

"Anytime, Red. Just anytime at all." Smoke lifted the reins and rode away.

The funeral of Aggie Feckles was an emotional, gut-wrenching time for all. Midway through the ordeal, Martha collapsed and had to be carried back to the doctor's office. Young Elias Brown had a very difficult time fighting back his tears. Just as the earth was being shoveled into the hole, Smoke cut his eyes and looked toward the north. Plumes of smoke were billowing into the sky.

"Max is burning you men out!" he called to Brown and his friends. "Let's ride."

They were too late, of course. It was miles to the collection of farmhouses and barns and other outbuildings. Brown had been completely burned out. Gatewood lost his house, but the other buildings were intact. Cooter lost his barn and smokehouse. Bolen's house was gone, and Morrison and Carson lost barns and equipment. All the farmers' cows and hogs had been shot, the chickens scattered and trampled.

"Goddamn a man who would do this!" Brown said. He

157

squared his shoulders and added, "That sorry son will not run me out. We'll rebuild."

"And we'll help you," Tom Johnson said.

"Your credit is good at my store," Marbly said. "For as long as it takes."

"I have money put back," Judge Garrison told the farmers. "I'm good for loans."

Sally and Victoria had ridden out in a buggy. Sally said, "Smoke, I'm going to wire our family's board of directors back east. I think it's time Barlow had a bank. I'll get the first steps in motion this afternoon."

Smoke turned and smiled at her. "Good, honey. That's a great idea."

"Your wife owns a bank?" Marbly asked.

"Her family is one of the richest families in the nation," Smoke told the startled crowd. "They own factories, banks, shipping lines, railroads . . . you name it. If Sally says put a bank in Barlow, a bank will be put in Barlow." He turned to Jim Dagonne. "Let's go pick up some tracks and see where they lead to. As if we didn't know."

But the direction the marauders took did not lead toward Hell's Creek. They went north for a couple of miles, then cut toward the northeast, toward the flathead range and the glacier country.

"What's up there, Jim?"

"Man, that is rugged country. I understand they's talk in Washington about making a big chunk of it a national park. It's about a million or so acres. And the weather is unpredictable as hell. Storms can blow in there—even in the summer, so I'm told—dropping temperatures fifty . . . sixty degrees. They's mountains in there over two miles high and impassable."

"You've been in there?"

"I've been on the edge of it several times. Continental Divide runs right through it."

"Anything between here and there?"

"Tradin' post of sorts up ahead on the Hungry Horse. Some pretty salty ol' boys hang around there."

Smoke nodded. "We'll follow these tracks as long as we

158

can. We'll supply at the post. The nick in that shoe is a dead giveaway. That'll hold up in court."

"You plan on bringing them back?"

"Not if I can help it."

The country was so rugged and unsettled that the men could not make the trading post that day. They camped along a creek and dined on fresh fish caught with their hands, Indian style.

"Where'd you learn how to do that?" Jim asked after watching Smoke catch their supper by hand.

"I was raised by mountain men, Jim. A very independent and self-sufficient bunch."

"I've met a couple of real old men who was mountain men. I saw something in their eyes that made me back off and talk right respectful to them."

"Wise thing to do. A mountain man isn't going to take much crap from anybody."

They ate until they could hold no more, then rolled up in their blankets, using saddles for pillows, and were up before dawn, making coffee and talking little until they'd shaken the kinks out and had a cup of coffee you could float nails in.

"Who runs this trading post?" Smoke finally asked.

"Don't know no more. Man by the name of Smith used to run it. He might still. Smith ain't his real name. He's a bad one. Have to be bad to run a place like that. Got him a graveyard out back of hard cases who tried to steal from him or brace him over one thing or another."

"Fast gun?"

"Nope. Sawed-off shotgun. And he don't hesitate none in usin' it, neither. He's got the worst whiskey you ever tried to drink. I think he adds snake heads to it for flavor. And I ain't kiddin'."

"I think I'll stick with beer."

"That would be wise."

They rolled their blankets in their ground sheets and were in the saddle as the sun was struggling to push its rays over the mountains.

They followed the tracks, and they led straight to the trading post on the north fork of the Flathead River. Both men had taken off their badges, had dusty clothing from the trail, and had not shaved that morning. Both of them had heavy beards, so they were beginning to look a little rough around the edges.

"If Smith is still here, is he going to recognize you?" Smoke asked.

"Probably. But he ain't gonna say nothing except howdy, 'til he figures out what I might be up to. How are we going to play this?"

"You just follow my lead."

"I's afraid you was gonna say that."

The men put their horses in the big barn behind the long, low trading post and unsaddled them, carefully rubbing them down and giving them a good bait of corn. *25 ceents a skoop,* the sign said.

"Yep," Jim said. "Smith is still here. You ever seen such outrageous prices?"

"It's the only game in town, partner."

"You called that right."

Smoke lifted the right rear hoof of each animal until he found the one with the chipped shoe. He smiled up at Jim. "We found our man."

"Men," Jim corrected. "I count six of them."

Smoke straightened up and, with a grin on his face, said, "Hell, Jim, don't look so glum. We got them outnumbered."

"If that's the way you count," Jim said soberly, "I shore am glad you don't count out my payroll!"

17

The men took the leather thongs off their guns and stepped up onto the rough porch. With Smoke in the lead, they entered the dimly lit old trading post. The smell of twist tobacco all mixed in with that of candy, whiskey, beer, and ancient sweat odors that clung to the walls and ceiling hit them. They walked past bolts of brightly colored cloth, stacks of men's britches and shirts, and a table piled high with boots of all sizes. They passed the notions counter, filled with elixirs and nostrums that were guaranteed to cure any and all illnesses. Most of them were based with alcohol or an opiate of some type, which killed the pain for a while.

Smoke and Jim stopped at the gun case to look at the new double-action revolvers.

"Pretty," Jim said.

"I don't like them," Smoke said. "The trigger pull is so hard it throws your aim off. And if you have to cock it, what's the point of having one of those things?"

"Good question," his deputy agreed. "They look awkward to me." Something on the nostrum table caught his eye and he picked up a bottle of Lydia E. Pinkham's Vegetable Compound. He read the label, blushed, and put the bottle down. "The things they put on labels. I declare."

"Sally swears by it. Says it works wonders."

"You ever tasted it?"

"Hell, no! I did taste some Kickapoo Indian Sagwa a couple of years ago, back east."

"Did it work?"

"It tasted so bad I forgot what I took it for."

Smiling, the men stepped into the bar part of the trading post and walked up to the counter, in this case, several rough-hewn boards atop empty beer barrels.

Smith flicked his eyes to Jim and they narrowed in recognition. But he said only, "Howdy, boys. What might your poison be on this day?"

"Beer," Smoke said. "For both of us."

Both Smoke and Jim had quickly inspected the heavily armed men sitting at two pulled-together tables near a dirty window at the front of the barroom.

"Hadn't been up here in a long time," Jim said after taking a pull from his mug. "I'd forgot how purty this country is. And how chilly the nights get."

"It do get airish at times," Smith agreed. "I got fresh venison stew on the stove and my squaw just baked some bread."

"Sounds good," Smoke said. "Jim?"

"I could do with a taste. Them cold fish we had for breakfast didn't nearabouts fill me up."

Smoke and Jim took their beers to a table across the room from the arsonists and began whispering to each other, knowing that would arouse some suspicion from the men who had torched the farmhouses and barns.

It didn't take long.

"What are you two a-whisperin' about over there?" one burly man called across the room.

Smoke looked at him just as the stew and bread was being placed on the table. "None of your damn business."

The man flushed and started to get up. One of his buddies pulled him back into the chair. "Let it alone, Sonny. They ain't worth our time."

"I ain't so sure about that," Sonny said, giving Smoke a good once-over. "I seen that face afore."

"That's Murtaugh talkin'," Smith whispered. "Watch your step, Jim. They're all bad ones."

"Now the damn barkeep's whisperin'!" Sonny yelled.

Smith turned and faced him. "It's my goddamn store, lunkhead. I'll whisper anytime I take a notion to."

"Who you callin' a lunkhead, you old goat?" Sonny hollered.

"You, you big-mouth ninny!" Smith fired back, moving toward the bar. There, he reached behind him and came around with a sawed-off shotgun in his hands. He eared back both hammers and pointed it at Sonny. "Now, then, mule-mouth, you got anything else you'd like to say to me?"

Sonny's complexion, not too good to begin with, lightened appreciably as he looked at the twin barrels of the express gun, pointing straight at him. Those around him took on the expression of a very sad basset hound, knowing that if Smith pulled the triggers, someone would be picking them up with a shovel and a spoon.

"I reckon not," Sonny finally managed to say.

"Good." Smith eased down the hammers and laid the shotgun on the bar. "That's just dandy. Use your mouth to eat and drink, and stop flappin' that thing at me."

With a scowl on his ugly face, Sonny turned away, but not before giving Smoke another dirty look.

The stew smelled good and tasted even better. The bread was lavishly buttered, and Smoke and Jim fell to eating.

"Bring us some of that stew," Murtaugh called.

"Dollar a bowl," Smith told him.

"A dollar a bowl! Hell, man, that's plumb unreasonable."

"Then go hungry."

"I'll take another bowl," Jim said. "That's fine eatin'."

"You better see the color of his money afore you dish up anymore grub to him," Murtaugh said. "He don't look like he's very flush to me."

"You worry about your own self," Jim verbally fired across the room. "I got money, and I earned it decent."

"What'd you mean by that?" the arsonist asked.

"Just what I said."

"You sayin' I ain't decent?"

"You said that, not me. Now hush up. I'm tryin' to eat, not jaw with you."

Murtaugh gave him a dirty look. "Maybe you think you're hoss enough to shut me up?"

"Just as soon as I finish eatin', mister."

"Anybody busts up furniture, they pay for it," Smith said.

"They started this war of words," Smoke pointed out. "All we did was come in for a drink and some food."

"That's right," Jim said, spooning stew into his mouth. "Sad state of affairs when a man can't even eat without havin' to listen to all sorts of jibber-jabber from lunkheads."

"Now, I ain't puttin' up with no saddle-bum callin' me a lunkhead!" Murtaugh stood up. He walked across the room. "I better hear some apologies comin' out of that mouth of yourn, cowboy," he said to Jim.

Jim grinned up at him. His right hand was holding a spoon, his left hand out of sight.

Jim belched loudly. "There's your apology, big-mouth. Catch it and carry it back acrost the room with you."

Murtaugh cursed and swung a big fist at Jim's head. But Jim anticipated the punch and ducked it, coming out of the chair and driving his fist into the bigger man's stomach. Murtaugh bent over, gagging. Jim grabbed the man by his hair and slammed his forehead onto the tabletop. Turning the stunned Murtaugh around, and grabbing him by the collar and the seat of his britches, Jim propelled him across the room, dumping him onto the table he had just exited.

"You boys best look after him," Jim told Murtaugh's buddies. "He can't seem to take care of hisself atall."

Sonny looked around him. Smith was holding the Greener, hammers back, pointed at him.

Jim walked bak to his table and looked at the spilled stew. "Get the money for this from Murtaugh," he told Smith. "It was his head that spilt it."

"I'll be damned!" Murtaugh said, and charged across the room at Jim, both fists whipping the air.

Jim picked up a chair and hit the rampaging Murtaugh in the face with it. The firebug hit the floor, on his back, and did not move. His face was bloody and several teeth had departed his mouth to take up residence on the floor.

"That does it," Sonny said, rising from his chair. He looked at Smith. "You gonna take a side in this?"

Smoke stood up, brushing back his coat, exposing his .44's. "Stay out of it, Smith. We're deputy sheriffs from down Barlow way. These men are wanted for arson and destruction of livestock. Any damage to your place will be taken care of."

"That's fair. I know Jim and you look familiar to me. Who you be, mister?"

"Smoke Jensen."

Sonny suddenly looked sick. And so did the other four with him.

"Have mercy!" Smith said.

"We ain't done nothin' to nobody and we ain't destroyed no livestock," Sonny said.

Murtaugh groaned on the floor and sat up. He blinked a couple of times and wiped his bloody mouth with the back of his hand. "What the hell's goin' on?"

"You're under arrest," Jim told him.

"Your aunt's drawers, I am!" Murtaugh's hand dropped to the butt of his gun at just about the same time Jim kicked him in the face. Murtaugh hit the floor again and this time he was out for the count.

Sonny grabbed for his gun and Smoke shot him in the belly. The outlaw stumbled backward and sat down hard on the floor, both hands holding his .44-caliber-punctured belly. He started hollering.

One of his buddies jerked iron and Jim took him out of the game with a slug to the shoulder.

The trading post erupted in gunsmoke and lead. The booming of .44's and .45's rattled the windows and shook the glasses behind the bar. Things really got lively when Smith leveled his Greener and blew one outlaw clear out of the barroom, the charge of rusty nails, ball bearings, tacks, and whatever else Smith could find to load his shells nearly tearing the man in two, picking him off his boots, and tossing him out a window.

One outlaw, gut-shot and screaming in pain, dropped his pistols and went staggering out into the other room. He died underneath the table holding five-cent bottles of Dr. Farrigut's elixir for the remedying of paralysis, softening of the brain, and mental imbecility.

When the dust and bird-droppings from the ceiling and gunsmoke began to clear the room, three arsonists were dead, one was not long for this world, and Murtaugh was again trying to sit up, blood from his broken nose streaming down his chin. The punk Jim had shot through the shoulder was leaning up against a wall, moaning in pain.

"My, my," Smith said, picking out the empties from his Greener and loading up. "I ain't seen such a sight in two . . . three years. Things was gettin' plumb borin' around here. Them no-goods really burn some folks out?"

"Five families," Smoke told him, punching out his empty brass and reloading. "All good people. I suspect Big Max Huggins paid them to do it."

"I'll talk," the shoulder-shot outlaw hollered. "It was Big Max who paid us to do it. I'll testify in court. I'll tell . . ."

Murtaugh palmed a hide-out gun and shot the man between the eyes, closing his mouth forever.

Smoke slammed the barrel of his .44 against Murtaugh's head, and for the third time in about three minutes, the outlaw went to sleep on the floor.

"Gimme ten dollars for the winder and you give whatever else is in their pockets to them folks that was burnt out," Smith said. "That fair?"

"Plenty fair," Jim said. "The families will thank you."

Smoke tied Murtaugh's hands behind his back with rawhide and straightened up. "We'll help you bury this trash, Smith. Then I'll get a signed statement from you attesting to the fact that you heard that one"—he pointed to the man with a hole beween his eyes—"confessing as to who paid them. You won't have to appear in court."

"Good enough," Smith said. "Shovel's in the back. I'll get my old woman to sing a death chant for them. She's Flathead. Does a nice job of it, too. Right touchin', some folks say."

Smoke put all the guns in a sack and tied it to a saddle horn, while Jim readied the horses for travel back to Barlow. The guns and horses and saddles they would give to the farmers who were burned out. The men had about five hundred dollars between them. That would go a long way toward rebuilding the homes and barns and smokehouses.

Morning Dove was still chanting her death song as they rode away.

18

Judge Garrison read the signed statement from Smith.

"Will that hold up in a court of law, Judge?" Smoke asked.

"It will in my court," the judge said with a smile. "Besides, both you and Deputy Dagonne heard one man confess. Don't worry, Smoke. Just remember the name of the town the jury is going to be picked from."

Both men shared a laugh at that. Smoke said, "Any further word about Max Huggins's background?"

"Yes, but unfortunately, we can't use any of it. Some of the parties involved are still too frightened to testify. Others have moved away or died. While the authorities east of here know Max is guilty, they can't prove it."

Smoke thought about that for a moment. "But Max doesn't have to know that, Judge."

The judge looked puzzled for a moment, then smiled. "Of course, you're quite right."

"Let me think about how we can use that information, Judge. We've got Max bumping from side to side now, let's see if we can keep him that way."

"Good idea. I have trial scheduled to start Thursday for those who tried to shoot up the town. I want extra security, Smoke."

"You've got it, Judge. How about Melvin Malone's case?"

"His is the first one I try. This is . . . unusual for a judge, Smoke. But I want to ask your opinion. I can put him in jail. I can put him to doing community work . . . public service work it's now being called. But putting him to work cleaning the streets is only going to anger him further. Jail? Probably do the same thing. Or I can fine him. What do you think?"

Smoke rolled a cigarette and lit up. Finally, he shrugged his shoulders. "The boy wants to kill me so bad now it's like a fire inside him. . . ."

"Is he that good?" the judge interrupted.

"I doubt it. He makes the mistake that so many would-be gunhandlers make: He hurried his first shot. I was born blessed with excellent eye and hand coordination, Judge. I was born ambidextrous." He smiled. "Sally taught me that word, by the way. The speed came with years of practice. I still practice. But I think the thing that keeps me alive—or has kept me alive all these years—is that I'm not afraid when the moment comes. I'm confident without being overly so. As to your original question . . . fine him and let him walk for all I care."

The judge nodded. "It might buy us more time, if you know what I mean."

"I do. Kill Melvin now, and Red is very likely to blow wide open. The town is growing stronger every day. In another two weeks, it would take an army to overrun it."

"That's correct. And we owe it all to you."

Smoke waved that away. "I just propped you people up, that's all. Gave you all a little talking to and jerked you around and around. You all did the rest."

The judge grinned and rubbed the side of his face. "I never thought I'd see the day when I appreciated a slapping around, but I do, boy, I do."

"See you around, Judge."

Smoke stepped out of the judge's chambers and walked the streets of town. People waved and called his name as he passed. No doubt about it, Smoke thought. These folks are going to fight for their town. And they're probably going to have it to do . . . very soon.

He walked back to the jail and stepped inside. Murtaugh started cussing him as soon as he heard the jingle of Smoke's spurs. "You'll never hold me in this cracker box, Jensen. Soon as I can get my hands on a gun, you're dead, hotshot.

You're dead, and that's a promise."

Smoke did not reply.

"I know a lot of things you don't, Jensen," Murtaugh kept flapping his mouth. "A whole lot of things."

Smoke waited.

Murtaugh laughed from his cell. "Have your trials, Jensen. Let that lard-butted judge bang his gavel and hand down his pronouncements. It ain't gonna make a bit of difference in the long run."

Murtaugh lay down on his bunk and shut his mouth.

Smoke got up and closed the door to the cell block.

"Have the others had anything to say?" he asked Sal.

"They've all been boastin' about us not keepin' them for very long. I been doin' some thinkin' about that. I think someone's gonna spring them after they've been sentenced."

"From the jail, you think?" Smoke asked.

Sal shook his head. "I don't know. I'd guess so. Max or Red ain't gonna take a chance of bustin' them away from the prison wagon when they come to haul them off to the territorial prison. That'd bring too much heat on Max, and he don't want that. So, yeah. I'd say they'll make their try just after these hard cases are sentenced."

"We have until Thursday to make some plans. The judge has requested extra security, so he thinks something is in the works, too."

Pete Akins hitched at his gunbelt. "Max could have at least seventy-five men ready to ride in ten minutes. He could pull fifty more in here in two . . . three days. The folks in this town are good people, and I mean that; I never did none of them no harm and they know it. They've accepted me. But they ain't gunhands, Smoke. If you know what I mean."

Smoke knew what he meant. Most of the men were good shots with a rifle. But few of them had ever killed a man close up. They had fought in the war; but that was, for the most part, a very impersonal thing.

Smoke tossed the question out, "How many men does Red Malone have on the payroll?"

"Thirty," Jim answered it. "He pays them all fightin' wages. And there ain't no backup in none of them. They ride

169

for the brand and that's it."

"So we're conceivably looking at anywhere from a hundred to a hundred and fifty men."

"Or more," Pete added.

Smoke paced the office in silence, deep in thought. Finally, he stopped and faced his deputies. "He's got to try to destroy the town. That's his only option. Killing me alone won't stop the movement now. He can't let Sally's people start up this proposed bank. That would bring the state and, in some cases, the federal government into it . . . if anything were to happen to it."

"Maybe there's another way to look at that, Smoke," Sal pointed out. "Maybe Max wants the bank to start up. Rob the bank, destroy the town, and haul his ashes out of the area and start up somewheres else. You can bet that he has someone in this town feedin' him information."

"Who?" Jim asked.

Sal shook his head. "That I don't know. It could be anybody. The swamper over at the saloon. The bartender, a store clerk . . . anybody who's hard up for money."

"Hell, that could be any one of a hundred people," Pete said. "Lemme tell you about Max. He's sneaky. He has one ear to the ground all the time. He hears about somebody seein' somebody else's wife, he holds that over their head. He finds out about somebody bein' wanted, say, back in Ohio, he uses that for leverage. Max can be smooth. He might have loaned someone in this town money when he first come here. Money's tight right now. Maybe they couldn't repay him like they said they would. Man, he could have half-a-dozen people in this town feedin' him information."

Smoke turned and looked out the window. It might be Jerry at the saddle shop. Lucy at the hotel. The boy down at the stable. One of the farmers scattered around this end of the county. One of Joe Walsh's hands. Then it came to Smoke; but he kept his suspicions to himself, hoping they would not prove true.

He left the office and walked over to the hotel. He sat with Sally for a long time in their suite, talking, exchanging ideas. At first she tought his suspicions to be perfectly horrible.

Then, gradually, she began to agree. When Smoke left, both he and Sally wore long faces.

Smoke walked the streets, looking hard into the face of every man and women he passed. Had to be, he thought. I didn't see it at first because I wasn't looking for it. But as he spoke and waved to another citizen, heading out of town, the family resemblance was just too strong to ignore.

There it was, staring him right in the face and saying good morning to him.

"You have to be joking!" Judge Garrison said, recoiling back in his chair.

"No. I'm ninety-nine percent certain. It has to be, Judge. Look at the person."

The judge drummed his fingertips on his desk. He shook his head and sighed. "Now that you mention it, I can see it. My God. I would have never put it together. It was all a sham on this person's part."

"It had to be, Judge. Looking back, it all went down too smoothly, with no arguments."

"And you propose to do what about it at this time?"

"I don't know. From all I've learned by association, this individual does not appear to be a bad person. Rather likable, actually. Let's just sit on this for the time being, Judge. See what develops."

"Just between us?"

"You, me, and Sally are the only three in town who know or who suspect."

"You think it's just this one person?"

Smoke sighed. "I hope so. But how can we be sure?"

"We can't."

Smoke stood up and put on his hat. He told the judge about Sal's suspicions as to when an attack to free the prisoners might take place.

The judge nodded his head in agreement. "I think he's right. They wouldn't want to attack the prisoner wagon from the territorial prison; that might bring the state militia down on their heads. They'll strike here, Smoke. Bet on it. We'll just have to be ready for it."

"We'll be ready," Smoke assured him. "I'm going to deputize all of Joe Walsh's hands and Brown and Gatewood and the other farmers in that area just in case Max tries a diversion to pull me out of town."

"That's a good idea. If trouble comes—and it would be a diversion—north of town, Brown and his friends could then legally handle it. Same with trouble south of town. I'll draw up papers making them full deputies. That will make it official and part of the record."

"The trial going to be in the new civic building?"

"Yes. I expect a large crowd to attend. Oh, by the way, the Marblys' dog had puppies about six weeks ago. Mrs. Marbly said to tell you to stop by and pick one out for Lisa Turner."

"I'll do that right now. See you, Judge."

Marbly grinned at Smoke. "I'm afraid they're mutts, Marshal. But they sure are cute. Come on, I'll show them to you."

"Mutts is right," Smoke said, squatting down by the squirming, yelping litter. "That one," he said, pointing. "The one with the patch around his eye."

"Her eye," Mrs. Marbly corrected.

"Whatever. I like that one."

"Lisa will love it. Tell Mrs. Turner she's paper-trained and completely weaned."

"Victoria will love that, I'm sure." Smoke picked up the puppy, who promptly peed all down his shirt from excitement and then licked his face to apologize, and carried the squirming mass of energy over to Dr. Turner's house.

Lisa was so happy she cried—she named the pup Patches—and ran out in the backyard to play.

Since it was not proper for a man to be alone in a house with a married woman, Vicky invited Smoke to take coffee with her on the front porch.

"I love everything about this town, Smoke," she said after the coffee was poured. "The people are so friendly and they accepted us immediately."

"Yes. They're good people. Where is Robert?"

"On a call out in the country. He left early this morning

and said he wouldn't be back until late. He wanted to check on the families who were burned out."

"Anything serious?"

Vicky laughed. "Not really. One of the kids came down with chicken pock and gave it to all the other kids who hadn't as yet had it. A lot of them are having an itching good time."

Smoke grimaced, remembering his own bout with chicken pock as a boy back in Missouri.

"Are you expecting trouble when the trial starts, Smoke?"

"I won't lie to you, yes, I am. Either during the trial or just after the sentencing. Security will be tight. Are you planning on attending?"

"I . . . don't know. I doubt it. I don't want Lisa to have to hear all that—there will probably be some pretty rough language at times—and if I went, I'd have to leave her alone, and I won't do that."

"I think that's wise. Sally isn't going to attend either. I'll ask her if she'll come over and stay with you. If there is trouble, Sally—as you've seen in the shooting classes—can handle a six-shooter with either hand. And won't hesitate to use one."

Victoria shook her head. "Sally certainly has changed since our days back at school."

"Out here, Vicky, one must change. Believe me when I say that the West will be wild for many years to come. People out here resist change; they fight it. It's the sheer vastness of the West that makes laws so difficult to enforce. Here it is 1883, and there are still many areas that remain largely un-explored. Millions of acres for outlaws to run into and hide. Oh, it's getting smaller with each year that passes. Law enforcement people are being linked by telegraph and train, but the gun still remains the great settler of troubles."

"When will you hang your guns up, Smoke?"

"When a full year passes and no one comes after me looking for a reputation. When newspapers and magazines and books no longer carry my name."

Victoria smiled. "What you're saying is, you will never hang them up."

"I'm afraid that's true."

"Would you like to hang them up?"

"Very much so." He looked at her and smiled. "For one thing, they're heavy."

She laughed aloud at that, then sobered. "What value do you place on human life, Smoke?"

"The highest value I can accord it, Vicky . . . for those who respect the rights of others; for those who can follow even the simplest rules of society. I don't prejudge on the basis of what a person has contributed to our society, but whether a person has taken away from it. None of us are obligated to create fine art or music, or invent things that better mankind. We're not obligated to do anything to improve society. What we are obligated to do is not take away from it." He waved one big hand. "There is an entire subculture out there with only lawlessness on their minds. To hurt, to steal, to kill, to maim, to destroy. They don't give a damn for your rights, or my rights, or Lisa's rights to live life and enjoy it in relative safety and comfort. They want what they want and to hell with anything else. They spit in the face of law and order and decency. If those types of people get in my way, I'll kill them."

Although the day was not cool, Victoria shivered. It did not escape the attention of Smoke.

"You think I'm half savage, don't you, Vicky?" he asked.

"I don't know what my thoughts are about you," she replied honestly. "You bring Lisa a little puppy and then talk about killing human beings. You are a philosopher and yet you've killed at least a hundred men. Probably twice that number. You respect law and order, and yet carry the name of gunfighter. I think you are a walking contradiction, Smoke Jensen."

He smiled. "I've been called that, too, Vicky."

"What are you, Smoke Jensen? The Robin Hood of the West?"

"I don't know whether I'm that or that fellow who went around sticking his lance into windmills."

"Don Quixote. No, I don't think you and Don Quixote have much in common. You get quite a lot accomplished . . . in your own rough way."

"It's a rough world, Vicky. There is a saying out here: A man saddles his own horse and kills his own snakes. Now, only a few species of snakes are harmful, and a rattlesnake will usually leave you alone if you don't mess with it. But these two-legged snakes we have surrounding us right now are the vicious kind. They are capable of thinking, know right from wrong, but still want to strike out and sink their fangs into anyone who gets in their way or tries to block their lawless behavior. They have had their chance to live decently. They looked at a decent way of life and chose to ignore it. And they've made that choice dozens of times. Nobody forced them into a life of crime. They chose it willingly. As far as I am concerned, that means they gave up any right to demand compassion when they're caught. If they face me, they are going to get a bullet."

"The West frightens me, Smoke. I like the people in this town. But even they carry guns."

"Then go back east, Vicky. Go back where you have a uniformed police officer on every street corner and it's getting to be when a criminal is caught, the punishment is light or nothing at all."

"But they're human beings, Smoke!"

"They're garbage, Vicky. Rabies-carrying rats whose diseased fleas are hopping onto everyone who gets close to them."

Smoke stopped talking as a tall stranger on a painted pony rode slowly into town. The stranger cut his eyes to Smoke, sitting on the porch, and smiled.

Smoke stood up. "Time to go to work, Vicky. Max is pulling in the heavyweights now."

"What do you mean?"

"That's Dek Phillips. A hired gun from down Texas way originally."

"Why is he here?"

Smoke stepped off the porch. "To kill me."

19

Victoria gasped and put one hand to her mouth. "But . . . you're the marshal! A deputy sheriff!"

"That doesn't mean anything to men like Dek. When this is over, Vicky—the war, I mean—and Max Huggins and Red Malone are either dead or have pulled out, go on back to Vermont or wherever you came from. Maybe I'm judging you hastily. But I don't think you're cut out for the West. Excuse me now, Vicky. I got to go stomp on the head of a snake."

"You're going to arrest him?"

"I'm probably going to kill him."

"But he hasn't done anything!"

"That's right. So I'll just crowd a little bit and see what he's got on his mind. If he wants to ride on out, I'll let him. Thanks for the coffee. See you, Vicky."

Smoke walked over to his office. Sal, Jim, and Pete were standing out in front. Dek's horse was tied to the hitchrail outside the saloon.

"We seen him ride in," Sal said. "You know him, Smoke?"

"I know him. From years back. He's a no-good."

"We agree on that," Pete said. "I'd hired on for fightin' wages down in Arizona some years back. I seen Dek shoot a nester woman in the back. I drew my wages and left. But give the devil his due, Smoke. He's good. He's damn good."

"I've seen him work. Yeah, he's good. But the problem is he knows it and it's swelled his head. He stopped working with his gun years ago, letting his reputation carry him."

"By the way," Jim said. "I been hearin' shootin' every mornin' for the past week or more. From outside of town. Real faint like. Sounds like someone practicin'. Reckon who that is?"

Smoke stepped off the boardwalk. "Me," he said. He walked across the dirt street to the saloon and pushed over the batwings, stepping into the dimness.

The bar had cleared of patrons when Dek walked in. His reputation was known throughout the West, and unlike Smoke, he liked all the hoopla. Smoke walked to the bar and faced Dek, leaning against the other end of the long counter.

"Jensen," Dek said. "I hear you been throwing a wide loop here of late."

"What of it?"

"Some folks don't like it. So they got ahold of me to cut you back to size some."

"And you figure you're the man for the job, huh?"

"I figure so."

"Anybody ever tell you that you were a damn fool, Dek?"

The gunfighter flushed, then fought his sudden anger under control and smiled at Smoke. "That won't work, Jensen. So save your little mind games for the two-bit punks."

"That's you, Dek."

Dek carefully picked up his shot glass and took a small sip of whiskey, gently placing the drink back on the bar. "You've had all those books written about you. I even seen a play some actors put on about you once. Made me want to puke."

Smoke waited. He'd played this scene many times in his life. Dek was working up his courage.

The barkeep said, "Can I pull you a beer, Marshal?"

"Yes, that would be nice. Thanks, Ralph. A beer would taste good."

Dek tossed a coin on the bar. "On me, barkeep. It's gonna be his last one."

"It's on the house," Ralph said. "And I 'spect the marshal will be comin' in tomorrow for his afternoon taste."

Dek didn't like that. His eyes narrowed and his left hand clenched into a fist. Slowly, he relaxed and picked up his whiskey. Another tiny sip went down his throat.

Ralph slid the beer mug up the bar and Smoke stopped it with his hand. He took a healthy pull, holding the mug in his left hand. He wiped his mouth with the back of his hand and took several steps toward Dek.

Dek watched him, the light in his eyes much like that of a wild animal, filled with suspicion.

Smoke stopped and said, "Why, Dek?"

"Huh? Why? Why what, Jensen?"

"Why do you want to kill me?"

"That's a stupid question! 'Cause there's money on your head, that's why."

"What good is it going to do you dead?" Smoke took another few steps.

"Huh? Dead? You're the one gonna be dead, Jensen. Not me. Now you're crowdin' me, Jensen. You just stand still. Back up and drink your beer."

Smoke took another step. He was almost within swinging distance. "You got a mother somewhere, Dek?"

"Naw. She's been dead. Now, dammit, Jensen, you stand still, you hear me?"

"No wife for me to write to?"

"Naw. Why the hell would you want to write to my wife even if I had one?"

"To tell her about your death, that's why." Smoke took two more steps.

"Jensen, you're crazy! You know that? You're as nutty as a road lizard. You . . ."

Smoke hit him in the mouth with a right that smashed the man's lips and knocked him spinning. Smoke jerked the man's guns from leather and tossed them behind the bar. He stepped back, raising his fists.

"Now, Dek. Now we'll see how much courage you have. Come on, Dek. You think you're such a bad man. Fight me. Stand up, Dek. I don't think you know how. I don't think you have the guts to fight me."

Dek cussed him.

Smoke took the time to pull riding gloves from behind his gunbelt and slip them on. He laughed at Dek. "Oh, come on, Dek. What's the matter? You afraid I might kick your big tough butt all over this town in front of God and everybody? You afraid somebody might see and laugh at you?"

"That'll be the day," Dek snarled, raising his fists. "You ain't about man enough to put me down."

"We'll sure see, Dek. But there is one thing that puzzles me."

"What's that?"

"Are you trying to talk me to death?"

Cursing, Dek charged Smoke. Smoke ducked a wild swing and tripped him. Grabbing Dek by the collar and by the seat of his pants, Smoke propelled him through the batwings and out into the street, Dek hollering and cussing all the way. On the boardwalk, Smoke gave a mighty heave and tossed Dek into the dirt.

Dek landed on his face and came up spitting dirt and cussing and waving his arms.

Smoke stepped in and gave Dek a combination, left and right, both to the face, which staggered the gunfighter and backed him up, shaking his head and spitting blood.

A crowd began gathering, grinning and watching the fun. The women tried to frown and pretend they didn't like it, but from the gleam in their eyes, they were very much enjoying watching one of Max Huggins's men get the tar knocked out of him.

"Knock his teeth down his throat, Smoke!" Mrs. Marbly hollered.

"Yeah," the minister's wife shouted. "Smite him hip and thigh and bust his mouth, too, Marshal."

Dek looked wildly around him. He looked back at Smoke just in time to catch a big right fist smack on his nose. The nose crunched and Dek squalled as the blood flew. Dek backed up, trying to clear his vision.

Jensen didn't give him much chance to do that. Smoke waded in, both big fists working. He busted Dek in the belly and connected with a left to the man's ear that guaranteed him a cauliflower for a long time . . . not to mention impairing his hearing for the rest of his life.

Dek connected with a punch that bruised Smoke's cheek and seemed only to make him stronger.

Dek suddenly realized that Smoke was going to cripple him; was going to forever end his days as a gunfighter, and was going to do it with his fists, not his guns. He looked for a way out. But several hundred people had formed a wide circle around them. There was no way out. He was trapped.

"Gimme a break, Jensen," he panted the plea. "I ain't never done nothin' to you to deserve this."

Smoke almost laughed at him. The man had been hired to kill him and was now asking for a break. Dek Phillips had killed women and children and brought untold grief and suffering to many, many others. And he was asking for a break.

Smoke gave him a break. He stepped in close and with one powerful fist broke several of Dek's ribs.

Dek yelped in pain and involuntarily lowered his guard. Smoke knocked him down with a left to the jaw.

Smoke stood over him and said, "You know what I'm going to do, Dek. Are you going to lay there like a whipped coward while I kick you to death, or get up and fight?"

Dek slowly got to his boots. "You're a devil, Jensen," he panted, blood dripping from his face. "You got to come from hell." He flicked a fake at Smoke but Jensen wasn't buying it. Dek swung a looping right that Smoke ducked under and danced away.

"Stand still, damn you, Jensen!"

Smoke's reply was a right to the jaw. Even those in the rear of the crowd heard Dek's jaw break.

Smoke began to deliberately and methodically ruin the man. He gave him his overdue punishment for all the good lives he had taken over the years, and for all the misery and heartbreak he had caused.

The crowd no longer cheered. They stood in silence and watched with satisfaction in their eyes as Max Huggins's man was beaten half to death in front of their eyes. Vicky Turner stood in silence, shocked by the brutality taking place in front of her eyes. Sally Jensen stood beside her. The wife of Smoke Jensen knew fully well what her husband was doing, and she approved of it. Men like Dek Phillips could not understand compassion because they possessed none.

They understood only one thing: brute force. That was the only thing they could relate to. And Smoke was giving Dek a lesson in it that he would never forget.

When Dek Phillips finally measured his length in the dirt and did not get up, Smoke walked to a horse trough and bathed his face and hands. He straightened up and said to Pete, "Tie him across his saddle and take him to the edge of Hell's Creek."

"The man is injured!" Robert Turner shouted. "He needs medical attention."

"Shut up, boy!" Joe Walsh spoke from the edge of the crowd. He had ridden up unnoticed and sat his saddle during the final minutes of the fight. "Dek Phillips just got all the attention his kind deserve." The crowd muttered their agreement with that.

Sal said, "This ain't back east, Doctor. The laws are still few out here. You're a nice fellow, I'll give you that, but you got some adjustin' to do if you're gonna make it out here. You might feel sorry for a rabid dog, but you don't try to comfort it. You just kill it. You best learn that."

His face stiff with anger, Dr. Robert Turner took Victoria's hand and left the street, walking back to his office.

Pete rode out, leading the horse with Dek Phillips tied across the saddle.

Joe Walsh told several of his hands to accompany Pete, to act as guards in case some of the scum at Hells' Creek tried to waylay him.

Smoke walked back to the hotel to bathe the sweat and grime from him and change into fresh clothing.

Henry Draper, editor of the *Barlow Bugle,* headed back to his office to write the story of how the mighty hired gunfighter Dek Phillips had fallen under the fists of Marshal Smoke Jensen. He knew he could sell the story to dozens of newspapers back east. The reading public loved it.

The crowds broke up into small groups, talking over and rehashing the fight. With each victory they were stronger as a town, becoming closer-knit. The advance party from back east was due in the next day, and soon they would have a bank. Max Huggins would continue trying to destroy them—they all knew that—but they all sensed he would fail.

And they owed it all to one man: Smoke Jensen.

Max Huggins had just come from the bedside of Dek Phillips. The horse doctor who had attended the gunfighter had said the man would probably live, but he would be marked forever. His jaw was broken, his ribs were cracked, one arm was broken, a lot of his teeth had been knocked out. And worse, the horse doctor said, Dek Phillips's spirit appeared to be broken.

"The trial will probably last two . . . three days," Val Singer broke into Max's thoughts. "It'll take a good two weeks for the prison wagon to get around to pickin' up the boys. By that time, the bank will be operatin'. We hit the bank, loot the town, lift us some petticoats and have some fun with the women, and then strike out for greener pastures. What'd you think, Max?"

Max was thinking about Smoke Jensen. For three weeks, the big man had been exercising, running several miles a day and working out. He might not be able to beat Smoke Jensen with a gun—and that was up for grabs, for Max knew he was one of the best with a short gun—but there was no doubt in Max's mind that he was the better fighter of the two.

But how much time did he have? His informant in Barlow had sent him word that Judge Garrison and Smoke Jensen were gathering up old arrest warrants on him from his days back east. Two or three weeks might be cutting it very close.

And his informant had also told him that old warrants were being looked at against Red Malone. If the authorities back east came through, the rancher would have to run with Max. And Max knew the man would never agree to do that. The man would stand his ground and die with a six-shooter in his hand. He was too bullheaded to do anything else.

With a deep sigh, Big Max turned his attentions to the group of outlaws in his office. "Yes," he said slowly. "We're out of time here. Smoke Jensen has beaten us. Red may not see it that way, but I do. Smoke has used fists and guns to bring civilization to our doorstep."

Max eyeballed the group, one at a time. Val Singer, Warner Frigo, Dave Poe, Alex Bell, Sheriff Paul Cartwright.

"We're all wanted men, maybe not under the names we're using now, but wanted nevertheless. Two or three weeks is going to be cutting it awfully close. But I understand that is the way it's going to have to be. Monies have to be in the bank before we hit the town. To hell with those in jail. If we can get them out during the raid, fine. If not, that's all right, too. Are we in agreement with that?"

They were in agreement.

"The next problem," Max said, "is where do we run to?"

Everyone had a different idea. Cartwright couldn't go back to California. He was wanted out there. Singer couldn't go east. He was wanted in six or seven states in that direction. . . . And so it was with them all.

Max waved them silent. "All right, all right! Enough. It might be best if we split up after the raid anyway. We'll pick a place to meet and divvy up the loot, and then split up. And boys," he eyeballed each of them, "I shall be personally leading this raid."

The outlaws all exchanged glances. Max had masterminded a lot of raids, but none of them had ever known him to lead one. They were curious, and Val Singer put that curiosity into words.

"I have plans for a certain lady in that town," Max said with a smile. "I want her to know a real man just once in her life . . . just before I kill her."

"Well, if you gonna be draggin' some squallin' petticoat around with you," Warner Frigo said, "I think it's best we do split up. We're gonna have enough money to divvy up to buy the best women in any crib in the world."

"Yeah," Dave Poe said. "That don't make no sense, Max. It's too risky. Once we're out of this area, when words gets out about harmin' a woman, they'll be posses lookin' for you all over the place. And you do have a tendency to stand out in a crowd," he added dryly.

"It'll die down. It always has before. Hell, don't you boys get righteous on me. You've all raped before. Besides, you don't even know who I have in mind."

"Sure we do," Alex Bell said. "Has to be the doctor's wife, Victoria Turner."

Max smiled. "Nope. Her name is Sally. Sally Jensen."

20

The trial of the outlaws and the arsonist went off without a hitch. Judge Garrison handed down the toughest sentences he could under the law and the territorial prison was notified. The returning wire said it would be two or three weeks before the wagon could come and pick them up.

Smoke noticed the now-familiar buggy rolling out of town, heading north. He walked to the livery, threw a saddle on Star, and headed out, staying to the high ground, which oftentimes ran parallel to the road but high-up.

He trailed the buggy to within a few miles of Hell's Creek and watched as Max Huggins rode out to meet it. Max and the driver of the buggy sat for a long time on a log, talking, Huggins with one big arm around the other person's shoulder.

That night he told Sally about it. She shook her head in disgust. "Things are just never what they seem to be, are they, honey?"

"This thing isn't, that's for sure. Problem is, I don't know what to do about it. No laws have been broken. The only thing broken will be the faith of the townspeople."

"And a broken heart when the other partner in the marriage learns of it," she added.

"Yeah. If they don't already know about it."

"I hadn't thought about that. Oh, Smoke, I just can't believe that. Just thinking about it makes me sick!"

"I'll have to face one or the other pretty soon, I reckon. And I'm not looking forward to that. Well, let's get off of it.

How's the bank coming along?"

"I just got word this morning. It'll open for business next Monday morning. The money will be coming in day after tomorrow. And it will be heavily guarded."

She handed him a telegraph and let him read it. He whistled. "That's a lot of money."

"Yes. And that will be too good an opportunity for Max to pass up."

"I wish you and Victoria would get out of here, Sally. The two of you go on back to the Sugarloaf."

She shook her head. "No. I'm staying. We'll leave together, Smoke."

He had expected that answer so it came as no surprise to him. "I'd say I have two weeks before Max hits us. Maybe three. But no longer. I think those rumors the snitch carried to him about those old warrants back east has him spooked. And I'm told that Red Malone is getting jumpy, too."

She smiled at him. "The Sugarloaf will look good, won't it?"

"You bet." He got up and found his hat. "I'm going to prowl the town for a while."

"Anything wrong?"

"No. I just want to check around."

"I'm going to read. If you're late, I'll leave the lamp low."

Smoke walked down the stairs and through the lobby, speaking to the night clerk at the desk. The Grand Hotel was full, for with the coming of the paper, a doctor, two lawyers, and a half-dozen new businesses, the town was experiencing a growth unseen since its inception.

The saloon was doing a land-office business and had hired two nighttime waitresses and a piano player. The piano player was banging out a tune, the melody floating on the night air.

Pete walked up, spurs jingling softly. "Horse tied out of sight down by the creek," he told Smoke. "I never seen the brand before. Fancy riggin'. Rifle is gone from the boot. We might have us a back-shooter in town."

"You tell the others?"

"Goin' to now."

"OK. Watch yourself."

Pete gone, Smoke stepped back into the shadows created by the storefront and lifted his eyes, inspecting the rooftops of the buildings across the street. He squatted down and removed his spurs, laying them behind a bench on the boardwalk.

Standing up, he freed his .44's and slipped into an alleyway, walking around behind the buildings. He paused at the alley's end, staying close to the hotel's outside wall. He listened, all senses working overtime.

Smoke watched a man come out of a privy and walk into the hotel, through the back door. The lamplight inside flashed momentarily as the door opened. Smoke closed his eyes to retain his night vision. He opened his eyes and walked on, slipping around the buildings.

He angled around Martha's Dress Shoppe and came out behind the cafe. A slight movement ahead of him flattened Smoke against the back wall of the cafe, eyes searching the darkness. He caught a faint glint of moonlight off what appeared to be the barrel of a carbine—short-barreled for easier handling. Smoke waited, muscles tensed. He pulled his right-hand .44 from leather and, with his left hand over the hammer to reduce the noise, cocked it.

The man behind the gun stepped away from the building, and for an instant, Smoke could see his face. It was no one he had ever seen before. The man was clean-shaven, his clothing dark and looking neat. The man took a step, a silent one. He wore no spurs.

Slowly, Smoke knelt down, carefully stretching out on the cool ground to offer the man less of a target. "You looking for me, partner?" Smoke softly called.

The man turned and fired, the slug striking the wood of the building some four feet above Smoke's head. Smoke fired, the .44 slug hitting the rifle and tearing the weapon from the man's hands. The gunman ran back into the darkness.

"Yo, Smoke!" Sal called from the street.

"I'm all right. Stay under cover. I'm thinking this man is not alone." Smoke rolled to his left as some primal warning jumped through his brain.

Two fast shots, coming from different weapons, tore up the ground where he had been lying.

Smoke caught the muzzle flashes of one of the guns and snapped off a fast shot. The gunhand screamed as the slug ripped his belly and sent him tumbling off the roof of the saddle shop. He hit the ground and did not move.

An unknown gunhand stepped out of his hiding place behind Smoke and leveled his pistol. Jim and Sal fired as one from the main street, both slugs striking the man, knocking him off his boots.

Smoke rolled and came up on his feet, behind a tree. Both his hands were filled with .44's, hammers back. A slug ripped the night, burning through the bark of the tree, knocking chips flying. Smoke stepped to the other side of the tree and fired twice, left and right guns working. The man doubled over, both shots taking him in the stomach. Smoke ran to him and kicked the dropped guns out of his reach. He knelt down beside the hard-hit man just as his deputies came running up.

"You're not going to make it," Smoke told the bloodied man. "Who hired you?"

The man grinned through his pain. "Told the boys we was gonna be buckin' a stacked deck comin' after you." He groaned. "But the money was just too good to pass up."

"Whose money?" Smoke asked.

"You go to hell!" the man said, then closed his eyes and died.

"This one's still alive!" Sal called, kneeling beside the man who had fallen off the roof. "But not for long. I think his neck's broke."

"Hell, that's Blanchard," Pete said, looking down at the man. "I thought he was in prison down in New Mexico." He knelt down. "Come on, Blanchard," he urged. "Go out clean for once in your life. This is your last chance, man. Who hired you?"

Two dozen people, men and women, in various dress, including nightshirts and long-handles, had gathered around.

"Huggins from over to . . . Hell's Creek," the dying man

gasped. "Pulled us up from Utah. We rode the train. Me and Dixson. Dee was . . . he rode over from Idaho."

"Dee Mansfield?" Smoke questioned.

"Yeah."

"That his horse down by the crick?" Sal asked.

"Yeah. He . . . Gettin' cold and I can't . . . move my hands."

Dr. Turner pushed through the crowd and knelt down, looking at the man. It was a quick look. Blanchard had died.

The doctor stood up and faced Smoke. "When is this carnage going to end, Jensen?"

"Whenever Red Malone and Max Huggins call it off," Smoke told him. He spotted the undertaker. "Haul them off," he said. "OK, folks, show's over. Let's break it up."

"No, it isn't," Tom Johnson said, walking up. "Melvin Malone just rode into town. He's calling you out, Smoke."

"Damn!" the word exploded from Smoke's mouth. "I knew that kid would cut his wolf loose someday." He punched out his empties and loaded up full. "Sal, clear the streets."

"I demand an end to this barbaric practice of justice at the point of a gun!" Dr. Turner said. "Just arrest him, Marshal. You don't have to kill him. You have the manpower to overwhelm him."

Smoke looked at the man in the dim light. "You . . . demand, Robert? Who in the hell do you think you are, anyway? Demand? Overwhelm him? How? He's come to kill, Robert, not talk. He'll shoot anyone who tries to disarm him."

"You don't know that, Smoke. That's just conjecture on your part. Law and order must prevail out here. It's past time."

"Why don't you go disarm him, then, Doctor?" Sal suggested.

"I . . . uh . . . I'm not a lawman," the doctor said, his face coloring. "That's your job."

"Yeah, right," Sal's reply was dour. "I think that was the reason I hung up a badge the last time I wore one."

Smoke turned his back to the doctor and walked away, his

deputies moving with him, the crowd following along.

"He's in the saloon," Tom called. "You goin' to kill the punk, Smoke?"

"I hope not," Smoke muttered.

"There might not be any other way, Smoke," Jim pointed out.

"I know. But I can always hope."

Smoke stepped up onto the boardwalk and pushed open the batwings. The piano player stopped his pounding of the ivories when he spotted Smoke. The waitresses moved as far away from the bar as they could get. The long bar was already void of customers. Only Melvin stood there, a whiskey bottle in front of him, his right hand close to the butt of his Colt.

"Come on in, Jensen," Melvin said. "I'll buy you a drink."

"You were banned from this town, Melvin. Leave now and I won't toss you in jail."

"You'll never toss me in jail again, Jensen. Me, or anyone else for that matter."

"Boy, don't be a fool!" Smoke snapped at him. He knew that his plan to move close enough to slug the young man was out the window. Kill was written on Melvin's face, and his eyes were unnaturally bright with the blood lust that reared up within him. "I've faced a hundred young hot-shots like you. They're all dead, boy. Dead, or crippled."

Smoke could tell that Melvin was not drunk. The young man had enough sense about him to lay off the bottle before a gunfight. Alcohol impaired the reflexes.

Melvin laughed at the warning.

Smoke was thinking fast. He had been warned that Melvin was very, very quick and very, very accurate, so any idea of just wounding the young man was out of the question. When Melvin dragged iron, Smoke was going to have to get off the first shot and make it a good one.

"Boy, think of your father," Smoke tried a different tact. "Your sister. Think what your dying is going to do to them."

"Me, dying?" The young man was clearly startled. "Me? Oh, you got it all wrong, Jensen. You're the one that's going to be pushin' up flowers, not me."

190

"Listen to me, boy," Smoke said, doing his best to talk some sense into Melvin. "You . . ."

"Shut up!" Melvin yelled, stepping away from the bar. "You're a coward, Jensen. You're afraid to draw on me."

A coldness touched Smoke. A coldness that was surrounded by a dark rage. It sometimes happened when he was looking at death. It was a feeling much like the ancient Viking berserkers must have experienced in battle.

"I tried, boy," Smoke's words were touched with sadness. "Nobody can say I didn't try."

"And that's all you're gonna do in this fight," Melvin sneered the words. "Try to beat me. You've had a long run, Jensen. Now it's over. Now my pa can stop worryin' about his back trail and we can get on with our lives."

"All but one of you," Smoke corrected the young man.

"Huh?"

"Your life is over."

With a curse on his lips, Melvin's hands flashed to his guns and he was rattlesnake quick. But Smoke's draw was as smooth as honey and lightning fast. Melvin got off a shot, the slug blowing a hole in the barroom floor. Smoke's first shot took the young gunslinger in the belly. Melvin's second shot grazed Smoke's shoulder, burning a hole in his shirt and searing his flesh. Smoke shot the young man again, the slug turning Melvin. Still he would not go down.

Melvin lifted his left-hand Colt and fired, the slug smashing the bar. Smoke shot him again and Melvin went down to his knees, still holding his Colts.

Smoke stepped through the swirl of gunsmoke and walked to the young man. He kicked the guns from his hands and stood over him.

"I beat Blackjack Simmons and Ted Novarro," Melvin moaned the words. "Holland didn't even clear leather against me."

"They were fast," Smoke spoke the words softly.

"But you . . ." Melvin gasped. "You . . ."

He toppled over on his face and began communicating with the afterlife.

Smoke punched out his empties and reloaded. "Jim, get

word to Red that he can come in and take his boy home. Just Red. Anybody else of the Lightning brand tries to enter this town, I'll toss them in jail or leave them in the dust."

The young deputy left the barroom and walked to the stable, saddling his horse for the night ride.

"Knowing Red as I do," Sal pointed out, "he just might come bustin' up here with all his hands, figuring to burn down the town."

"If he does, it'll be the last thing he'll ever do," Smoke said. He looked around the barroom. "I want ten men on guard at all times tonight. Take some water and biscuits with you when you go to the rooftops. Go home and get your rifles." He looked at the barkeep. "Shut it down, Ralph."

"Will do, Marshal. I'll clean up and then get my rifle to stand a turn."

"Thanks, Ralph."

The body of Melvin Malone was carried to the undertaker and the lamps in the saloon were turned off. The men of the first watch were getting in place on the rooftops as Smoke, Sal, and Pete walked the boardwalks of the town, rattling doorknobs and looking into the darkness of alleys.

Smoke passed Robert Turner on the boardwalk as the man was going home. The doctor did not speak to the gunfighter.

"Yonder goes a scared man," Sal said. "Something about that fella just don't add up to me."

Pete said, "I been thinkin' the same thing. He looks familiar to me, but I swear I can't place him."

"Think of Max Huggins for a moment," Smoke told the men.

"What do you mean, Smoke?" Sal asked.

"Max Huggins is Dr. Robert Turner's brother."

21

Smoke swore his deputies to silence about the true identity of Dr. Turner, then went to the hotel to catch a few hours' sleep. He was up long before dawn. Smoke dressed quietly, letting Sally sleep, then went down to the jail to bathe his face and hands and shave. He walked out onto the silent boardwalks and leaned against a support pole. Jim had arrived back in town after delivering the news. He said Red did not take the news well. Smoke sent the man off to bed and then rolled a cigarette, waiting for the arrival of Red Malone.

Just at dawn, the hooves of a slow walking horse drummed over the wooden bridge at the south end of town. It was Red Malone, and he had come alone.

Red reined up and stared at Smoke thrugh the gray light of dawn. The man's face was hard and uncompromising. "I come to get my boy, Jensen."

Smoke jerked a thumb. "He's over at the undertaker's, Red."

"I'll get my boy buried proper, Jensen, and then you and me, we'll settle this."

"Why settle anything, Red? Your boy came to me, looking for trouble. Thirty . . . forty men heard me practically beg him not to draw. He was a grown man and he made his choice. He tossed the dice and threw craps. Bury your boy and put the hate out of your heart."

Red stared at him for a long moment. Then, without

another word, he turned his horse's head and rode slowly up the street, toward the undertaker. A few minutes later, Melvin was tied across the saddle of his pony, the horse carrying its owner for the last time.

As he rode slowly past Smoke, Red turned his head and said, "I'll be back, Jensen."

"I'll be here, Red."

Smoke waited until the sounds of horses had faded to the south, then walked across the street to the hotel dining room for breakfast. Red was going to work himself up into a murderous rage, then gather all his hands and attack the town. He would get with Max Huggins and work it all out. Max and his men would attack from the north, Red and his bunch from the south. Smoke was sure of it.

After breakfast, Smoke walked up and down the town's streets, telling people what he felt was coming at them. They had all felt that sooner or later they would be attacked. They took the news stoically. Benson, the blacksmith, summed up the town's feelings. "We'll be ready, Marshal."

The town braced for trouble, and Smoke went to see Dr. Robert Turner.

The doctor met him at the door. "If you're hurt, I'll treat you, Smoke; I'd do that for any man. But other than that, you are not welcome in this house."

"I see," Smoke said, standing on the small porch. "Does that include my wife, too?"

Robert hesitated. Women were held in high esteem back east, but nothing compared to the way they were almost revered out here in the wild West. "Sally is welcome here anytime, of course."

"You just don't like my barbaric ways, is that it, Doc?"

"Something like that, yes. All this killing is quite unnecessary, you know."

"No, I didn't know that, Doc. What am I supposed to do when a man confronts me with a gun? Kiss him? Let me tell you something, Doc. This will probably change over the coming years, and in a way it'll be a sad thing when it does; but out here, a coward can't make it. Now, there is a reason for that. If a man is a coward, then there is a good chance that he's also a liar and a cheat. Not always, but often that's true. You see, Doc, out here, a man's word is his bond. If a man's word can't be trusted, what good is he? So no man wants the title of coward branded on him. Too much goes with it. Are you beginning to understand what I just said?"

"Of course, I understand it. It's still stupid, primitive, and barbaric."

"Victoria home?"

"No. She went shopping."

"That's good. 'Cause I just don't believe she knows the game you're playing."

Robert stared at him for a time. The doctor's eyes were unreadable. "I don't know what you're talking about, Jensen."

"You're a liar."

Robert didn't back up. "I'm no gunhand, Smoke. And I certainly can't whip you with my fists, so I'm not going to try. Does that make me a coward?"

Smoke chuckled. "No. But I didn't call you that to provoke a fight. That's a bully's way. And I'm not a bully. I called you that to get your attention. Have I got it?"

"Yes. I believe you could say that." Robert stepped out onto the porch and waved Smoke to a chair. "What's on your mind?"

"Your brother, Max Huggins."

Robert was so shaken he missed the seat of the chair and went tumbling to the porch floor. Smoke helped the man up and into the chair. Robert was ghost-white and his hands were trembling.

"You want me to get you a drink of water?" Smoke asked.

"That would be nice. Yes. Would you?"

"Sure." Smoke went into the kitchen, pumped a glass full of water, and took it to the man.

Robert drank the glass empty and sighed heavily, as if a load had been taken from him. "How did you find out about Max?"

"By looking at the two of you and guessing. I knew someone had been leaking information out of town, so I followed you one day. Now, then, what do you intend to do about it?"

The man shrugged. "Victoria doesn't know, Smoke."

"All right. Neither Sally nor I believed she was a part of it."

"How many people know?"

"Me and Sally. Judge Garrison. My deputies."

"When the townspeople find out, I guess I'm through in Barlow, right?"

"I imagine so. You and Victoria, you're not cut out for this kind of life, Robert. The West is not for people like you. It's still plenty raw out here. You and Victoria, you both want all the pretty things that are scarce out there. Women wear gingham out here, not lace. Coming up here from train's end, me and Sally took our baths in creeks. I can't work up a picture in my mind of you and Victoria doing that. Killings are common out here, Robert. Not as common as they used to be, but people will still travel a hundred miles to see a good hanging."

The city doctor shook his head at that and grimaced in disgust.

"And then there is the little matter of your brother to take into consideration."

"Max is my brother. Can't you understand that?"

"He's also a thief, a rapist, a murderer, and God only knows what else. And accept this, Doc: I intend to kill him."

"Judge, jury, and executioner, right, Smoke?"

"Sometimes that's the way it has to be, Robert. And you're no better than Max, are you, Robert?"

"What do you mean by that?"

"There was no old rancher that you befriended back in the city, was there, Robert?"

The doctor's silence gave Smoke his reply.

"I suspected as much. Max killed that rancher and then had the letter forged. The letter you showed your wife."

"He never said, and I never asked."

"Didn't you even care?"

"Yes," the doctor's reply was spoken low. "Yes, I cared. I came out here in hopes of changing my brother, making him see that what he was doing was wrong. Evil. Our parents died two years ago, four months apart. They left quiet a sizeable estate; it all came to me. Of course, they had written Max out of the will years before. I even offered Max half of the estate."

"Sally thought you were a poor struggling doctor."

Robert laughed, a bitter bark that held no humor. "Hardly. I assure you I have plenty of money."

"And Max told you he would change his evil ways and become a fine upstanding citizen." It was not a question.

"Yes, he did, and I believed him."

"All that crap you told Victoria, that she wrote to Sally, about Lisa and Victoria being lusted after by Max. All that was a lie?"

"No. No, it wasn't. He told me he wanted my wife. And he told me he would use Lisa to have her."

"And you still defend the sorry no-good? Jesus Christ, Robert, what have you got between your ears? Mush?"

"I owe him my life, Smoke. Three times, I owe him. And I owe him my family fortune."

"You want to explain that?"

"A gang of thugs set on me when I was a boy. They had knives. Max whipped them. Every one of them. Later, when I got a—a woman in a family way, her father had me cornered, with a gun. Max killed him."

Smoke looked at the man, amazement in his eyes. "You're a real swell fellow, Robert. You know that?"

Robert could not miss the sarcasm in Smoke's tone. "She was just trash. So was her father."

"You did see the child through school, I hope?"

"Of course not. Don't be ridiculous. I told you, she was trash. Anyway, she moved away. I have no idea where she and the brat might be."

Smoke took off his hat and shook his head in disbelief. Robert was as bad, in his own way, as Max. He wondered if Victoria knew about any of it. He didn't think so. At least, he hoped not, for Sally's sake. "Go on, Robert." Smoke put his hat on and leaned back in the chair, rolling a cigarette. "It's such a heartrending tale."

"Yes. It really is, isn't it?"

Smoke looked at him to see if the man was serious. He

was. Smoke sighed and waited.

"The third time Max saved my life I was in college. He was on the run from the law—had been for years—but he was back east at the time. I had a rather unpleasant experience with a brother. . . ."

"You have another brother?"

"Oh, no. This was a fraternity brother at school."

"What the hell is that? Never mind. I don't want to know."

"I beat the young man quite severely about the head with a brick. It was over a woman, of course. Max finished him off for me."

Smoke was jarred right down to his boots. The good doctor, Robert Turner, was crazy. Insane. Smoke had read of people who had, or professed to have, two or three or more personalities. This was, he believed, the first time he'd ever met one of those people. He sincerely hoped he would never meet another.

"Finished him off? What do you mean, Robert?" Smoke knew exactly what he meant, but he wanted to hear the words out of Robert's mouth.

"Killed him, of course. Oh, the young man was dying anyway. Max just took the brick and beat his head in with it. I was appalled, of course. I abhor violence of any kind."

"Yeah. I can sure see that."

"It was in the dead of winter. And my heavens, but it was cold. Max took the body and threw it into the river, after tying several heavy objects to it. We're brothers, you know. Brothers help each other."

"Yeah. Right."

"It was just after that when my father got into his . . . ah . . . predicament. Max took care of that, too. Then he headed west. He always kept in touch with me, though. We're brothers, you know."

"How did he take care of your father's . . . ah . . . troubles?"

"Killed my father's mistress. She was attempting to blackmail Father. That would have done poor Mum in had she ever found out about it."

"I'm sure it would have, Robert." It's just about doing me

in listening to it, he thought.

Robert sat up straight in his chair and clasped both hands to his knees. "Well, my good fellow. I certainly am glad we had this little chat. I feel so much better now that I realize what an understanding man you are." He stood up, a broad smile on his face. "I must go see my patients now. They need me, you know? It's such a nice feeling to be wanted."

Robert walked back into the house, took his doctor's bag, and got into his buggy, clucking the horse forward. Smoke sat on the porch and watched the doctor drive out of town.

"The man is nuts," Smoke said. "Crazy and dangerous. Very dangerous."

He was sitting on the porch when Vicky strolled up, her arms filled with packages. She did not seem surprised to see Smoke sitting there. He helped her with her packages, then waited on the porch for her to come out of the house.

"Are you waiting for Robert?" she asked.

"No. I had a long chat with Robert. He just left. I was sitting here . . . ah . . . sort of catching my breath after our conversation."

"Whatever in the world do you mean, Smoke?"

Smoke did not know how to handle this. He was not the type of man who relied on finesse. His way was straight ahead and get the job done.

He shook his head and stood up. "Nothing, Vicky. It was just that our conversation got a little deep for me. Medical stuff."

"Oh! Are you ill? Is Sally all right?"

"Both of us are fine. Where is Lisa?"

"Playing with a friend." She smiled. "Don't worry. The kids are well guarded."

Smoke nodded. "Vicky, could I ask you some questions without your getting angry?"

"Why . . . of course." She studied his face. "It's Robert, isn't it?"

"Ah, yeah. It is." Smoke really didn't know how to get into this.

"He's a good man, I believe. But a very strange man at times. It's . . . and please don't think I'm criticizing him or

199

talking behind his back; I've tried to discuss this with him. . . ." She paused. "It's almost as though he is several different people in one body. Do you know what I mean?"

"Yes, Vicky, I do."

"I've been worried about him ever since we came out here. My goodness, I haven't even told this to Sally. You're easy to talk to, Smoke."

"Has his . . . ah . . . behavior been sort of odd, Vicky?"

"Why . . . yes. That's it. You've noticed it, too?"

"Oh, yeah. I sure have. He sort of . . . ah . . . rambled, I guess you'd call it, while talking with me."

She stared at him for a moment, then rose from the chair and walked to the edge of the porch. She stood for a moment, looking at the mountains in the distance. Smoke could hear her sigh. "I don't know what to do, Smoke," she said. "I don't have a penny of my own money. I am totally dependent upon Robert. He has violent mood changes. I'm frightened of him, and so is Lisa." She turned to face Smoke.

"I know he used to meet Max Huggins in town. I thought that very odd. And I have no ides what they discussed. Except . . ." she flushed deeply, ". . . me."

"And Lisa," Smoke said, taking a chance.

"Yes. Max came to the ranch lots of times. Robert would laugh and joke with him. Usually outside, away from me. But sometimes in the living room. I never could understand the . . . well, call it a bond between them."

"They're brothers, Victoria."

She fainted, falling off the porch.

22

Smoke yelled at a passing boy to run to the hotel and fetch Sally, then go to his office and tell his deputies to get over here.

The boy took off like he had rockets on his feet.

Smoke picked Vicky up and placed her on the couch in the living room. He was dampening a cloth at the kitchen pump when Sally ran in.

"What happened?"

"She fainted after I told her that Max Huggins and Robert were brothers."

"I'm surprised she didn't have a heart attack. Give me that cloth and go outside."

Smoke went outside and sat on the porch. Sal, Jim, and Pete had just arrived, out of breath from unaccustomed running in high-heeled boots. They were typical cowboys; anything that could not be done from the hurricane deck of a horse they usually tried to avoid.

"What's up, Smoke?" Pete asked.

He brought his men up to date. Judge Garrison rolled up in his buggy and joined the men in the front yard.

"That poor woman," the judge said. "She certainly has a heavy cross to bear."

"Judge," Smoke said, "can you get Robert declared insane?"

"All I have to do is sign my name to a piece of paper. He'll be taken to the state hospital for the insane."

One of Joe Walsh's hands rode up and dismounted. "Say, Smoke, I just seen Dr. Turner headin' north toward Hell's Creek. He was putting the whip to that horse of his. He was shoutin' and cussin' as he drove. Damn near ran me down. I hollered and asked him what was the matter. He said he had to get to his brother. What brother's he talkin' about? I didn't know he had any kin out here."

"We just found out that he and Max Huggins are brothers," Smoke told him.

The cowboy's eyes bugged out and his mouth dropped open. "Holy crap!"

Smoke turned to the judge. "Get all the legal action going that needs to be done, Judge. Committing Robert, and seeing to it that his estate is in Victoria's hands."

"Easily done, Smoke. I'll have the paperwork done in an hour and wire his banks back east. You get into his strongbox or files and find out where and how much. Have the papers sent to me."

Smoke walked back into the house.

Sally had opened Victoria's bodice and placed a cool cloth on the woman's head. Her eyes were open and she seemed alert. Smoke pulled a chair up close to the couch.

"I'm sorry, Vicky," he said. "But I just didn't know how else to tell you."

"It's all right, Smoke. I'm glad you did. It answers a lot of questions I had in my mind. Now I can see the family resemblance."

Smoke told her what the cowboy had seen. "Judge Garrison is going to have him committed, and we're going to get Robert's estate in your hands. I need to know where he keeps his documents, bank books, and so forth."

"I'll show you." She fastened a few buttons on her bodice and sat up on the couch.

"You best lay back down," Smoke told her.

"No." She smiled and stood up. She was steady on her feet. "If I'm to be a western woman, I've got to learn to be strong."

Smoke returned the smile. "I thought you were leaving, heading back east?"

"I'm staying," Vicky said. "I want my daughter to be raised out here. The town needs another schoolteacher, and that is what I was trained to be."

Sal had entered the room. He took one look at Vicky's

open bodice and blushed. Turning his back to the woman, he said, "I sent Pete over to fetch your girl, ma'am. They'll be along directly."

"Thank you, Mr. . . ."

"Just Sal, ma'am."

Vicky buttoned up her bodice. "You may turn around now, Sal."

"Thank you. I feel sorta stupid standin' here talkin' to a wall."

"That was kind of you thinking of Lisa."

Sal blushed. "Wasn't nothin', ma'am."

"It is to me, I assure you. Well!" She patted her hair and got herself together. "I have to assume that Robert is not coming back. So I think what I'll do is this: If you all will leave me alone for a time—Sally, will you look after Lisa for a few minutes? Good, thank you—I'll have myself a good cry and then start putting my life back in order."

Sal was the first one out the door. Women made him nervous, unpredictable creatures that they were.

"Man ought to be horsewhipped leavin' a good woman like that one back yonder," Sal said to Smoke as they all walked back to the office.

Sally looked at Smoke and winked at him. "Sal, what are your plans when we leave here?"

"Why . . . I don't rightly know, ma'am. Why do you ask?"

"The county is going to need a sheriff," Smoke picked up on what his wife was leading up to. "And you've been a fine deputy. How's about I recommend you to Judge Garrison."

"You mean that?"

"Are you interested?"

"Sure. But how 'bout these boys?" He jerked his thumb at Pete and Jim.

"Well," Smoke said with a smile, "I think Pete is going to try his hand at ranchin', seeing as how he's been tippy-toeing around the Widow Feckles, the both of them making goo-goo eyes at each other."

Pete's face suddenly turned beet-red. "I just remembered something. I got to go see about my horse," he said, and walked across the street.

"How about you?" Sal asked Jim.

"I like this deputy sheriffin'. Sure beats thirty a month and found sleepin' in drafty bunkhouses. It's fine with me, Sal."

"Good. It's settled then. Judge Garrison has papers declaring the election of Cartwright to have been illegal, and the man has no more authority. He's going to post election notices starting tomorrow. And you're going to be the only candidate."

"What are you gonna do?" Sal asked, clearly startled at the rapid turn of events.

"Retire from law enforcement and hang around to see the fun. A badge is too restrictive for me, Sal. I like room to roam."

"In other words, you're gonna take the fight to them."

"Why, Sal," Smoke said with a serious look on his face, "you know I wouldn't do anything like that."

"He occasionally tells tall tales, too, Sal," Sally told him.

"Judge Garrison did what?" Max jumped to his feet.

"Declared my election as sheriff illegal and they had an election down to Barlow yesterday," Cartwright said. "Sal is the new sheriff."

"He can't do that. We weren't advised of any election."

"Yes, we were." Cartwright held out a piece of paper. "One of the boys found this tacked to a tree just outside of town."

Max snatched the paper from him and squinted. "Hell, you can't read it without a magnifying glass!"

"That's sure enough the truth and that's what I done, too. It's a legal paper, telling the citizens of Hell's Creek about the election."

Max sat down and cussed. Loud and long. He wadded up the notice and hurled it across the room. He had never before been stymied at every turn, and it was an unpleasant sensation that he did not like.

"Well, you can still be town marshal of Hell's Creek."

"Big deal," Cartwright said sarcastically. "We got no protection now, Max. We don't know what's goin' on in Barlow now that your brother moved in with you. And the boys is gettin' right edgy."

"About what, Paul?"

"They're wantin' to hit the town now and get out. The bank's in place, ain't it?"

"Not yet. Monday morning is still the target date. We'll double our money if we wait until everybody there has dug up the money they've buried or pulled it out of mattress ticks. Tell the boys to calm down."

Cartwright left and Max turned in his chair, looking out his office window. His main concern right now was what he was going to do with Robert. His younger brother was getting unpredictable. He was like a goose, waking up in a new world every morning. Most of the time he was lucid, but other times he was crazy as a loon. Of course, he had always known his brother was nuts, walking a very fine line between genius—which he was—and insanity—which he certainly was.

But he was family, and family looked out for each other. As best they could, that is.

"You just sign right here, Victoria," Judge Garrison said, "and Robert's estate will be under your control."

Victoria signed and she became executor over Robert Turner's estate, thus insuring that she and Lisa would not be thrust penniless into the world.

Sal was now the officially elected and legal sheriff of the county, and Smoke had turned in his badge.

While Smoke respected the law, he was also well aware that there were hard limits placed upon it when dealing with the lawless. As a private citizen, he had shed himself of those limits. Now he could meet Max Huggins and Red Malone on an equal footing.

Smoke bought supplies at Marbly's General Store—including a sack of dynamite—and made ready to hit the trail. In addition to his .44 Winchester, he carried a Sharps .56 in another saddle boot. Two days after the election, Smoke kissed Sally good-bye and swung into the saddle. Star was ready to go; the big black was bred for the trails and was growing impatient with all this inactivity.

"I won't ask how long you'll be gone," Sally said.

"Two or three days this time around. I'll be back in time to see the bank open."

He headed north, toward Hell's Creek, to see what mischief he could get into. He had heard rumors that Big Max Huggins thought himself to be unbeatable as a bare-knuckle fighter. Smoke knew that the man could be formidable; just his size would make him dangerous. But Smoke also knew that many big men rarely knew much about the finesse of fighting, depending mostly on their strength and bulk to overwhelm their opponents.

The trick would be to catch Big Max by himself. Smoke didn't trust anyone left in Hell's Creek not to shoot him after he whipped Max—and he knew he could whip him. He'd take some cuts and bruises doing so, for Max was a huge and powerful man. But Smoke had whipped men just as big and just as tough; men who knew something about boxing.

Smoke stayed off the road, keeping to the mountain trails, enjoying the aloneness of it all. He rested and ate an early lunch above a peaceful valley, exploding with summer colors. Deer fed below him, and once he spotted a grizzly ambling along, eating berries and overturning logs, looking for grubs. Squirrels chattered and birds sang their joyful songs all around him.

Then suddenly it all stopped and the timber fell as silent as a tomb. The deer below him raced away and the grizzly reared up on his hind legs, testing the air. The bear dropped down to all fours and skedaddled back into the timber.

Smoke had picked a very secure position to noon, with Star well hidden. He did not move; movement would attract attention faster than noise.

Soon the horsemen came into view, about a dozen of them, riding through the valley. Smoke moved then, getting his field glasses out of the saddlebags and focusing in on the men, being careful not to let the sun glint off the lenses.

He knew some of them—or had seen them before. They were hired guns—hired by Max Huggins. The men were riding heavily armed, carrying their rifles across the saddle horns. Smoke could see where many of them had shoved extra six-shooters behind their belts.

The route they were taking would lead them straight to the farm complex of Brown and Gatewood and the others.

Those families had taken enough grief from Huggins and Red Malone and their ilk, Smoke thought, returning to Star and stowing the binoculars.

He decided he'd trail along behind the hired guns and add a little spice to their lives as soon as he was sure what they were up to.

Smoke decided not to wait when he saw the men reach into their back pockets and pull out hoods. They reined up and slipped the hoods over their faces.

They were about three miles from the farm complex. No man elects to wear a hood over his face unless he's up to no good; but still Smoke held his fire. He was looking down at a pack of trash, that he knew. But so far they had done nothing wrong.

He left them, riding higher into the timber and getting ahead of the gunslingers. On a ridge overlooking the valley where Brown and the others were rebuilding, Smoke swung down from the saddle and shucked the Sharps .56 from its boot. He got into position and waited.

He didn't have long to wait. The raiders came at a gallop, riding hard and heading straight for Brown's farm, guns at hand.

Smoke leveled the Sharps and blew one outlaw from the saddle, the big slug taking the man in the chest and flinging him off his horse, dead as he hit the ground.

Brown, his wife, and their two sons had been working with guns close by. The four of them, upon hearing the booming of the .56, dropped their hammers and shovels and grabbed their rifles, getting behind cover. They emptied four saddles during the first charge, and that broke the attack off before it could get started. The outlaws turned around and headed back north. They had lost five out of twelve, and that had not been in their plans.

They were about to lose more.

They headed straight for Smoke's position, at a hard gallop. Smoke leveled the Sharps, sighted in, and squeezed the trigger. Another hooded man screamed and fell from the saddle, one arm hanging useless by his side, shattered by the heavy .56 caliber slug. He stood up and Smoke finished him.

The hooded raiders were riding in a panic now, not

knowing how many riflemen were hidden along the ridges. Smoke lifted the Sharps and sighted in another, firing and missing. He sighted in another man and this time he did not miss. The raider pitched forward, both hands flung into the air, and toppled from the saddle.

Smoke walked back to his horse, booted the rifle, and mounted up, riding down to see if any of the outlaws on the ground were still alive. Two of them were, and one of them was not going to make it. The second man had only a flesh wound.

Smoke jerked the hoods from them and glared down at the men. "You'll live," he told the man with the flesh wound. He cut his eyes to the other man. "You won't. You got anything you'd like to say before you die?"

Brown and his family had gathered around. The sound of the galloping horses of the farmer's neighbors coming to their aid grew loud. Soon the men of the entire complex had gathered around the fallen raiders.

"How'd you know?" the dying man gasped out the question, his eyes bright with pain, his hands holding his .56-caliber-punctured belly.

"I didn't," Smoke told him. "I was having lunch on the ridges when you crud came riding along."

"What'd you gonna do with me?" the other outlaw whined.

"Shut up," Smoke said. "You get on my nerves and I might just decide to hang you."

"That ain't legal!" the man hollered. "I got a right to a fair trial."

Cooter snorted. "Ain't that something now? They come up here attackin' us, and damned if he ain't hollerin' about his right to a fair trial. I swear I don't know where our system of justice is takin' us."

"Wait a few years," Smoke told him. "I guarantee you it'll get worse."

"I need a doctor!" the gut-shot outlaw hollered.

"Not in ten minutes you won't," Gatewood told him.

"What'd you mean, you hog-slop?" the outlaw groaned the words.

"'Cause in ten minutes, you gonna be dead."

He was right.

23

Smoke helped gather up the weapons from the dead raiders. Brown and the others in the farming complex now had enough weapons and ammo to stand off any type of attack, major or minor.

"They got their nerve comin' back here," Cooter said as they dug shallow graves for the outlaws.

"And we'll keep comin' back," the outlaw trussed up on the ground said. "Until all you hog-farmers are dead." He had regained his courage, certain he was facing death and determined to face it tough.

"You're wrong," Smoke told him, stepping out of the hole and letting one of Cooter's boys finish the digging. "Take a look at these men around you, hombre. Even without my guns, they'd have stopped the attack. I don't know whose idea this was, but I doubt if it was Max's."

The young man on the ground glared at him but kept his mouth closed.

Smoke had an idea. "Can you read and write, punk?"

"Huh?"

"You heard me. Can you read and write?"

"Naw. I never learned how. What business is that of yours?"

Smoke walked to his horse, dug in the saddlebags, and found a scrap of paper and the stub of a pencil. He wrote a short note and returned to the outlaw. Folding the paper, he tucked it into the raider's shirt pocket and buttoned it tight.

"That's a note for Big Max. You give it to him, and to him

alone. I'll know if you've showed it to anyone else." That was a lie, but Smoke figured the outlaw wouldn't. "You understand?"

"You turnin' me loose?"

"Yeah. With a piece of advice. And here it is: Get gone from this country. Give the note to Max and then saddle you a fresh horse, get your kit together, and haul your ashes out of Hell's Creek. We know Max and Red are going to attack the town. That is, if the old arrest warrants on his head don't catch up with him first. And they might." Another lie. "The town is ready for the attack, hombre. Ready and waiting twenty-four hours a day. We know the bank is tempting. But don't try it; don't ride in there with them. The townspeople will shoot you into bloody rags. There's nigh on to six hundred people in and around Barlow now. Six hundred." That was also a slight exaggeration. "And there are guards standing watch around the clock, ready to give the call. It's a death trap waiting for you."

"You say!" the outlaw sneered, but there was genuine fear in his voice that all around him could detect.

Smoke jerked the man to his feet, untied his hands, and shoved him toward his horse, who had wandered back toward its master after running for a time. Pistols and rifle and all his ammo had been taken from the raider.

"Ride," Smoke told him. "And give that note to Max."

The man climbed into the saddle and looked down at Smoke. "I might take your advice. I just might. I got to think on it some."

"You'd be wise to take it. I'm giving you a break by letting you go."

"And I appreciate it." He tapped the pocket where Smoke had put the message. "All right, Smoke. I'll give this to Big Max, and I'm gone. You'll not see me again unless you come around a ranch. That's where you'll find me . . . punchin' cows."

"Are there any kids in Hell's Creek? Any decent women?"

The man shook his head. "None at all. There ain't nothin' there 'ceptin' the bottom of the barrel—if you know what I mean."

210

"Good luck to you."

"Thanks." The man rode north, toward Hell's Creek.

Smoke swung into the saddle. "Before you boys bury that crud, go through their pockets and take whatever money you find. You earned it."

"Don't seem right, takin' money from the dead," Bolen said.

"They won't need it," Smoke assured the man. "Near as I can figure out from reading the Bible, there aren't any honky-tonks in hell."

Big Max Huggins opened the folded piece of paper and read. He read it again and began cussing. He ripped the small note into shreds and did some more fancy cussing. All of the cussing leveled at and centered around Smoke Jensen.

The note read: MAX, YOU STUPID, HORSE-FACED PIECE OF HOG CRAP. MEET ME TOMORROW AT THE WEST SIDE OF THE SWAN RANGE BY THE CREEK. NO GUNS. I'M GOING TO STOMP YOUR FACE IN WITH FISTS AND BOOTS. COME ALONE IF YOU HAVE THE GUTS—WHICH YOU PROBABLY DO NOT HAVE, BEING THE COWARD THAT YOU ARE.

Max let his temper rage for a few moments, then began to calm himself. He sat back down behind his desk and smiled. Max had killed men with his fists and felt very confident that he would do the same with Smoke Jensen.

This is what you've been training for, isn't it? he thought. Yes, of course it is. How to play it? The fight will be rough and tumble, kick and gouge. That isn't what you meant and you know it! he mentally berated himself.

Jensen had slighted his courage, for a fact.

Max folded his hamlike hands behind his head and leaned back in his chair. How to play it? Well, there was only one way: He would play it straight. He would go alone.

Jensen had tossed down the challenge; Jensen had implied that he did not have the courage to meet him alone. Well, he'd show that damn two-bit gunfighter a thing or two about courage.

Jensen had chosen well, Max thought. He knew exactly where Smoke would be: on the flats just above the creek. Good level place for a fight.

Max would go in alone, but he would be armed; to do otherwise would be foolish. Once there, both men would shuck their guns together, each in plain sight of the other. Then, Max smiled, I will beat Smoke Jensen to death with my fists.

Smoke camped on the flats. On the afternoon before the fight—if Max showed up, and Smoke felt confident he would—Smoke prowled the area, picking up and throwing away every stick and rock he could find. He walked the area a dozen times, looking for holes in the ground that might trip a man. He memorized the natural arena. Then, sure he had done everything humanly possible, he cooked his supper and made his coffee. He rolled into his blankets just after dark and went to sleep with a smile on his lips.

What he was doing he knew was foolish. It was male pride at its worst. But when two bulls are grazing in the same pasture, one is going to be dominant over the other; that was nature's way. And Smoke had been raised too close to the earth to attempt to alter nature's way.

The fight would really accomplish nothing of substance. Smoke knew it, and Max probably knew it, too. If he didn't, then the man was a fool.

Smoke knew that what he ought to do was to kill Max Huggins just as soon as the man stepped down from the saddle. But that wasn't his way, and Max probably realized it. If Max came, and came alone, then he was going to follow the same rules.

It promised to be a very interesting fight.

Smoke was up at dawn, boiling his coffee and frying his bacon. He ate lightly, for he knew the fight might take several hours until the end, and he did not want to fight on a full stomach.

At full light he looked out over the flats, and far in the

distance he saw a lone rider approaching. From the size of the man, he knew it had to be Max Huggins. He lifted his field glasses and scanned the area all around Max, to the rear and both sides. He could pick up no sign of outriders. Big Max was coming in alone.

Max rode up to the flats and dismounted. He was wearing two guns, tied down. Smoke stood up from his squat and hooked his thumbs behind the buckle of his gunbelt.

"How do we play this, Max?"

"It's your show. You call it."

"First we untie, then we unbuckle and put them over here, next to my bedroll."

"That sounds good to me."

The men untied, unbuckled, and laid their guns on the ground, next to Smoke's bedroll.

Smoke pointed to the battered coffeepot and two tin cups. "Help yourself. It's fresh made."

"Thanks. That'll taste good." Max squatted down and poured two cups. With a smile, he handed one cup to Smoke and said, "If it's poisoned or drugged, then we'll go out together."

"It's neither," Smoke said, and took a sip of coffee. "It's just hot."

The men sipped and stared at each other in silence. Max broke the silence. "How'd you put it together about Robert?"

"Family resemblance is strong. Then I followed Robert one day and saw you together."

"He's quite insane, you know." It was not a question.

"Yes, I know. What are you going to do with him?"

"I honestly don't know, Smoke."

"Judge Garrison has legal papers ordering him committed to the asylum."

Max's face hardened. "Robert will never be confined in one of those places. They're treated worse than animals in there."

"You better think of something to do with him after you're gone."

"Oh? Am I going somewhere?"

"Yes. You're either going to leave this area voluntarily, go to prison, or I'm going to kill you."

Max chuckled, then laughed out loud. "Damn, but you are a gutsy man, Smoke Jensen. If the circumstances were different, I could really like you."

"There is nothing about you that I like, Max."

Max chuckled again, and it was not in the least forced. "That's a shame. I'm going to both enjoy and regret beating you to death."

"Don't flatter yourself. I've whipped bigger and better men than you in my time."

Max cut his eyes, looking at Smoke. The man was all muscle and bone. Max upgraded his original estimate of Smoke's weight. His arms and shoulders and chest and hands were enormous. Max probably had a good sixty pounds on the man, but he guessed accurately that Smoke would be quicker and able to dance around with more grace than he.

"I'm not surprised that you came alone," Smoke said.

"I do have some honor about me," Max replied stiffly.

"Honorable men do not make war against women and children. Neither do they rape young girls."

"Aggie was a mistake," Max admitted. "But both Robert and I—we get it from our father—have hot blood when it comes to girls. It's a failing, I will admit."

Smoke wondered how many young girls had suffered and died at the hands of the man he faced. And once again the thought came to him: I ought to just shoot him.

Smoke sipped his coffee, holding the cup in a gloved hand, and stared at Max Huggins from the other side of the fire.

"I guess it's about that time," Smoke said.

Both rose as one and tossed the dregs of their coffee to the ground. They tossed the cups to the ground and walked away from the campsite. Max flexed his arms and wiggled his hands and did a little boxing shuffle with his feet.

"That's cute," Smoke told him. "Where'd you learn that? From a hurdy-gurdy girl?"

"You're going to be easy, Jensen. That's one of Jem Mace's moves."

"Somehow I think he did it better. You looked kind of stupid."

Max stepped in quickly and tried a right at Smoke's head. Smoke sidestepped, but not to the side that Max anticipated, and the left that followed the right almost jerked him off his boots when it exploded against thin air.

"Damn, you're clumsy," Smoke told him.

Max charged in and Smoke was forced to back up. Smoke knew that if Max connected solidly with that big right, it would hurt. Max drew first blood with a sneaky left that bloodied Smoke's mouth; but Smoke moved away too quickly for the right he threw to connect. Smoke's left did connect against Max's belly and it was like hitting a tree.

He danced back and let Max follow him. Neither man had as yet worked up a sweat or was even breathing hard. Both of them knew that this fight could last a long time.

Max snaked a right in that almost connected. Smoke smashed a left uppercut that jerked Max's head back and stopped him for a couple of seconds. Before he could fully recover, Smoke danced away.

Blood was leaking out of one side of Max's mouth as he followed Smoke around the flats. Smoke suspected the big man had bitten his tongue due to that uppercut.

Suddenly Max dropped his fists and charged, trying to catch Smoke in a bear hug. What Max got was a combination left and right to his face, followed by a boot to his knee that staggered him. Before he could catch his balance, Smoke had hit him twice more, both times on the face. Max felt blood running down from his nose and the sensation infuriated him. He stepped in and busted Smoke on the jaw with a hard right, and then a left to the belly that hurt the smaller man.

Smoke backed up, shaking his head, for Max had a punch like the kick of a mule.

Max sensed victory too soon, but with good reason. Never had he had to hit a man Smoke's size more than twice to put him down. He stepped closer to put the finishing touches to one Smoke Jensen, and Smoke knocked the crap out of Max Huggins.

The hard right fist connected flush on the side of Max's jaw and put the big man down on the grass. He was astonished! He wasn't hurt, just simply astounded that Jensen had actually knocked him down.

Max was further astonished when Smoke backed up, allowing the man to get to his feet. Smoke was fighting ring rules.

"Just as long as you do, Max," Smoke said after correctly reading the man's expression.

Max nodded and stepped in, raising his fists. So it was boxing that Jensen wanted, hey! Well, he would sure oblige the man.

Both men were wary now, each of them knowing the other could do plenty of damage. They circled each other, Max with his fists held high, Smoke with his left fist held wide from his body and his right fist just in front of and to one side of his head.

He's no boxer! Max thought gleefully. Not with a stupid stance like that. Now I have him. Now I have him.

What Max got was a left fake that he brushed aside and a powerful right that barreled through and busted him flush on the mouth. He felt his lips split and the blood gush. The left that he had brushed away caught him a smashing blow on the side that hurt the big man, backing him up.

Smoke pressed in, hitting the man with a flurry of blows to the arms and shoulders as Max could do nothing but cover up until he caught his wind. And the blows were bruising.

Smoke pounded the man's arms, hurting and bruising them, taking some of the power from them. Max finally had to lower his guard and shove Smoke from him. The move got Smoke off him for a moment, but it also earned Max a smashing blow to the head.

Max saw an opening and took it, handing Smoke a one-two combination to the head. The blows popped Smoke's head back and bloodied his mouth. The left had caught him above the eye and opened a cut.

Smoke backed up, shook his head, and then plowed right back in, pressing the attack. He drove a right fist in that caught Max on the nose, and the big man felt the already injured nose break. The blood poured. Smoke didn't let up. He smashed a left and right to Max's head that rocked the big man back on his heels. Max got in a hard right that shook Smoke down to his boots, staggering him.

Max jumped at Smoke, intending to boot the man to the ground. One boot did catch Smoke on the leg, bruising the flesh but not putting him down. Smoke countered with a kick of his own that caught Max on the shin and brought a yelp of pain from the man. Smoke jumped in and blasted another left and right. The left took Max on the side of the jaw and the right hit him flush in the mouth.

Max grimly spat out part of a broken tooth and came on, both fists held high.

Smoke hit the man in the belly and took a left hook to his head for that move. Max followed the hook with a heel-drop that sent Smoke to the ground. Max tried to kick him. Smoke rolled away and came up on his boots, a hard light in his eyes.

Max had expanded the fight, moving away from ring rules with that attempted kick. If that were the way the man wanted it, so be it.

Max swung a looping right. Smoke caught the forearm and wrist and threw the man to the ground, then stepped in and gave Max a vicious kick to the kidney that brought a howl of pain from him. Smoke brought his balled fist down hard on Max's neck just as the man was trying to get up. The blow knocked him flat on the ground. Smoke went to work with his boots, stomping and kicking. One boot caught Max flush in the mouth, and the force of the kick shattered the big man's front teeth, top and bottom.

With a scream of rage and pain, Max flung out his hand and caught Smoke's jeans leg, tumbling the smaller man to the ground. Smoke rolled and came up on his boots before Max could get to his feet and apply the boots to him.

For a full minute the men stood toe to toe and slugged it out, with each of them giving and receiving about the same amount of damage. But Smoke could tell the bigger man was losing some of his power. Max was fighting with his mouth open now, sucking in air in great gasping gulps. Smoke had known nothing but hard work all his life. Max had spent the last fifteen years either sitting behind a desk, planning his evil, or sitting at a poker table, cheating those who played the game of chance with him.

Smoke sent a crashing right fist through Max's guard, a punch that knocked the big man to the ground. Smoke stepped in and kicked the man in the butt just as he was trying to get to his feet. The butt-kick knocked Max sprawling, sliding facedown in the dirt and the grass.

"You know what I'm going to do, don't you, Max?" Smoke asked, standing over the man. Max tried to get to his feet and Smoke kicked him in the butt again, knocking the big man down to the ground.

"I'm going to rearrange your face, Max." Smoke walked around to the front of the struggling giant of a man. "When I get tired of hitting you, I'm going to kick your face in."

Max knew he was whipped, knew Smoke was going to stomp him into the ground. "I've had enough," the big man said, blood dripping from his mouth.

"I imagine Aggie said something along those lines, didn't she, Max?"

"She was trash! Nester trash."

Smoke kicked him in the belly with all the power he could get behind the boot. Max's body arched upward off the ground and he screamed in pain.

Smoke backed away and let the man struggle to his feet. Big Max stood before him, swaying slightly. "Fight, you sorry bastard," Smoke told him.

Max lumbered forward and walked into a straight right that he felt all the way down to his toenails. Smoke followed that with a left that turned Max's head and loosened teeth. Smoke didn't let up. He began to work on Max's belly, driving hammer blows to the man's guts. Max backed up, unable to throw a punch that would stop Smoke Jensen. He landed several punches, but they had no power behind them.

Smoke shifted his area of punishment. He began working on Max's face. The face of Big Max now began to resemble a raw side of beef that someone had worked over with a sledgehammer. His nose was flattened, one ear was swollen and pulpy, his mouth was a ruined mess, and both eyes were closing. Still Smoke Jensen continued to punish the man.

Max searched frantically around him for a weapon—a club, a rock, anything! He found nothing. Smoke had carefully cleared the area. He tried to run and Smoke pursued him, leaping onto his back and riding the man around the area like some sort of beast of burden. It was the most humiliating thing that Big Max Huggins had ever been forced to endure.

Max finally collapsed onto the ground, his strength gone. Smoke stood over him. The smaller man had taken his licks. One eye was almost closed, and blood was leaking from his nose and mouth. But he was on his boots and ready to fight.

Max heard the words: "You got a choice, Big Man," Smoke told him. "You either get up and fight, or as God is my witness, I'll kick you to death."

Max struggled up. He turned and faced Jensen, lifting his fists. Max charged in a last-ditch effort to grab the smaller man and break his back.

Smoke stepped to one side and buried his fist into Max's belly, doubling the man over and bringing a painful retching sound from his mouth. Smoke's fist struck the man on his ear and Max experienced a roaring in his head. Another fist came up, seemingly from the ground, and slammed into his battered face. That was followed by a right fist that crashed into his nose. Smoke's fist hammered his lower back and smashed into his rib cage, sending waves of pain through the man as his kidneys took the brunt of the blows.

Max was beyond mere pain. This was an agony new to him. He had been moved into a sea of solid hurt. It was nothing like he had ever experienced before. His shirt had been torn from him sometime during the fight, and his upper torso was bruised and bloody.

Still Smoke Jensen would not back off. Big Max Huggins stood like a giant oak that was being battered by the elements, his huge arms hanging by his sides. He could not find the strength to lift them.

Smoke knocked him down and Max painfully climbed to his boots to face his tormentor. He turned in time to catch another huge right fist to his already ruined and swollen mouth.

Through eyes that were now nothing more than swollen slits, Max could see Jensen smiling at him. He had never seen a smile that savage on Smoke's face. Jensen's eyes were cold, killing cold. Max watched as Jensen measured him. He knew with a soaring feeling of relief the fight was soon to be over.

Smoke started his punch somewhere down around his ankles, and when the gloved fist exploded against his head, Max's world turned black.

The big man lay stretched out on the ground. Unconscious.

24

Smoke muscled Big Max across his saddle and tied him there. He looped Max's gunbelt on the saddle horn and slapped the horse on the rump, sending it on its way back to Hell's Creek.

Smoke packed up and headed for the high country, making camp not five miles from Hell's Creek. He had plans for that town. Smoke ached all over and his hands were swollen. He looked for and found the plants he sought, carefully picking them and boiling them in water, then soaking his hands. He stayed snug in the camp for two days, resting and eating and treating his hands until the swelling had gone down and he was ready to go.

Smoke had spent the time in the hidden camp not only resting and treating his hands and the cuts on his face, but also capping and fusing the dynamite, tying them into three-stick bombs. Star was rested and restless and eager to hit the trail.

At dawn of the third day after the fight on the flats, Smoke swung into the saddle and pointed Star's head toward Hell's Creek. He had it in his mind to destroy that town and as many people in it as possible.

The startled gun hands who watched as Big Max's horse walked slowly up the muddy and rutted main street of Hell's Creek could not believe their eyes. They were further astonished—and some a little frightened—when they untied Max and lowered him to the ground.

To a man, none of them had ever seen a person beaten so badly as was Max.

Robert Turner snapped out of his befuddlement of the moment and slipped back into his role as doctor. He ordered Max carried to bed and ran for his bag. Robert had taken one look at his brother's battered body and knew the big man was hurt—how seriously he would know only after a thorough examination.

"Not seriously," he finally said with a sigh, leaning back in the chair by his brother's bed. "No ribs are broken that I can detect, but his face will never be as it was. Smoke Jensen did this deliberately. This is the most callous act I have ever witnessed. Jensen deliberately set out to destroy my brother's handsome looks."

Robert looked around at the outlaws. "Well, my mind is made up. I have never believed in violence, but this"—he looked down at the sleeping Max, the sleep brought on by massive doses of laudanum—"has to be avenged."

Val Singer seized the moment, guessing what this crazy galoot had in mind. "What do you plan to do about it, Robert?" he asked.

"Why . . . I plan to step into my brother's boots and lead the raid against Barlow, that's what. What do you think about that, Mr. Singer?"

The outlaw leaders had to fight to hide their smiles. Of course, they'd let sonny-boy here lead the raid. Of course, they'd go along with it. For with Max out of the picture, they could ravage the town, rob the bank, and would not have to share a damn thing with Big Max Huggins. And before they left the country, they would kill Robert Turner.

So much for honor among thieves.

"That's a damn good idea, Robert," Dave Poe said. "I like it. I really do. When do you think we ought to hit the town?"

"Tomorrow morning, just as the bank opens."

"I like it," Alex Bell said.

Smoke had left his horse in timber on the edge of town, and he worked his way up a dry creek bed, coming out behind a privy. He ducked back down as two men walked to the outhouse, chatting as they walked.

"This time tomorrow, Larry," ond of them said, "Barlow ain't gonna be nothing but a memory, and we'll have had our fill of women and be a damn sight richer."

"Yeah, and we won't have to share none of it with Big Max. That's what makes it so rich to me."

Smoke listened, wondering what was going on. Tomorrow! They were going to hit the town tomorrow?

"Goofy Robert said he'd give Max enough laudanum to keep him out for a day and a half. He'd give it to him just before we pull out."

"Who's gonna kill that nut?"

"Hell, who cares? Sometime during the shootin' one of us will plug him. I've got me an itch for some of them women in that town."

"Me, too."

The men stepped into the two-holer and closed the door. Smoke made his way back up the wash, swung into the saddle, and headed for Barlow.

He stopped at Brown's house to rest his horse and to tell the farmer to warn the others about the raid the next day.

"You want us in town, Smoke?" Brown asked.

"No. I want you men to load up full and be prepared to defend yourselves in case they decide to attack you first, although I don't think they will."

"We'll be ready." He smiled, his eyes on Smoke's bruised face. "Who won the fight?"

"Big Max is still unconscious," Smoke told him with a grin.

"Glad to hear it."

Smoke mounted up and headed for Barlow. He hit the town at a gallop and yelled for people to gather around him. "It's tomorrow morning, people," he shouted, so all could hear. "The men of Hell's Creek are going to hit the town at nine o'clock, to coincide with the bank opening. Start gathering up guns and ammo, and make certain the pumper is checked out and the fire barrels are full."

He swung down from the saddle and handed the reins to the boy that helped out at the livery. "Rub him down good and give him all the corn he wants, boy." Smoke handed the

223

boy a coin and Star was led off for a well-deserved rest.

Smoke stepped up on the boardwalk in front of the sheriff's office, while others gathered up the rest of the townspeople. Smoke stayed in hurried whispered conference with Sal, Judge Garrison, and Tom Johnson for a few minutes, until the whole town was assembled in the street.

Judge Garrison, Sal, and the mayor agreed with his suggestions, and Smoke turned, facing the crowd. "All right, folks," he said, raising his voice so all could hear. "Here it is. There is a good chance that a rider was sent out to Red Malone's spread before I slipped into Hell's Creek and overheard the outlaws' plans. Red will probably attack us from the south at the same time the raiders hit us from the north. We've got to be ready to hit them twice as hard as they hit us. Jim has already left to warn Joe Walsh and his people. I told Jim to tell Joe to stay put and guard his ranch. Red hates him as much as he hates us. So it's going to be up to us to defend this town and everything you people have worked for. That's all I have to say, except start getting ready for a war."

The crowds broke up into small groups, each group leader, already appointed, waiting to see where they were supposed to be when the attack came.

"Tom," Smoke said, "you and your group take the inside of the bank. Take lots of ammo and water."

"Will do, Smoke," the mayor said, and moved out to get ready.

"One group inside Marbly's store. Toby, you and your people will defend the hotel. Benson's group will take the livery. Ralph, you and your bunch will fight from the saloon. The rest of them know where to be and what to do. Let's start getting ready."

Sal looked at Smoke's battered face and commented, "Need I have to ask who won the fight?"

"Big Max didn't," Smoke said, then walked toward the hotel for a hot bath, a change into fresh clothes, and to rest beside Sally.

"I'd give a pretty penny to have seen that scrap," Sal said.

"Yeah," Pete Akins agreed. "He must have hurt him bad

for Max not to be leadin' the raid come the morning."

"How many men are we facing tomorrow?" the owner of the cafe asked.

"Nearabouts a hundred from Hell's Creek," Pete told him. "Maybe more than that. And all of Red Malone's bunch. We'll have them outnumbered, but bear this in mind: Them we'll be facin' is killers. Ninety-nine percent of the townspeople ain't." He looked hard at the cafe owner and at the other group leaders. "You pass the word, boys: Don't give no mercy, 'cause you shore as hell ain't gonna be gettin' none from them that attack us."

Smoke took a long hot soak in their private bath in the suite, then napped for an hour. He dressed and began cleaning his guns, loading rifle, shotgun, and pistols up full. He took his spare pistols out of wraps and cleaned and oiled them, loading them up. They were old Remington Frontier .44's, and Smoke had had them for a long time. He liked the feel of them, and was comfortable and confident with them in his hands.

"Early in the morning," Smoke told his wife, "you go get Victoria and Martha and the kids. Bring them back up to this suite. We'll be up long before then—the cafe and hotel dining room is going to open about four o'clock to feed those that don't eat at home—and we'll rearrange the furniture in this suite to stop any bullet. I'll have a boy start bringing up water to fight any fires that might start. Their plan is to destroy the town, so they'll be throwing torches."

Sally sat at the table with her husband, oiling and cleaning her own guns. "Vicky doesn't know anything about pistols," she said. "But Martha does. We'll have rifles and shotguns ready. How about Robert, Smoke?"

He shook his head. "I don't want to kill him, honey. I can't justify killing a crazy person unless there is just no other way out."

"I've been reading that there is some new treatment for the mad. But insane asylums are just awful."

"I know. I mean, I've heard they are. Chain them down

225

like wild animals until they die." He rose from the table and buckled his gunbelt around his lean waist, tying it down. "I'm going to roam the town."

Everybody was pitching in to secure the town. The new bankers just arrived from the East were nervous about the upcoming fight but doing their share in carrying water, moving barricades in place, and anything else they were asked to do. And Smoke could also read excitement in their faces.

Sal caught up with him. "Where are you going to be come the mornin', Smoke?"

"I'll be lone-wolfing it, Sal. Moving around. Did you see to it that everybody had a red bandana?"

"Everybody that will be behind a friendly gun will have one tied around their right arm. They was a darn good idea of yours. That's gonna help keep us from shootin' our own people."

"The dust and smoke are going to be bad when it starts. So I would suggest we water down the main street just before the bank opens. What do you think?"

"Another good idea. I'm gonna miss you and Sally when y'all pull out."

"You'll handle it, Sal. And, Sal? . . ."

The sheriff turned to face him.

"Martha and Vicky and the kids will be with Sally in our suite come the morning. So you won't have to worry about Victoria."

Sal blushed and headed across the street. Smoke smiled and continued his walking tour.

The saloon had been turned into a fort, as had the livery stable and barn. Marbly's store was barricaded, and anything that might be broken had been taken from the shelves and stored in wooden boxes. Smoke nodded his approval and walked back to the hotel. The waiting was going to be hard.

"Way I see it," John Steele said to Red Malone, "we just ain't got much of a choice."

"We have no choice," the rancher said. "We both have warrants on us in other states. The town has to be destroyed,

226

and everybody in it dead and buried in deep graves. We'll toss the bodies into the fires and burn them before we bury them. The authorities, if any show up, won't be able to prove a damn thing."

"Some of our men rode out today, right after the rider from Hell's Creek left. Said they wasn't havin' no part of killin' women and kids."

Red snorted his disgust. "We don't need them. We're better off without them."

What neither of them knew was that the hands who had left in disgust over making war against women and kids were riding toward Barlow, to join the defenders of the little town.

"After Barlow is burned out," Red said, "the outlaws will scatter to the wind. We'll ride and burn down Hell's Creek. We'll blame everything on Max's bunch. Hell, we can even say that we sided with the townspeople in trying to fight them outlaws off. We'll take some of our own men dead, for sure. We can point their graves out to the invesigators as proof."

"That still leaves Joe Walsh and his crew," the foreman pointed out.

"We'll deal with them. We've got them outnumbered three to one. Soon as Barlow is done and over, we'll ride for the Circle W and clean out Walsh and his crew."

John smiled a death's-head grin. "Then we can wipe out all them damn hog-farmers and other nesters, and the valley will once again be ourn."

"Yeah." Red rubbed the stubble of beard on his jowls. "And some of them nester girls ain't that bad looking. We can have some fun with them." He laughed. "Be just like old times. . . . Hey, John, remember them days?"

John Steele joined in the laughter. The men were in high spirits as they walked out of the house to sit on the porch.

"Just let me get Jensen in gunsights," Red said. "All I need is one shot. Front or back, it don't make no difference to me."

The town of Barlow rolled up the boardwalks early that

evening. Far earlier than usual. Everyone wanted to get a good night's sleep before the storm struck the next morning.

Red's Lightning hands who had rebelled against fighting women and kids had ridden in, holding up a white handkerchief—well, it was almost white—and Smoke, along with Judge Garrison and Mayor Johnson, met them in the street.

"We done quit Red," the spokesman for the group said. "We ain't havin' no part in killin' women and little kids. If you want our help, we're here."

"How do we know you weren't sent in here by Red to start shooting us in the backs come the attack in the morning?" Tom asked.

"That's a good question," the hired gun said. "And I don't know how to answer it."

"I do," Sal said, stepping off the boardwalk and into the street. "Howdy, Cobb."

"Howdy, Sal. We all right proud of you, you bein' elected sheriff and all. Me and Benny and Hale and Stacy here, we got to talkin' about that this mornin'. After that no-good from Hell's Crick come talkin' to Red this mornin' about killin' the women and kids and burnin' this town down. We couldn't do that, Sal. You've ridden some trails with us; you know we're not that kind of men. Oh, we've hired our guns out—just like you've done, for fightin' wages. But there ain't none of us ever made war agin' nobody 'ceptin' grown-up men. And we ain't about to start now. Smoke, I guess that's the only answer we can give you."

Smoke smiled and nodded his head. "It sounds good to me, boys."

"Me, too," Judge Garrison said. He wore two guns belted around his expansive waist. Two old Remington .44's—the Army model. Both guns looked to Smoke as if they'd seen some action. "There'll be stars in your crown for this, boys."

Stacy shifted in his saddle. "I don't know about that, Judge. I just don't want no more black marks agin' me in the Judgment Book. The Good Lord knows I got aplenty of them already."

"You boys stable your horses and meet me in the hotel

dinin' room," Sal said. "Glad to have you with us."

"Right will prevail, Smoke," Judge Garrison proclaimed. "Sometimes it just takes an outsider to prod those oppressed into action."

Smoke looked at the .44's belted around the judge's waist. "When is the last time you fired those, Judge?"

The judge smiled. "I came out of the War Between the States a colonel, Smoke. Of cavalry. I had my law degree when I enlisted. I fought through nearly every major campaign." He smiled. "With Lee. I graduated VMI, sir."

"Then I won't worry about you, sir."

"Coming from you, that is high praise. Tell me, since I haven't had a chance to ask, how did you leave Max Huggins?"

"Unconscious and tied across his saddle."

The judge walked away, shaking with laughter. His booming laughter could be heard up and down the main street of Barlow.

25

Smoke was up and dressed for war long before dawn. He wore his customary two pistols in leather, his two spares were tucked behind his gunbelt, and he carried an American Arms 12 gauge sawed-off shotgun, a bandoleer of shells slung across his chest, bandit-style.

He and Sally had breakfast before the sun was up, and then he walked Lisa and Victoria back to the hotel, Lisa carrying her puppy, Patches, in her arms. Pete escorted Martha Feckles and the boy to the suite, and the women made ready for war.

The men tied red bandanas around the upper part of their right arms. Since there were no females among the raiders who were riding to attack them, the women dressed in their customary attire. More than a few of them, including Mrs. Marbly, Victoria, Sally, and Martha, wore men's britches.

Sal's eyes bugged out when he saw Victoria. "Lord have mercy!" he said. "What's next?"

"The vote," Smoke told him.

"You have to be kidding! Votin' is men's business. Women don't know nothin' about pickin' politicians."

"You'd be surprised," Smoke said.

Smoke walked the town, inspecting each water barrel—and there were many. He checked to see if the buckets were ready in case of fire. They were. He checked each store that was to house fighters. They were ready and willing, even if many of them were scared. Mrs. Marbly, a very formidable-sized lady, had found herself a pair of men's overalls, and when she bent over, she looked like the rear end of a stagecoach. But she handled the double-barreled shotgun like she knew what she was doing. Smoke concluded that he wouldn't want to mess with her.

Pete was still in shock after seeing Mrs. Marbly in men's overalls, bent over.

"Close your mouth, Pete," Smoke told him. "Before you suck in a fly."

Jim was stationed two miles out of town, on a ridge, a fast horse tied nearby. As soon as he spotted the dust of the raiders, he was to come hightailing it back into town and give the warning.

Smoke walked to the north end of the town and leaned up against a hitchrail. He rolled him a cigarette and lit up, waiting for the action to start.

He looked back up the wide street. It was void of any kind of life. The horses were stabled safely and the children's pets were in the house, out of harm's way.

Smoke watched as a water wagon rolled down the street, then back up, watering the wide street to keep down the dust. He clicked open his watch: eight-thirty. He walked on down the street, coming to a nearly collapsed old building; a relic of a business of some sort that had failed. This was the last building on either side of the street. Smoke stepped up on the porch and pushed open the door. Rusty hinges howled in protest. He stepped inside and looked in both rooms of the structure. He tried the back door, working it several times to make certain he could exit that way. There was not a windowpane intact in any frame, so he did not have to worry about being cut by flying glass. He sat down on the dusty floor and waited.

At eight-forty-five, Jim came fogging into town from his post. Smoke heard him yell, "Here they come, folks. And there's plenty to go around." He rode into the livery stable and disappeared.

Smoke eared back the hammers on the sawed-off and knelt by the window. Moments later, he could feel the vibration through the floor, the faint thunder of hundreds of hooves striking the ground.

As the pack of outlaws drew closer, Smoke stared in amazement. Robert was leading the bunch. He wore a pith helmet, the leather strap tied under his chin, and was waving a sword. God knows where he had found either article in Hell's Creek.

The raiders, more than a hundred strong, thundered into town. Smoke let Robert and a few behind him gallop past, then he gave both barrels of the sawed-off to the outlaws.

The hand-loaded charge of nails and buckshot cleared a bloody path in the middle of the outlaw horde. Smoke dropped the shotgun and jerked out his Colts, cocking and firing as fast as he could; deadly rolling thunder erupted from the small collapsing building on the edge of town. Horses began milling around, confused and frightened and riderless. Bodies lay in the street.

A wounded outlaw, his hands filled with guns, staggered up on the porch. He spotted Smoke and leveled his guns. Smoke gave him two .44 slugs in the chest and the man's days of lawlessness were over.

Smoke quickly reloaded his Colts, shoved fresh shells into the express gun, and ran out the back door, turning to his right.

"Red and his bunch are attacking from the south!" he heard the faint shout over the roar of battle.

Smoke ducked into the space between a home and a business and ran to the street. A hatless and bearded man stepped off the path and turned to face Smoke. Smoke pulled the trigger of the sawed-off, and the force of the charge lifted the outlaw off his boots and knocked him out into the street. Smoke ran to the edge of the street and gave the other barrel to a cursing raider. Blood smeared his saddle and the man hit the street, dead.

Smoke filled both hands with Colts and began emptying saddles. From the sounds of shotgun fire coming from the bank building, and the number of bodies littering the street in front of the bank, the Easterners were having a duck shoot and doing a damn fine job of holding their own.

Smoke stepped back and reloaded the pistols and the shotgun.

"Forward, men!" he heard Robert shout, the cry coming

from behind him. "Slay the Philistines."

Smoke turned around. Robert was charging him on horseback, waving his sword. Smoke ducked the slashing sword that could have taken his head off and swung up behind Robert as the frightened horse reared up, dumping both men on the ground. Robert lost his sword and Smoke gave him a one-two combination that dropped the man to the ground, out cold. Smoke tore the pith helmet off and used the leather chin strap to bind Robert's hands behind his back. He used the man's belt to securely bind his ankles, then rolled the doctor under a building. Smoke picked up his shotgun and stepped back into the fray.

Two raiders, apparently having lost their appetite for any further battle, came racing up the street, heading north. Smoke stepped out and gave them both barrels of the sawed-off. Two more saddles cleared.

Smoke stepped up on the boardwalk and ran toward the center of town, reloading the shotgun as he went. He turned down an alleyway and entered the hotel through the back door, muttering curses because the rear of the building was not guarded.

Just above him, on the second floor, Warner Frigo had kicked open the door to the presidential suite and was looking down at Lisa, huddled on the floor, holding her puppy close.

"Well, now," the outlaw said with a sneer. "Won't you just be a juicy little thing to have."

He holstered his guns and reached down for her, lust in his eyes.

"You'll hurt no more children and kill not another child's pet," Warner heard the woman say.

He looked up. Sally stood in the foyer, holding a sawed-off in her hands, both hammers eared back.

Warner's lips peeled back in an ugly smile. "I'll have you after I taste little-bit here."

"I doubt it," Sally said, then pulled both triggers. The force of the blast knocked Warner off both boots and sent him flying into the hall. He hit the hall wall and slid down to the carpeted floor. The wall behind him was a gory mess.

Smoke looked up as the shotgun went off. If anyone had tried to mess with Sally, they picked the wrong woman. He went up the stairs to check it out.

He saw Warner's body and stuck his head into the foyer. "Everybody all right in there?" he called.

"Just dandy," Sally said. "Would you please remove that garbage from the hall, darling?"

"Sure." Smoke dragged Warner's body down the hall and threw him out the second-story window. The downward hurtling body hit Sid Yorke and knocked him out of the saddle. The outlaw stared in horror at what was left of Warner Frigo.

He looked up at Smoke, standing behind the shattered window, grinning down at him. Sid lifted his pistol, and Judge Garrison, standing in his office, fired both Remington .44's, the slugs knocking the man to his knees. The outlaw died in that position, his hands by his side. His hat fell from his head. The wind picked it up and sailed it down the street.

Sal stepped out from his position just as John Steele was rounding a corner.

"Hey, John!" Sal called.

The foreman of the Lightning whirled in a crouch, both hands by his holstered guns.

"You always bragged how good you was," the newly elected sheriff said, his voice carrying over the din of battle and the whinnying of frightened horses. "You wanna find out now?"

John dragged iron. He was far too slow. Sal put two slugs in his belly before Steele could clear leather.

"I guess now you know," Sal told him.

"You sorry . . ." John gasped the words. He never got to finish it. The foreman fell off the boardwalk and landed in a horse trough.

"Have to remember to clean that out," Sal muttered.

Judge Garrison went out the back door of his office and came face to face with Paul Cartwright. The judge smiled at the man. "You used to love to lord it over me, Paul. You have guns in your hands. Use them!"

The deposed sheriff's guns came up. Judge Garrison lifted

his Remington Army Model .44's, and the muzzles blossomed in fire and smoke. Paul Cartwright fell backward, dead.

The judge reloaded and walked up the back of the buildings, conviction and courage in his eyes.

"Gimme all your goddamn money, you heifer!" Frank Norton yelled at Mrs. Marbly.

Mrs. Marbly lifted her shotgun and blew the outlaw out the back door.

"Nice going, mother," her husband said.

Larry Gayle knew it was a losing cause. He had been thrown from his rearing, bucking horse and was now cautiously making his way out of town . . . on foot. He'd find a horse. To hell with Barlow, Max Huggins, and the whole mess. There had to be easier pickings somewheres else was his philosophy.

"Going somewhere, Larry?" the voice spun him around.

Pete Akins stood facing him.

Larry lifted his Smith & Wesson Schofield .45 and got off the first shot. It grazed Pete's shoulder. Pete was much more careful with his shooting. He shot Larry between the eyes. He walked to the prostrate and very dead outlaw and looked down at him. He shook his head.

"Whoo, boy. You was ugly alive. Dead, you'll probably come back to haunt graveyards."

Ted Mercer stood facing Smoke Jensen. The outlaw felt a coldness take hold of him. His Colt was in his hand, but he was holding it by his side. Could Jensen beat him? He didn't know. He really didn't want to find out.

"You can drop that iron and walk," Smoke told him. "Change your life. It's up to you."

"You're only sayin' that 'cause you know you can't beat this."

"You're wrong, Ted."

"Your guns are in leather!"

"Drop it and walk, man. Don't be a fool."

"I think I'll just kill you, Jensen." Ted's hand jerked up. He felt a dull shock hit him in the belly, another hammerlike blow beat at his chest. Impossible! he thought. No man is that fast. No man is . . .

Smoke walked up and looked down at the dead outlaw. "I gave you a chance," he said.

Fires had been started by the raiders, but they had been quickly put out by the ladies of the bucket brigades. The plans of the outlaws were put out as quickly as the flames. Lew Brooks jumped his horse over the body of a friend and went charging between buildings. Judge Garrison stepped out and gave the outlaw a good dose of frontier justice, not from a law book but from a .44. Lew hit the ground, rolled over, and came up with a .45 in his hand. Judge Garrison imposed the death sentence on the man, then calmly reloaded and walked up the alleyway.

Jake Stringer knew that John Steele was down and dead, along with several other Lightning men. He didn't know where Red Malone was. He tried to calm a badly spooked horse and climb into the saddle. But the horse was having none of that. The animal jumped away and left Jake on foot.

"Damn that hammerhead!" Jake swore. "I ought to shoot it."

"Why not try me?" Jim Dagonne said.

Jake turned. Jim's guns were in leather, as were his own. A smile creased his lips. "I enjoyed whuppin' you with my fists, Jim. Now I'm gonna enjoy killin' you."

Jim was no fast gunhand, but he was a dead shot. Jake cleared leather first and his shot went into the dirt at Jim's boots. Jim plugged the man just above the belt buckle. Jake sat down on the ground and started hollering.

Jim walked to him. He could see where the slug had exited out the man's back, right through the kidney. "You ain't gonna make it, Jake. You got anyone you want me to write?"

"I didn't even know you could write," Jake said, then fell over on his face and closed his eyes.

Ella Mae, Tom Johnson's wife, was struggling with a man who had less than honorable intentions on his mind. He ripped her bodice open and stared hungrily at her flesh. Momentarily free, Ella Mae ran to the kitchen, jerked up the coffeepot from the stove, and threw the boiling contents into the man's face.

237

The outlaw screamed and went lurching and staggering through the living room, finding his way out the front door, his face seared from the boiling coffee. He stumbled out into the street and was run down by another wounded outlaw, trying to get out of the death trap named Barlow. The burned outlaw fell under the hooves and lay still.

Clark Hall made the bank and hurled himself through the door. He came up on his boots just in time to face several men with shotguns. He had time to say one word: "No!"

Three sawed-off shotguns roared, and Clark Hall was literally torn out of his boots and thrown out into the street.

The shooting stopped. An eerie silence fell over the town. Smoke stepped out into the street, the Remington Frontier .44's in his hands. The moaning of the wounded drifted to him.

Judge Garrison took charge. "Gather up the wounded, and we'll patch them up as best we can and then try them. We were forced to use frontier justice to stop this, but there'll be no unauthorized hangings. From now on we go by the book."

Ralph from the saloon was dead. Shot through the head. Toby at the hotel had taken a slug through his shoulder. Several other citizens were wounded, but Ralph was the only fatality. The streets and alleys of the town were littered with dead and wounded. Guns lay everywhere one looked and riderless horses milled around, not knowing what to do or where to go.

Henry Draper came out of his office at the newspaper, wearing two huge Dragoons belted around his waist. That would account for some of the booming sounds Smoke had heard and also some of the hideous wounds he'd seen. Draper set up his camera and began preparing for shots of the carnage. This was great stuff. The newspapers back east would eat it up.

Tom Johnson had wandered the main street, counting the dead and wounded. "Red Malone's not here," he said, walking up to Smoke and a group of others.

"How about his men?" Sal asked.

"Most of them are dead. I saw two of them riding out

north early on. Looked like they were clearing the country."

"You have enough to do here for three men, Sal," Smoke said. "Besides, this is personal between me and Red. I'll get him. And I'll bring him in alive if I can."

"You better find him before Joe Walsh does," Jim said. "Joe told him years ago that if he ever caught him without his private army with him, he'd kill him."

"There is that much bad blood between them?" Smoke asked. "I knew they didn't like each other. . . ."

"Man, yeah!" Jim said. "He helped found this town—Joe, I mean. Him and Red don't like each other at all."

"Well, I'll be!" came the shout. "Here's that so-called preacher from up at Hell's Creek. He had him a torch and was right in the middle of it all."

"Dead?" Pete called.

"I'll say. Plugged through and through."

Smoke walked the littered street, looking at the dead and wounded. But Alex Bell, Ben Webster, Nelson Barrett, Al Martin, Dave Poe, and Val Singer were not among them. That left a lot of very bad men still on the loose, but Smoke doubted that they would ever return to Barlow.

He walked to the hotel, kissed Sally and petted Lisa's puppy Patches, then told his wife, "I'll be back. I'm going after Red Malone."

"I'll go down and help with the wounded."

"See you when I return."

As Smoke was riding out, Jim said to Pete, "I wonder if he'll bring Red in alive."

Pete spat on the ground. "Not if Red tries to draw on him."

26

Smoke rode easy, knowing there was no hurry. Red Malone was not about to run. But he wondered about Max. What would the big man do—that is, if he were still alive? Or had his renegades returned to Hell's Creek after their failure in Barlow and killed him? And that was highly likely.

Smoke rode on, keeping Star in an easy canter, sometimes walking him. But the big horse loved to run and they ate up the distance. He was soon on Lightning range and, within minutes, facing three Lightning cowboys. One of them was wearing a bloody shirt, due to a bullet graze on his arm.

"The people of Barlow are signing warrants right now, boys. Best thing you can do is just ride and keep on riding. If you think Sal and his deputies won't come out here to get you, you're flat wrong."

The cowboys looked at each other, then back at Smoke. One said, "You'll let us ride?"

Smoke jerked a thumb. "Ride on."

"I'll tell you this much," another said. "Red is alone. Except for that no-account daughter of his. But you won't take him alive."

"Thanks. But I'd hate to kill a man in front of his daughter."

One of the cowboys laughed. "Smoke, that girl is as low and mean-spirited as her pa. She don't give a popcorn poot for him. All she wants is the ranch. I believe she'd kill him herself if she got the chance."

241

"Thanks. I hope I don't see you boys again."

They grinned. "You won't!"

They rode out, taking trails that would skirt the town of Barlow.

When Smoke rode into the yard, Tessie was sitting on the porch. A shotgun lay on the porch floor. At the sight of him, she started bawling and squalling. As he drew closer, he could see that her dress was torn. She stopped crying long enough to expose more skin. Then she resumed her blubbering.

Smoke sat his saddle for a moment, staring at the young woman. "Where's your father?" he asked when there was a break in the hollering.

"He's dead!" she squalled. "In the house. He tried to attack me. He went crazy. I had to defend my honor!" She began a new round of wailing.

Smoke swung down from the saddle and walked up onto the porch. He really didn't know what to expect; maybe a trap. He just didn't know.

He opened the screen door and the smell of blood hit him hard. He walked through the house until he found Red, dead, sprawled in front of a safe in his study. The door was open, and greenbacks and small sacks of gold lay on the floor and in the safe.

Smoke grunted. Red Malone had been shot in the back at close range.

"Ohhh!" Tessie hollered from the front porch. "I'm shamed forever. My own father tried to as-sault me. Oh, the dishonor and disgrace of it all." She started blubbering.

Smoke looked down at Red. "I hate to say it, Red, but even you probably deserved better kids than you had."

He walked outside. Tessie honked her nose into a bandana and said, "What am I gonna do with this big ol' ranch? Why, I'm just a woman; I can't handle men's work."

"I certainly don't envy you, ma'am. Don't you have anybody else left on the ranch?"

"Just the cook. She's gone visitin' friends for the day. I suppose I could get her to help me bury Pa. You think he'll keep 'til late this afternoon?"

"I expect so, ma'am." Smoke stepped into the saddle.

"Are you just gonna leave me here all alone with my poor dead father? I could sure use some comforting." She batted her eyes at him. It was the most grotesque thing Smoke had ever seen—and he had seen some sights in his time.

"I'll explain to the sheriff what happened," Smoke said as he backed Star up. Damned if he was going to turn his back to this woman. "I'll sure do that."

When he had backed Star to the point where he was reasonably sure she could not hit him with the sawed-off, Smoke gave the big black his head. Star took off like the wind. The horse wasn't real thrilled with Tessie, either.

When Smoke arrived back in town, he told Judge Garrison and Sal what he'd seen out at the Lightning spread. Neither man seemed very surprised.

"She'll take every dollar from the safe, sell off the herds, and be gone in a month," the judge prophesied. "And good riddance to bad baggage."

Smoke looked around. Most of the bodies had been tossed in wagons and were being hauled off to be buried in a mass grave. Half the men in town were working with shovels at the gravesite.

"Wagons coming," Jim announced, pointing to the north.

As the wagons neared, Judge Garrison said, "Saloon girls, gamblers, and assorted riffraff from Hell's Creek. Rats leaving a sinking ship."

"No," Smoke said. "A burning one. Because that's what we're going to do in the morning."

"Suits me," Tom said. "I'll ride with you."

"Keep moving," Sal told the lead wagon. "And don't stop until you're in the next county. And he won't want you, either, 'cause I'm fixin' to wire the sheriff and tell him about you scum."

One of the ladies of the evening, sitting in the back of the wagon, gave him a very obscene gesture with a finger.

"I'll jerk you out of that wagon and hand you over to the good ladies of this town," Sal warned her. "And they'll shave your head and tar and feather you."

The shady lady tucked her finger away and stared straight ahead.

The wagons rumbled out of sight.

"Why wait until the morning?" Pete asked. "Hell, Smoke. Let's ride up there and put that town out of its misery right now."

Smoke was curious to see what had happened to Big Max. "All right. Let's ride."

The band of men had stopped at Brown's farmhouse and asked if the farmers wanted any of the lumber in the town before they put the torch to it.

To a man, they shook their heads. "Thanks kindly, but no thanks," Gatewood said. "We just want shut of that den of thieves and whores and hoodlums."

The men rode on, Smoke, Pete, Tom Johnson, Judge Garrison, and half a dozen more of the town. They were heavily armed, for no one among them knew what awaited them in Hell's Creek.

Desolation.

As they topped the ridge overlooking the town, they could all sense the place was empty, completely void of life.

"Let's check it out," Smoke said.

The men inspected every building. The town was deserted. Thre was no sign of Big Max Huggins. Smoke looked at the safe in Max's quarters. The door was open and there was no sign of forced entry. So Max had found the strength to open it and ride.

Smoke found a coal-oil lantern, lit it, and tossed it into the squalor that someone had once lived in . . . and from all indications, it had housed several women. The building was quickly ablaze. The other men were doing the same with coal-oil-soaked rags. Soon, the fierceness of the heat drove them back.

In half an hour, the town of Hell's Creek, Montana was no more than an unpleasant memory.

The men headed back toward Barlow, for a hot bath, a

good meal, and some well-deserved rest. The day's events would alter their lives forever. For the good.

All that was left for Sally and Smoke were the good-byes to the people of Barlow and the ranchers and farmers out in the county. In the short time they'd been there, a lot had happened and they had discovered some friendships that would last forever.

Robert had been transferred to the territorial mental asylum and the doctors there had given him very little hope of ever recovering.

Through Sally's help, the new bank had agreed to loan Martha and Pete the money for a down payment on the Lightning spread. The two were married the day before Smoke and Sally were due to pull out.

Tessie Malone left the country the very day she sold Lightning to Pete and Martha.

Much to Sal's embarrassment, Victoria announced that the newly elected sheriff had proposed marriage to her and that she had accepted. Victoria had also accepted a position of teaching at the new school.

The other new schoolteacher in town, a cute little redhead, was making goo-goo eyes at Jim Dagonne. Bets were that he'd be roped and hog-tied before summer's end.

Smoke and Sally had said their good-byes to Joe Walsh and his wife.

The town of Barlow had been quiet for a week. Not one shot had been fired, not one fist had been swung in anger. Sal commented that it was just too good to last.

That proved true when one of Joe Walsh's hands came fogging into town, pale as a ghost and so excited he could hardly talk. He'd found Smoke Jensen's body on the trail. Sally Jensen was missing.

27

Smoke was not dead, but had the bullet that grazed his skull been one millimeter more to the right, the slug would have blown out his brains.

He was back on his feet the next day, over the protestations of the new doctor in Barlow, and strapping on his guns.

Every able-bodied man in Barlow had been on the search for Sally and her kidnapper or kidnappers. They had ridden back into town at dawn, weary. They had lost the trail.

All Smoke could remember was that he and Sally and the packhorse had ridden down the edge of Swan Lake, intending to pick up the Swan River and follow it south to the railroad. They had stopped to water and rest their horses when Smoke's head seemed to explode.

That's all he could remember.

He swung into the saddle and pointed Star's head south, intending to backtrack. He had a headache, but other than that, he felt fine.

"You're sure you don't want some help?" Sal asked.

"No. A big posse is too easy to spot. Besides, Sally will leave messages along the way; messages and markers that would make sense only to me. It's Big Max, I'd bet on that. I was instrumental in bringing down his little empire, so now he intends to destroy as much of what I hold dear as possible. See you, Sal."

Smoke rode easy, down to the south end of the lake. There

he dismounted and began searching the area, using tactics taught him by the old mountain man, Preacher. He worked in ever-widening circles, on moccasin-clad feet. By mid-afternoon he had picked up the trail—the true one, not the one that had been deliberately left for the posse.

The trail headed north by northeast. The lead horse was carrying a heavy load. That would be Max Huggins. Smoke recognized the hoofprints of Sally's mare. If they stayed on this trail, Smoke surmised, they were heading for glacier country.

Smoke doggedly stayed with the trail, taking his time, being careful not to miss a thing. He found where they'd camped at the base of and on the east side of Mt. Evans. Sally had left three stones in the form of an arrowhead, pointing toward the Flathead River.

Smoke followed, his head no longer aching and his strength having returned. He kept his fury under control—barely. He met a lone hunter, and the man took one look into Smoke's eyes' and felt the chill of death touch him. The hunter backed off the trail and let Smoke pass with just a nod of his head.

The man would tell his grandkids that he had once seen Smoke Jensen on the prod, and that it was not a sight he ever wanted to see again.

On the east side of the South Fork Flathead, Max had met up with the tracks of a dozen riders. Probably the remnants of Max's gang, Smoke thought. Several miles farther, one rider had left the bunch. Smoke left the trail and circled. He picketed Star and worked his way back a bit on foot. He smiled when he saw who had stayed behind to waylay him.

It was the young man who had taken to calling himself Kid Brewer; the young man with a few pimples on his face who had made the obscene gesture at Smoke after the window-washing incident.

"Waiting for me, Kid?" Smoke called from behind the young man.

Kid Brewer whirled, his hands frozen over the butts of his tied-down guns. Smoke Jensen stood facing him, a Winchester pointed at his belly.

"You really shouldn't have taken a part in the taking of my wife, punk," Smoke told him. "Coming at me is one thing; taking my wife is something entirely different."

"Yeah," the young gunhand sneered at him. "So what do you think you're going to do about it?"

Smoke shot him. The .44 slug from the rifle struck the young man in the right elbow, knocking him down and forever crippling his gun hand. He lay on the cool ground, moaning and calling for his mother.

Smoke walked down to him and placed the muzzle of the rifle on the gunhand's left elbow. "If you think I won't leave you permanently crippled in both arms, you're crazy. Talk to me, punk."

Brewer looked up into the coldest eyes he had ever seen in all his young life. They so chilled him he momentarily forgot the pain in his shattered right arm. He began talking so fast Smoke had to slow him down.

When he had finished, Smoke smashed Brewer's guns, threw him on his saddle, and when the young man had stopped screaming after the jolting pain in his arm from the toss had lessened, Smoke gave him some advice. "If I ever see you again and you're wearing a gun, I'll kill you." He slapped the horse on the rump and the pony took off at a fast canter. Brewer was still screaming when Smoke mounted up.

Smoke backtracked and once more picked up the trail. He found where they had nooned and discovered Sally had taken stones and spelled out: O K. With a smile that would have backed up the devil, Smoke swung into the saddle and rode on.

He left the obvious trail and rode up into the high lonesome, into the east slopes of the Rockies. He dismounted and took his binoculars, carefully scanning the area below him. He scanned it once, then twice, and then a third time. He picked up the thin tentacle of smoke on the third try. He studied the area below him until he felt he had found a way in. He mounted up and headed down into the valley.

Nelson Barrett was enjoying a cup of hot coffee. His pleasure abruptly lessened when he felt the cold steel of a big Bowie knife against his throat. What made it even worse was

249

the dark stain that suddenly appeared in the crotch of his dirty jeans.

"Talk to me, pee-pants," Smoke whispered. "And I'd better like what you have to say. 'Cause if I don't, I'll stake you out and skin you alive."

"Your woman's awright!" Nelson blurted. "There ain't nobody touched her. I swear it, man!"

"You were left here to do what?"

"Kill you!"

"Well, now. Is that a fact? What do you think I ought to do with you?"

"You let me ride, you'll never see me again, Smoke. As God is my witness, I promise you that."

Smoke took the knife from the man's throat and Nelson made a grab for his gun. Smoke jammed the big blade into the man's back and ripped upward with it. Nelson Barrett fell face-first into the small fire.

Smoke wiped the blade clean on Nelson's shirttail and poured himself a cup of coffee. He drank it slowly, then carefully put out the fire. He left Nelson where he lay and mounted up.

He crossed the Middle Fork of the Flathead River and rode into the area that would someday become the Glacier National Park. Smoke slipped into a jacket, for it had turned cold.

He plunged into a wild, beautiful wilderness. His thoughts turned to Preacher and how much the old man would have enjoyed the beauty of this rugged, lonesome country.

Then his thoughts lost all trace of beauty and turned savage and ugly as he followed the trail of Max Huggins and his dwindling gang of thugs and punks and human crap. He thought he heard a voice from out of the dark tangle of vegetation and pulled up, dismounting. He picketed Star and moved forward, both guns in his hands.

Al Martin, Dave Poe, and Ben Webster squatted around a campfire, boiling coffee and frying bacon.

"I cain't understand why Big Max don't go ahead and take the woman," Al said. "I would have."

"'Cause he'd have to knock her out cold to do it," Ben

replied. "And that ain't no fun."

"He ought to just go 'head and shoot her," Dave opined. "She ain't never gonna be what Max wants her to be."

"I say we go on and kill Jensen, if that is him behind us, then kill Max, take his money, and have our pleasures with the woman," Al said. "There ain't nobody ever gonna find her body in this place."

Smoke stepped out and ruined the men's appetites. Both .44's belched flame and death, destroying the tranquility of the lovely forest in the high-up country.

Smoke dragged their bodies away from the fire and dumped them down a ravine. He pulled the picket pins of their horses and set them free. Smoke got Star and unsaddled him, rubbing the animal down and allowing him to graze for a time.

By that time, the bacon was done and the coffee was ready. Smoke drank and ate, sopping out the grease in the frying pan with a hunk of stale bread.

Smoke rolled him a cigarette and leaned back, enjoying the warmth of the fire. He poured another cup of coffee. If his calculations were corret, all that remained were Max, Val Singer, and Alex Bell. He moved away from the fire, laid his head on his saddle, and went to sleep.

He slept for a couple of hours, then rose and began circling the camp. He found another stick message from Sally. Three sticks laid out side by side, with four sticks next to them, in the shape of a crude D. Triple Divide Peak. Had to be.

Ol' Preacher had told him about this country, as had other old mountain men, and like most outdoorsmen, Smoke retained that knowledge in his head, a mental map.

He saddled up and took a chance, cutting straight east for a time, then turning north just west of what he felt was the Continental Divide. If he was right, and Max and what was left of his gang were not too far ahead of him—and he didn't think they were—he would make Triple Divide Peak ahead of Max.

Smoke pushed Star that day, but it was nothing the big horse couldn't take and still have more to give. Man and horse traveled through country that seemed as unchanged now as it was when God created the earth.

And Smoke could not understand why Max, with his love of cities and towns, hurdy-gurdy girls and parties, had chosen to come here, into this cold and vast wilderness.

He concluded that Max, like his brother Robert, had a streak of insanity running through him.

Smoke made camp that evening between Mt. Thompson and Triple Divide Peak. He loved this country, this high lonesome, where bighorn sheep played their perilous games on the face of seemingly untraversable mountains. Where cedars grew so tall they seemed to touch the sky. Where far below where he camped, heating his coffee over a hat-sized fire, he could see herds of buffalo roaming.

It all seemed just too peaceful a place for what Smoke had in mind.

But peaceful or not, he had come to find Sally, and get Sally he would. He rolled up in his blankets and went to sleep. Tomorrow was going to be a very busy day.

Smoke was up before dawn. He did not build a fire. He watered Star and left the big horse to graze. Below him, by one of the many small lakes that were scattered like jewels in this wilderness, he had spotted a campfire. Leaving his boots and spurs behind, Smoke slipped into his moccasins and picked up his rifle. He had it in his mind that he and Sally would be riding toward the Sugarloaf come noon.

Smoke moved through the thick underbrush and damp grass like a wraith. His clothing was of earth tones, blending in with his surroundings. From his high-up vantage point, Smoke had seen the second fire. That would be where Max and Sally were camped. Max had chosen to make his stand—if that's what he had in mind—on the flat of a sheer drop-off, maybe a thousand feet above where his two remaining gunmen were camped, waiting for Smoke Jensen.

"Let us not disappoint you, gentlemen," Smoke muttered. "I do hate to keep people waiting."

"No word from any of them we left behind," Val Singer said to Alex Bell. "That means that Jensen got them."

Bell said nothing for a moment. He sipped his coffee, warming his hands on the tin cup. He was cold, he was uncomfortable, and he was scared. All along the way up into this godforsaken country, they had left good men behind them; men left there to take care of Smoke Jensen. But Jensen had taken care of them, it seemed. The man was a devil. Straight out of hell. Had to be.

"Let's get out of here, Val," he finally spoke. "To hell with Max and the woman. Let's just ride."

"It's too late," Val said, the words soft.

"What the hell do you mean?"

"Jensen's here."

Alex looked wildly around him. He could see nothing, only the seemingly impenetrable tangle of brush that was all around them. "I don't see nothin'. I don't hear nothin'."

"No," the gunfighter said, standing up and working his guns in and out of leather. "You wouldn't with Jensen. But he's here."

Alex stood up, loosening his guns. "You're beginning to spook me, Val."

"We shoulda left when Jensen showed up. We shoulda just pulled out and got gone. Now it's too late."

"That's right, Val," the voice came from the underbrush. "Now it's too late."

Alex Bell jerked iron and emptied one gun into the thick brush.

Laughter was his reply.

"Come out here and fight, damn you!" Alex screamed.

A .44 slug from a Winchester doubled him over, the slug taking him just above the belt buckle. The second slug turned him around and dropped him to the cold ground. His gun fell from numbed fingers.

Val Singer had not moved. He stood tall, his right hand close to the butt of his Colt. He waited.

Alex Bell moaned on the ground. Val ignored him.

Smoke stepped out of the brush. He carried the rifle in his left hand, his right hand by his side.

Val said, "I guess we do it now, don't we, Smoke?"

"I reckon."

"No point in my sayin' I'd just ride on out and leave you be?"

"Nope."

"You're a hard man, Smoke."

"Yep."

Val cussed him.

Smoke waited, tall and tough and cold-eyed.

Val jerked iron and Smoke shot him twice in the belly, once with his Colt and once with the .44 rifle. Smoke walked to the fire and poured a cup of coffee. He made a sandwich out of the nearly burned bacon and some bread wrapped in a cloth. He cut his eyes to Val Singer.

"We all make mistakes," the gun-for-hire said, his eyes pain-filled as he lay on the ground, both hands holding his punctured belly.

"Indeed you did."

"Gimme some coffee, Smoke."

"You're gut-shot. Worse thing in the world for you is liquid."

Val laughed bitterly. "I'm a good two hundred miles from a doctor. You think I don't know I've had it?"

Smoke poured Val a cup of the strong brew and handed it to him.

"Thanks," Val said. He took a sip of the brew and then screamed as the pain rose in waves.

To the west and above them, Sally had been working for several hours, rubbing the rawhide that bound her wrists against a rock. She felt the rawhide part and then, keeping her hands behind her, began to work circulation back into her hands.

Max turned to look at her. His face was a ruin. Smoke had destroyed the man's handsome looks with his fists. Madness shone in his eyes; madness combined with a burning hatred for Smoke Jensen.

"You heard the shots?"

"Yes."

"I'm next."

"I'm sure."

Max tried to smile. The broken bones in his face twisted his smile into a grimace. "I've got about an hour before Jensen can work his way up here. So I'll have you and then

254

throw you off this cliff."

"I'm cold," Sally said. "May I scoot closer to the fire?"

"May I?" Max said mockingly. "My, how proper. Yes, Sally, you may."

Sally scooted to the fire's edge. Max turned his back to her, looking down into the valley below. Sally reached around and quickly untied the rawhide that bound her ankles, but left the rawhide looped around her boots.

Alex Bell sighed once and then died.

"Well, that's the end of it," Val managed to say, his voice thick with pain. "That's the last one of us 'ceptin' Max. And I 'spect you'll nail him, too. You gonna bury us, Smoke?"

"Nope." Smoke ate his sandwich and sipped his coffee.

"You just gonna leave us for the buzzards and the bears and the wolves?" The outlaw could not believe that Smoke really meant that.

"Yep."

"That ain't decent!"

"You're not a decent person, Singer. There is nothing decent about you."

"I was drove to a life of crime!"

Smoke laughed at him. "That's all horse-crap and you know it, Val. You chose your life-style willingly. So don't go out with a lie on your lips."

"I guess," the outlaw said, his voice weak. He looked around him and laughed bitterly. "All them books them folks back east write about the glamorous life on the hoot-owl trail. They don't know nothin'. All the outlaws I ever seen, me included, were dirty and hungry and cold and miserable ninety-nine days out of a hundred. But there ain't no point in wishin' I could change it, is there?"

"No, there isn't."

"Smoke?"

Smoke looked at him.

"You're a good man, Jensen. You got a good woman. I wish you both the best."

"Thanks, Val. You want to be buried with your boots on?"

"No. Gonna be hot enough where I'm goin'." He laid his head on the ground and closed his eyes.

Smoke waited for death to take the man.

"Max?" Sally whispered. She had taken a good-sized chunk of burning wood from the fire and stepped up behind the man. One end of the fire-brand was blazing hot.

Max turned and Sally hit him in the face with the burning end, then jammed the blazing wood into his open mouth. Max dropped his rifle and screamed, backing up. His boot hit a rock and sent him tumbling over the edge of the cliff. He screamed for a thousand feet.

Silence fell over the wilderness.

Sally rubbed her aching ankles and wrists, then set about making fresh coffee and slicing bacon. Her man would be along in about an hour.

Smoke rode into the flats and dismounted. He held his woman in his arms for a long time. She pushed him away and expelled breath. "What took you so long?"

"I buried Val Singer. Are you all right?"

"I am now. Come on, eat. I made fresh coffee."

The sun burst out of the clouds and mist of mid-afternoon. Sally looked across the fire at Smoke Jensen. "No point in starting out now. We can wait until morning."

"Oh? You have something in mind?"

She came to him and whispered in his ear.

Smoke took her in his arms. "Now that's the best suggestion I've heard in a long time."